The Fossil Hunter

IRENE SANDELL

DOUBLE MOUNTAIN PRESS

The Fossil Hunter

Irene Sandell

Double Mountain Press

Copyright © 2025 by Irene Sandell

ISBN: 979-8-218-74519-6 Paperback

Cover design by Cathy Cashdollar

Illustrations and product development by GaryGroup.press

To my grandmother Dora Velma Rhea and my mother Lydia Velma Robinson.

Their gentle kindness, grace and strength bridged three centuries.

Meredith

2015

I read once that an earthquake is caused by the slipping of a single grain of sand, deep in the earth. One grain slides against another, and that motion causes a thousand others to move until that tiny movement has changed the course of a million others and reshaped the very surface of the earth.

When I read that I was a child, and it bothered me. It made me feel unsafe, as if I could not be sure of even the very ground under my feet.

Chapter 1

No matter that it was the 5th of October, it was hot! Meredith Bannon leaned toward the car window trying to catch a breeze, but the air still felt stiff with heat. She glanced up in the rearview mirror and pushed her hair back from where it was clinging to her forehead. She just felt sticky all over, and her thighs were glued to the vinyl car seat. Meredith clenched her jaw in defiance. She wouldn't think about the broken a/c, or the cracked windshield, or the paper-thin tires. Those problems had seemed superficial at first, but now all these engine noises had begun, and it was too late for second guessing. She had to live with her mistake. Ten more miles;

that was what she would think about. Just let this 'junker' make ten more miles, and then the poor thing could die.

The road toward Troubadour, Texas rolled out before her through broken prairie. What grass that she could see was scattered over bare ground in all directions and flat-topped mesas faded to blue in the distance. The lacy leaves of mesquite trees added an accent of green as though an unseen artist had brushed a hint of color across the land. Home. Meredith drew a deep breath. After all these years, even with all her reservations about coming back, it still felt like home.

She smiled to herself. She had hardly set foot in this country since her grandmother died; rarely thought about it. And she had certainly never entertained the idea of coming back to stay; not until now. But no doubt about it, it was a majestic and harsh and foreboding place.

She glanced down at the car seat beside her. The envelope was there, almost everything she had left in the world, and a note clipped to the front showed the lawyer's address. Ten miles, even less now, and the gas tank was half full.

A water tower appeared on the horizon accenting the skyline. Scattered houses with bare ground yards popped into view huddled along the road, white wooden or stucco structures, stained reddish brown by wind-blown sand. It was as if nothing had changed in the years she had been away.

Meredith glanced one more time at the address, *Taylor Street, one block off the square. How had she remembered that little factoid?*

She eased into a parking space and turned off the ignition while the car did that annoying rattle, clatter, cough thing as if it were refusing to die. Embarrassing, but she glanced around and gratefully realized there was no one to hear it but her. A quick look in the rearview mirror and a toss of her hair; deep breath, here goes. The car door gave out a metallic groan as she opened it. One more insult. She peeled her legs away from the car seat and shook her skirt tail loose as she stood up. Not too bad. Meredith fluffed her hair once more and slammed the door, as it gave out another loud grinding complaint.

The girl at the front desk smiled as she walked in.

"I'm Meredith Bannon. I . . ."

"Yes." The girl jumped to her feet. "Mr. Miller is expecting you." She motioned toward his door. "I'm Sara Lee Fisher. My mother went to school with you, --- Emma Compton?" The question in her voice was asking if she remembered.

Meredith smiled. "Oh really. How is your mother?"

The smile faded. "She passed away last year." Blank silence. "Cancer," she whispered.

"I'm so sorry."

The girl nodded. "She always spoke highly of you."

Meredith moved toward the inner office door. There it was, that niggle of panic in her gut. Coming back here was not a good idea! "Thank you for sharing that with me," she managed to say. She had no idea who Emma Compton was. No memory.

The office door opened, and Sol Miller was standing there. "Meredith." He reached out to take her hand. "Good to see you. Come on in here." He pulled her into the office, and they stood staring at one another. She recognized him well enough. He'd gained quite a lot of weight from the skinny kid she had sat by in grammar school, and what hair he had left was grey, but the eyes and the smile were the same. And what did he see? What was he thinking? She had put on a few pounds herself, and even though she colored the grey in her hair she still found a fair share of wrinkles staring back at her from the mirror each morning.

After a moment, he said, "It's been a few years, hasn't it?"

"Yes. A few," she said, and they both laughed softly.

"Have a seat." Sol moved around behind his desk. "I was glad to hear from you. We had a hard time tracking you down." He settled himself in his chair.

"I'm sure you did. I don't have much connection here now." She sat down as he directed. "And my name has changed." Her heart seemed to be beating like a hammer.

"Yes, that was a challenge." The pause that followed hinted questions he wanted to ask, but he apparently thought better of it. Instead, he took a deep breath as if stage one was over, and then tapped the folder on his desk. "Now we can get this all settled." He flipped it open. "Did you read through the papers I sent you?"

Meredith nodded.

"Any questions?"

"No . . ., well maybe just one. Is there anything of the estate left?"

Sol blinked. "Yes, of course." He tapped the pages in front of him. Your grandmother's will was very clear. The house and property were to be yours, but your mother could live there as long as she wanted, and you were not to intervene. Now that your mother has passed, you are free to do what you wish with the property."

There was an awkward pause while Sol busied himself ruffling though his papers. "So, all we need to do is get your signature on this and give you the keys."

"How much property is left?"

Sol looked up from his work. "Not a lot, I'm afraid. Your grandfather sold the majority of the place in his lifetime. Your grandmother sold off parcels of the remaining land over the years to cover expenses and taxes. Then, after your mother died, and I couldn't find you, I had to make some decisions to settle any debts. It's all in my letter there. Of course, you need to talk to Lucas at the bank about anything else.

"I understand." Meredith brushed his words aside with a hand motion, and he nodded.

"The good news is the house is free and clear. There's about 200 acres left behind the house, so that's something. The bad news is the house hasn't been updated much at all. Grace Durham wasn't one for spending her money loosely and your mother, as you know, was no different. You've got running water, electricity, and propane heat. That's it."

Meredith studied his expression for a moment. He wasn't joking, or even being sarcastic. Amazing. Her mother did nothing in her whole life except spend money loosely, but obviously, he didn't realize that. Like so many others, Audrey had played him for a fool.

"Are the lights on?"

"Yes, the lights are on."

"And the plumbing is in good order?"

He smiled. "Well, it's old, but everything still works." He turned the pages around and handed her a pen.

Meredith studied the papers for a second. There was her mother's signature; Audrey Durham Fancher. She never had bothered to change her name. She laid the papers on Sol's desk and added her name, Meredith Grace Fancher Bannon, and smiled at the irony. She was tired of changing her last name, also. She handed the papers back, and Sol studied them before he closed the folder and leaned back in his chair.

"So what do you plan to do with the place?"

Meredith smiled. "I plan to live there." And she enjoyed the surprise, maybe shock even, she saw in his eyes. She did love being mysterious.

"I see. Well, then you've got your work cut out for you, I guess." He gave her a smile, but it was a thin one. "After your mother died, ah, we cleared everything out of her room." He stared in silence for a moment, as if expecting her to comment. "We left everything else just as it was."

"Did my mother die there at the house?"

"The sheriff found her." Sol took a deep breath. "She died in her sleep apparently."

"I see," Meredith nodded, but she had no more to say.

Sol rose and came around his desk. "And there's one other thing. I have your grandmother's trunk. It wouldn't have been safe out there at the house." He pointed behind her to the corner of the room. "I brought it in this morning since you were coming."

Meredith looked back when he motioned, and there it sat. She would have known it anywhere. That battered wooden box with the metal bindings sat perched on a dolly with red bungee cords stretched across it, as much a shock as if she had seen her grandmother sitting there.

"I can take it out to your car for you, if you like", Sol offered. "It's rather bulky."

She thought of her car and how piled it was with all her stuff. "I'm not sure I have room. I have all my things out there. The car is pretty full."

"Oh, sure. I was thinking you would be leaving today, but sure. I understand. Since you're staying, there's no rush, I guess."

"I'll come back tomorrow."

"Better yet, I'll bring it out this evening if you're going to be at the house. How about that? My wife would love to meet you."

She hesitated only a moment. "That would be nice of you. I'll be out there. I have a sleeping bag, so I was planning on camping out tonight." She laughed, but it sounded forced, even to her.

If Sol was shocked, he didn't show it. "Then that's what I'll do." He walked her to the door. "Maxine was a couple of years behind us in school, but she remembers you. Shoot, I guess just about everybody from back then remembers you." Meredith didn't know how to respond to that. A jumble of thoughts flashed through her mind. *Everybody?* echoed in her head.

Sara Lee Fisher stood up as they came out, still smiling. "Nice talking to you. We'll be seeing you, I'm sure."

Meredith smiled back as she opened the front door, "I'm sure you will." They stopped on the sidewalk, and she watched as Sol looked her car over. To his credit he didn't show any reaction.

"We'll be out around six, if that's ok."

"Sure, see you then." She stepped off the curb, very conscious of Sol still standing there.

Her driver's door opened and closed with its grinding screech. *Please God, let this thing start, just one more time; just one.* Meredith turned the key. Nothing. She turned it again and pumped the gas pedal. A gurgle, a rattle and reluctant roar, and the motor came to life. *Praise the Lord!* She waved at Sol as she backed out and headed west. She could see him in the rearview mirror, watching her drive away.

Meredith stopped for gas on the way out of town. No sense in chancing it any further. While the pump gurgled away, her phone rang. It was Rachel.

"Hello dear."

"Mom." The voice sounded very far away. "So, you made it fine?"

"Yes, no problems at all. I told you I would call if this car gave out on me."

They both laughed. "You should have waited and let me drive you instead of wasting your money on that old wreck."

"I know, I know. You told me, but I'm a big girl. I can handle this."

"Yes, I know." There was a slight pause, and Meredith knew her daughter was counseling herself not to nag.

"So, how's the house?" Rachel said instead. "Have you seen it yet?"

"I'm on my way out there now. I'll give you a report later. When are you coming down?"

"I don't know." There was another pause. "I'll be in California for another week at least, but I'll get down there as soon as I can. "

"How's the job going?"

"Busy. You know, everyone needs everything yesterday."

"I know you can handle it, my dear." They both laughed softly.

"Yes, I can. Now let me know if you need anything."

"I will. I love you."

"I love you too, Mom."

Meredith slipped the phone back in her pocket and closed the gas cap. What she had ever done in her life to deserve her daughter, she was not sure. Responsible, successful, nothing like her father, thank God. Maybe Rachel's personal life was a little unsettled, but she was doing better than her mother.

Seventy-three years old and still trying to get my life straight, pretty pathetic.

The car gratefully cranked right up and only grumbled a little as she pulled away from the station.

Chapter 2

The old house was still the most imposing thing on the west side of town. Meredith caught sight of the roof top over the trees as she reached a clearing, and when she turned into the lane, she noted that the front elevation still commanded the view. The only difference was that several houses and one or two mobile homes had sprung up along the road, cluttering the landscape with tricycles on the front walks and pick-up trucks in the yards. Neighbors had inched closer to the house, but not too close. It still stood alone, just as she remembered. a wide veranda with large white columns at the front and scattered windows wrapped around the rest of the house.

She eased the car up to the white picket fence around the yard and shoved her contrary door open one more time as the motor put up its protest. Then silence wafted around her, and the only sound was the sizzle of car tires on the highway a half mile away. Meredith stood transfixed for a few minutes. The place was timeless. Nothing had changed in all these years. A light breeze ruffled her hair, and she turned her face toward it. Even on this hot day, there was always still a breeze here on the hill.

It took a little force to push the gate open, testifying that the hinges hadn't been moved lately. She followed the gravel path to the porch remembering helping her grandmother spread those rocks. *If you want something done right, you must do it yourself,* she could hear Grace saying, even now.

The front steps creaked under her weight, and the slats in the porch were rumpled and uneven. The screen door protested when she pulled it back, but the key Sol had given her slipped easily in the lock. She turned the ornate oval knob and pushed the door back as the sound it made echoed around the room. A musty closed-up smell was her first impression; that and the hollow sound her footsteps made on the wooden floor. The only thing in the entry hall was an old coat rack.

Without moving from the front hall, she craned her neck to look into the side rooms, the parlor on one side, the dining room on the other, then past the staircase down the hall toward the kitchen. The place looked like a time capsule. The furniture in the parlor looked just as she remembered, except for a slight powdering of dust. Her grandmother might have just walked out of the room. The only thing missing were pictures on the walls. Just dark patches where they had hung stared back at her. Same in the dining room. The table and chairs and sideboard were still there. Her mother had changed nothing else apparently in her 13 years of occupation. A dirt dauber buzzed by her head, attracted by her body heat, and she waved it away.

Down the hall, past the stairs, she could see the curling edge of yellow linoleum on the kitchen floor. Her footsteps echoed around her as she walked down the hall, passing the door to the room her grandmother always called the library. Meredith turned the knob and and tried to open the door, but something was in the way. She peeked through the crack she had managed to make, but the room was dark, and she could see nothing familiar. *Worry about this later,* she counseled herself and moved on to the kitchen.

That room had more life to it. An oil cloth covered table and two chairs sat in the middle of the room. The old red and white checkered cloth looked festive compared to the rest of the house. A small array of cabinets covered one wall arranged around a window, and there was a sink in the center with a tiny drip marking time. The stove was new, or at least newer than the one she remembered, gas by the look of it. Sol had said she had propane. The refrigerator was new, also. A major improvement over her grandmother's old icebox with the water pan underneath to catch the melting ice block. The refrigerator door stood slightly open. Someone had thoughtfully cleaned it out and left it open to the air so no mold would form. So far so good.

Looking out the window, she could see the barn. From here it seemed to be holding up. The roof looked good, and the corral fence was standing. Someone, probably Sol, was seeing to it that the sparse grass and weeds around the house was being kept at bay. She would have to remember to ask about that.

She backtracked to the stairs and started up. Everything seemed smaller to her than she remembered. This house had felt like an ocean of space to her as a child, but now the stairs seemed narrow and the ceiling low. At the top of the landing she stopped and surveyed the area. All the doors were closed, but her old room drew her attention first. She turned the knob and pushed the door back. This room was empty, not even shades on the windows. She could see watermarks on the faded wallpaper where rain had penetrated by some circumstance, and again, there were dark splotches here and there on the walls where pictures had once hung. The closet door was open, showing an empty space. All traces of her years in this room were gone.

Back out in the hall, she tried the door to the room her grandmother had always called the guest room. It was her mother's room when she was there. The room was empty, also. Nothing left. Sol had said that they had cleared out her mother's room. The space felt as lonely to her now as it had all those times when her mother had gone away. Her grandmother's voice crackled in her memory. *She'll be back, Meredith. Never you mine. People are who they are.* She turned her back as she had done so many times before.

Her grandmother's room was last, opposite the stairs, a little removed from the other two, and she opened the door expecting the same blank space. Grace Freeman was never one for frills. But instead of the emptiness, the room held a massive wooden bedstead, Grace's bed. The shock of memories brought tears to her eyes, unexpected. How many times had she crept into this room and scuttled her way into Grace's bed? She remembered the sweet smell of her grandmother's talcum powder and the welcome arms that took her in. *Don't you worry child. People are who they are,* she would whisper in her ear and then kiss the top of her head. A huge wardrobe chest sat across the room. When she opened it, it was empty also. The furniture got left behind because it was probably too big to wrestle down the stairs, she guessed.

Meredith backed up and sat on the bed and then let herself fall back on the sagging mattress to stare at the ceiling. So, she was here. The mattress ticking was scratchy, and a puff of dust circled her head, dancing in the light from the window. *Ugh! There was so much work ahead of her.* She took a deep breath. *Another chapter? How many times had she reinvented herself?* She dragged herself to her feet and went out to unload the car.

The rest of the day flew by as she gathered up her life, one box or bag at a time and carried it in. The stack almost filled the hallway by the time she was finished. She took a break in there somewhere and went looking for the bathroom. It was just off the kitchen at the back of the house, and she was glad to note that the water was on and the plumbing worked. In the kitchen she plugged in the fridge and waited to hear the hum of a motor. It also worked. She was on a roll here. She unloaded her cooler into the fridge and ate some cheese and ham, noting there was still plenty left for dinner.

Meredith was sorting through boxes according to where they needed to go in the house when she heard a vehicle drive up and realized the afternoon was gone. A heavy truck door slammed, then another, and when she got to the front door, Sol, and his wife were coming up the gravel path. He was pulling the dolly behind him. Meredith went out on the porch to meet them, and the woman smiled up at her from the front walk. Meredith noted that she looked as soft and rounded as her husband, her hair perfectly sculpted into a 1960's helmet of curls.

"Hello there," Meredith called.

"Here you go." Sol bumped the dolly up the steps one at a time and settled it on the porch.

Meredith offered her hand to the woman. "I'm Meredith Bannon. It's nice to meet you."

"Call me Maxine," the woman whispered. She had a rather timid smile.

"I'll just leave the trunk on the dolly here," Sol said. "You can put it wherever you want and bring the dolly by sometime. You might have a use for it around here while you're moving things."

"Thank you, that's very thoughtful." Meredith looked around the porch. "I'm sorry I can't offer you a chair, I'm . . . ."

"No problem." Both he and his wife looked stumped for anything else to say.

"Well, if you don't mind sitting on the steps here, I'll go get us something to drink. I've got some cold water in there."

"That will be nice," Sol said, and his wife smiled again.

Meredith scurried in to get the bottles of water. They were fairly cold still from her cooler, and the fridge was cooling down. When she got back out to the porch Sol and Maxine were arranged on the steps waiting patiently. Meredith joined them.

"I've been so busy this afternoon that I didn't realize how late it was until I heard your truck."

"Yeah, I ran by the house and picked Maxine up. Are you getting settled?"

Meredith smiled. "Not so much, but the car is unloaded. That's something."

Maxine was studying her with a squinted look. "Are you going to be all right here? I would think you would want to stay at the motel out on 37. It's very nice."

Meredith could hear the judgment in the woman's voice. *Are you so poor as this, she was truly asking.*

"No, I'll be fine. I'm anxious to be in my own space."

Maxine smiled sweetly. "Well, I just think it's wonderful that you are coming back here to live. This old house has been vacant too long."

Meredith glanced around the porch. "This is where I grew up. It's home to me."

I remember you." Maxine said. "You always had the prettiest clothes."

Meredith felt an old pang of warning. *Was this person one of those girls?*

"All the rest of us had dresses that our mothers made, but your dresses were store bought. I still remember that," Maxine added.

"My mother couldn't sew," Meredith offered. Sol smiled, but Maxine didn't.

"I got to know your mother a little," Sol put in, "After she moved back here when Grace died, you know. She was a quiet person. Kept to herself mostly," he added. The look on his face hinted that he wasn't sharing all he was thinking, she thought.

"Yes, I guess she was," Meredith agreed. There was silence for a few minutes. She would certainly not let herself be dragged into a discussion of her situation with her mother. "So, you came back here after law school?"

Sol nodded. "I joined Judd Marshall's firm. You remember him, I guess"

"Yes, I do. Are there many others from our class still here?"

"Several. Do you remember Thomas Waggoner?"

She nodded.

"He owns the auto parts house. He took over the Granger's business when Mr. Granger died. His wife used to be Betty Lynn Ford. You remember her, I guess. She was a few years behind us in school."

Meredith smiled and nodded. She had no idea who Betty Lynn Ford was. This small town game of 'remember everyone' was going to be tricky. She would have to find an old yearbook and study up a little. The truth was that she had spent most of the last 50 years forgetting Troubadour, Texas.

Silence filled the conversation space for a few minutes.

"We were noticing your front walk here." Sol pointed toward the ground. "What are those things laid out along the edge there? Not just rocks, are they?"

"No, they're fossils," Meredith explained. "My grandmother loved those things. You can sometimes find them along the creek banks out here. When I found one, I would wag it home to her."

"Fossils?' Maxine asked. "Fossils of what?

"Ancient sea creatures. Those that look like a big snail shell are called ammonites. "

"Really! And they are found around here?"

Meredith nodded. "Yes, Grace knew quite a lot about them."

"Really!"

"How old would you say?" Sol asked.

"I'm not sure, but old. Prehistoric times."

"How about that. Sea creatures."

"Yes, this whole area was once a great sea at one time, apparently. At least that's what Grace told me."

"How about that," Sol repeated.

They all three looked at the path in silence.

Sol stood up. "Well, I guess we need to get going." He took Maxine's hand and helped her up.

"Thanks for bringing the trunk out."

"No problem. There ought to be some interesting stuff in there, I think."

Meredith glanced at the trunk. "Yes, I'll have to go through it. "

"There's a letter in there to you from your mother. I forgot to mention it today, but I put it there with the other things so it wouldn't get lost."

Meredith froze. A high-pitched ringing like a warning siren sounded in her ears. *A letter?*

"Thank you," she managed to say. "I'll look for it."

"Call me if you have any questions on anything." Sol stepped off the porch.

Maxine put out her hand. "We look forward to seeing you at church real soon."

Meredith shifted her attention to Maxine and managed a smile. Her mind was whirling from learning about the letter. Dealing with Maxine was more than she could handle right now, but she still could feel the barriers going up as they stood there.

"I'll get your dolly back to you."

"No problem, take your time." Sol called back over his shoulder.

She watched as the Millers climbed into their truck and pulled away. Then, as they disappeared down the lane, Meredith turned back to look at the trunk, and an old lonely feeling wormed its way into her mind. She was an outsider here, and she always had been. What in the hell was she thinking, coming back? But she already knew the answer to her own question. She didn't have anywhere else to go. She had to make a go of it this time.

And now a letter, Audrey's last words. That would be like her mother, getting in one last round of lies and excuses that she would never have to defend. Meredith looked at the trunk. Hadn't they said it all long ago? She took a deep breath and forced it out slowly. *Not right now, Audrey. Not today.*

But the memories washed over her as she went back to sorting boxes, and it was 1953 again.

Meredith heard her grandmother calling her. How could she not? But she ignored her as long as she could. Even when her mother's voice chimed in from an upstairs window, she still sat in the hayloft with her knees drawn up, and her arms clamped around them, her jaw clenched. She didn't want to go in, didn't want to listen to all the same excuses and lies and promises.

"*Meredith Grace!*" *Grandmother was reaching the boiling point when she used her middle name. Meredith took a deep exasperated breath and climbed down the ladder.*

Her grandmother was standing on the back porch, arms akimbo. When she saw Meredith emerge from the barn, she turned and disappeared into the house. As Meredith followed her in, she could hear her mother on the stairs.

"*Mama, we go over this every time. I have to go. It's my job. She has to understand that. I don't have any control on where the airline sends me. You both know that.*"

"*Well, you need to tell her, Audrey. Don't just leave her hanging.*

Meredith could hear the suitcase bumping down the stairs. "*I will. I will. There was just no time to do it. I'll explain it when I get back. She'll understand. She isn't a baby anymore, you know. She's ten years old.*" *Her mother stopped on the last step when she saw Meredith in the hall.*

"*There you are darling! Come give me a kiss. I have to go.*" *She gathered her daughter into a hasty hug.* "*Now you be good and mind your grandmother, and I'll bring you back something wonderful from New York. What would you like?*"

"*I don't know.*"

"*Something special! Something none of these other girls around here have ever seen. Right? Oh, here's Charley.*" *Bye Mama, bye darling.*" *And she was gone. Out the door and into*

Charley Thompson's car, doors slamming and gravel spitting from under the tires. Meredith and Grace stood watching until the car disappeared from sight at the end of the lane.

Grace squeezed her shoulders. "Want some lemonade?"

Meredith followed her to the kitchen. "Did Momma say when she will be back?" She studied her grandmother's face carefully for any clues.

"No, she didn't." Grace busied herself with the lemonade.

"Usually she says," Meredith persisted, but Grace didn't respond. "Probably a week, do you think? She said New York." Still no response. Meredith took the glass she offered. "Aren't you having some?"

"Most certainly." Grace poured another glass and set the pitcher back in the ice box. They sat down at the table and silence closed in for a bit.

"So, you think about a week this time?"

Grace sat her glass down. "Honey, I don't know. I'm sure she'll come home as soon as she can. People are who they are, darling. She'll always come back to you."

"Why does Charley Thompson always drive her to Dallas?"

"Well, he's salesman from Dallas, and this is part of his territory. He's just nice enough to give your mother a ride when he can."

The girls at school asked me if he was Mama's boyfriend."

Grace's head snapped back as if she had been struck. "Don't listen to those silly girls, honey. Don't pay them any mind."

"Do you think Mama has a new boyfriend?"

"I don't know. Why ask that?"

"I don't know. Did you know my father?"

"No, remember, I never met him. Your parents were married during the war, and your father was killed before he could come here."

"In the war?"

"Yes. Grace hesitated. "You already know all this, honey."

Meredith ducked her head. "I know."

"How 'bout another glass?"

Meredith shook her head and pushed her empty glass away. "I think I'll go see about Mickey."

"Well, stay close to the house if you go riding, so you can hear me when I call."

Meredith let the screen slap shut behind her and jumped off the side of the porch. Something was wrong today. Something was different. She knew that much.

Mickey was lazing in her stall, but her ears perked up when Meredith entered the barn. "Hey girl. Want to go for a run?" She led the horse out of the stall and stepped up on a wooden crate to climb on bareback. Mickey sauntered out of the barn and stopped by the gate so Meredith could lean down to open it. Then they were gone. Slow at first, then a trot, and by the time they turned the corner at the water trough they were flying along; open prairie before them, wind in their hair. No worries, just sunshine.

After a short run, Mickey slowed to a walk. It was wonderful out here. Meredith could see for miles to the blue hills in the distance that marked the boundary of her family's land at one time. Thousands of acres, her grandmother said. Meredith looked back at the house. It looked stately from here. All white in the sunlight with the widow's walk perched on the top, so her grandfather could survey all of his land from there, her grandmother had explained. Her grandfather, she had never known him either. All the men in her life disappeared long ago, her grandfather, her father. Just faded photographs and someone else's memories.

She rode down to the creek on the north side of the pasture and let Mickey put her feet in. The silence was wonderful, just a soft breeze and the whisper of tires on the highway some distance away. Their land lay in a v shape with the house at the point and the pasture spreading out to the west, bounded on each side by a road. Roads to places she had never been. But someday she would go. She would stop sitting here waiting for her mother to come back, stop wondering what was over the rise. Someday.

The memory was as fresh as though it had just happened. Meredith shoved another empty box out of the way. Out the window she could see it was getting dark. Tomorrow was another day, as they say. She ate a little more of the ham and cheese from the fridge and headed up stairs.

Chapter 3

The first thought that crossed Meredith's mind the next morning was that she had to invest in some window shades. The light through the window next to the bed could not be denied. After the excitement of yesterday, she had just thrown her sleeping bag across Grace's bed and fallen immediately asleep. Now she shielded her eyes from the glare and studied the high ceiling above her. From this angle the room looked huge. The wallpaper was faded and water stained in spots, the same as the rest of the house. She sighed. She would have to live with the shabbiness for now. *You're on your own, kiddo.*

Darin's face flashed before her. *Lord what a mistake! Another mistake. Husband number four! How could she be so stupid again and again. He had seemed different, though, in the beginning. Sweet, attentive, brought her flowers for no reason. Her career was going well then, and he needed someone to take care of his life while he sorted himself out. God! How stupid!* She sat up suddenly and stormed off to the bathroom downstairs. *Never again!* She would never be suckered in by any more needy men. *Never! New page!*

She washed up quickly in the tiny bathroom, ate a little ham and bread, and headed back to tackle the pile in the hallway, carrying kitchen utensils and dishes to the kitchen and covering the tabletop in boxes. Computer and office files went to one side. She would decide all that later. Clothes she carted upstairs and stacked the bags in the bedroom. Midway through it all, she realized she had to make some decisions about the parlor and dining room, and the library. No telling what was in there! Pushing bags and boxes around from room to room was not progress.

At noon she finished off the last of her food stores and a cold bottle of water. She needed to fire up that old car out front and venture out to the store, but she wasn't looking forward to it. Of course, by dinnertime she knew she would regret not going. Stalling for time, she stared out the back door at the barn and corral. It looked more inviting than a trip to town. Might as well take a break and go check it out.

On the screened-in porch she discovered a treasure, a wooden rocker, sun faded but sturdy looking. She sat down for a moment, relaxing into its frame, and felt as though she had found an old friend. As a child she had read about a thousand books on this porch scrunched up in this old chair. Sitting in this friendly space, her optimistic side gained ground and gave her courage. She patted the arms of the chair. Check out the barn!

Birds fluttered up from the corral lot when she opened the gate and again when she lifted the latch on the barn door and swung it open. She hadn't been near this place since Mickey died. She could never bear the emptiness at the time. That horse had been her salvation in a lonely childhood. Now the place felt just as lonely, but welcoming in some way, like an old friend. In the hush she could hear mice scurrying about and birds fluttering in the hayloft above. Old ropes and halters still hung on pegs by the stalls. Again, this place was a time capsule where nothing had moved for forty or fifty years. Well, something maybe. There was a utility vehicle of some sort at the back of the area. Someone had been here. She walked back to inspect it. Not her mother's, for heaven's sake. She couldn't imagine Audrey ever even venturing out the back door of the house, much less getting on one of these 4wheeler things. Maybe someone had rented the barn and pasture at one time.

She swung the door back to the tack room and let her eyes adjust to the darkness. A saddle was hanging by a rope in one corner. Her grandfather's, she remembered. It had always been there. She saw that first, but then the rest of the room came into focus. The place was stacked with cardboard boxes. She also recognized a small table that had sat by Grace's bed. There were four wooden chairs stacked on top of each other, a small bookcase, and a pile of wooden crates, a jumble of them. A gold mine!

She started untangling legs and corners and hauling pieces out into the light. They were covered in cobwebs and dust, and badly in need of paint, but she could fix that. Yes, this could be done! She lifted a corner of one of the wooden crates. It contained framed pictures. Gracious! These need to be in the house. The heat would destroy them. She flipped carefully through the crate. They were the pictures she remembered that her grandmother had displayed in the parlor. A collection of family pictures, Grace as a young mother holding her daughter, and another one was large portrait of her grandfather. Also, a newer picture of her grandmother and her at her college graduation.

And one of her paintings! She stopped in astonishment. "My Heavens!" Grace had kept this all these years! It was a watercolor she had done when she was about four or so. Her grandmother had covered a tabletop with newspaper out on the back porch and then covered her up with in an old work shirt. She laid out paper and watercolors and a glass of water. The memory brought tears to Meredith's eyes. Painting had been one of her favorite activities. and her grandmother always encouraged her. Grace had sketched out a big pot of flowers that day for her to color in, and somehow she had managed not to dribble paint everywhere. Meredith looked over her efforts from seventy years ago and smiled. The painting really was quite good, actually. Grace had made over it a lot and whisked it away so she couldn't keep adding more paint to it, she said later. Then she framed it, and it had hung proudly in the parlor all the years after that. Meredith smiled through her tears.

The crate was too heavy for her to lift so she carefully pulled out the framed pictures and carried them inside. The cardboard boxes she ignored. They were probably just old magazines or something. Grace tended to save those for some reason.

The rest of the day was spent wiping off the chairs and tables and wrestling them in the back door. The chairs went in the kitchen. She did struggle up the stairs with the bedside table and set her desk lamp on it, and even rigged a blanket across the windows to blot out the next sunrise. Next, she dragged the mattress off the bed and attempted to give it a good beating; actually a fairly futile endeavor. Then she dragged it back, flipped it over and put on sheets. She was exhausted by the time she was finished, but at least tonight she would sleep in a normal bed.

Meredith heard the crunch of gravel as a car rolled up out front. Interesting. After living in cities for the past fifty years surrounded by noise, now, all of a sudden, a single car door slam could get her attention, because here in the country, the company had to be for her. Out the bedroom window she looked down on an older looking women getting out of a car, no one familiar. She went down to the front door and watched her come up the walk.

The woman stopped to catch her breath on the top step and flashed a big smile. "Hello Meredith."

"Amy?" That smile. It had to be her.

"Well, at least you recognized me." The woman laughed. "I've changed so much ..."

Meredith reached out and grabbed her in a big hug. "Amy Warren. My heavens! It's so good to see you!" She held her out at arm's length and then hugged her again.

Amy was laughing and trying to catch her breath all at the same time.

"Come on in. Come in." Meredith pulled her in the door. "I didn't know you were here. This is wonderful?"

"Five years now", Amy managed to get out. "I moved back after my husband died." She paused and studied Meredith's face. "My lord, I'd know you anywhere girl. You haven't changed a bit." She pushed at her shoulder. "You haven't even gained weight. I hate you!"

They both dissolved into laughter.

"You look good, yourself. Come on back to the kitchen. It's a mess, but there's chairs back there. How did you find me?"

"Are you kidding? In Troubadour? Word is out all over. Anytime our population goes up, it's news."

"How about some cold water? That's all I've got to offer right now"

"Wonderful."

"Let's take it out to the back porch. It's cooler out there." Cradling the water bottles, Meredith dragged a kitchen chair behind her and directed Amy to the rocker. "I'm so glad to see you! What's it been? Forty years? Fifty?"

Amy grimaced. "Fifty or so I'm afraid. Right after graduation?"

They both took a deep breath and shook their heads.

"So," Amy clapped her hands together. "We have some catching up to do."

"I would think so. You go first." Meredith handed her the water bottle.

"No, I think it's going to take a long time to do all this. I've got a better idea." Amy patted her arm. What are you doing for dinner tonight?"

"Not a thing planned. In fact, I'm out of food. I fiddled around all day today and never got to the store."

"Okay then, I'm taking you out to dinner as a welcome home. What do you think?"

Meredith looked down at her work clothes, cobwebs and all. "Not like this."

"Then do what you have to do, girl." She motioned with her bottle of water. "I'll be right here."

Between rushing to change and getting to the café, there wasn't much conversation. Meredith was still in a daze over Amy's arrival. Her dearest friend in her memory, Amy was her only close girlfriend in high school. What a breath of fresh air. It felt as though no time had passed. They could still be sixteen and going out for a burger. After all her uncertainty about coming home, this was a wonderful gift.

They ordered. It was a tiny little Italian place. Something different for Troubadour, Meredith was thinking, but welcome. Amy produced a bottle of wine from her purse, and the waitress brought glasses. Yes, things had changed. They laughed about the relaxed morals as they ordered.

"So," Amy took a deep breath. "Fifty years, my friend."

Meredith shook her head. "Doesn't seem possible, does it?"

Amy raised her eyebrows. "Only when I look in the mirror." She poured the wine. "So where have you been all these years?"

Meredith hesitated. Was she up to all this? Spilling details?

"Or would you rather I go first? "Amy ducked her head and peered over her glasses.

"You go first." Meredith agreed. "Last I heard you were in Dallas."

"Yes, let's see. I was at SMU. Dropped out after my sophomore year and got married." She rolled her eyes. "Trenton Howard. He had graduated and gotten a job in Seattle, and I couldn't bear to let him go. We packed all our possessions in the back of his Chevy and struck out West. Then the twins were born; boys, and I got busy being a mother. Three years later our daughter came along" She paused. "What else to say? It all just rushed by. I went back to college when the kids were all in school. Trent encouraged me. I finished my art history degree and went to work as an assistant director of a small museum. Great fun, not too demanding. Got to do some traveling over the years."

The waitress brought their food, and they were distracted for a bit, commenting on the food between bites.

"So, you've been in Seattle this whole time?"

"Until Trent retired. We opted for drier climes and moved to Prescott Arizona, a wonderful place. I thought we were settled, but after four years Trent died suddenly; massive heart attack, they told me. He had never had any warning that I knew about. He was on the golf course and just collapsed."

"I'm so sorry."

Amy shrugged. "It would have been what he wanted, I guess. No warning, no pain, doing something he loved. But it threw me for a loop, I can tell you. I wandered around the house peering out windows. Almost fifty years of my life were built around that man, and I had no idea what to do next. The kids were great, but they have their own lives, and they are scattered all over. My daughter, Julia and her family live in New Jersey. She's a doctor, and her husband is a lawyer. They have two children. The twins are doing their own thing. Brad is career navy. He's been in Hawaii for the last three years, and who knows where next. Bart is a lawyer in Idaho. He and his wife are into the great outdoors and skiing."

She took a sip of wine. "For two years I hung on in Arizona, feeling like a fish out of water. Extra woman at all the events and dinners, and I hadn't lived there long enough to feel connected to the place. So, five years ago I made the big decision to come home. I inherited Mom and Dad's house after they passed away, and it had just been sitting here rented out for years. It's been good here. I'm a Texas girl, it seems. Sprinkling of old friends, lots of new ones.

"Trent sounds like a wonderful person."

Amy smiled. "He was. Oh, he was about as difficult as most men, I guess." She laughed softly. "An A type personality, always in charge, but he was great company, always up for an adventure. We traveled a lot, and he was the rock of Gibraltar when you needed him. I've got to tell you, my world has been thrown into a spin for the last five years, but you know, you must move on. That's what he would be saying if he were here. So here I am."

The waitress came back to ask if everything was okay. They were about the only customers left in the place, and she seemed disappointed that they didn't need anything.

"Your mother was living here when I first moved back," Amy said.

"Yes, she moved back here after Grace died."

"Actually, I think your mom died the year I came back. There was some talk about it. She was a recluse, I think. Stayed isolated, I believe everyone said. But you weren't involved with her?"

Meredith didn't answer for a few minutes. Was it time? If she could tell anyone in the world, it would be Amy.

"Not in several years." Meredith shifted in her chair. "You know, my mother always vowed that she would pay for my college. That was her first excuse for working away from here and traveling all the time. She was going to take care of me. Save me from this life in Troubadour." She paused again. "But after I got accepted for college, her story changed. She had had some financial setbacks, and she just couldn't afford to help out, she told me. But, she promised, she would contribute as much as she could.".

Meredith paused to set her glass down. "My grandmother told her she understood. She would take care of it all. And after Audrey left, Grace hugged me and told me not to worry. She said she had never fully believed Audrey would come through on the college promise anyway. She said she had been saving for just this moment and not to worry. I was just to concentrate on school. It wasn't much of a shock for me either. I guess I just knew to never count on my mother for anything." Meredith took a deep breath and continued.

"College was like a dream come true. A new life, a whirlwind of new people. The dorm was huge. Everything seemed huge compared to Troubadour."

Amy nodded her head in agreement, and Meredith went on. "There was always someone to walk to class with, talk to, eat with. In those first weeks we spent hours with all the girls on our floor getting acquainted, long talks into the night. Where was everyone from? What were their majors, their dreams? Everyone seemed as excited and anxious as I was.

My roommate, Mary, was from Houston and said she was planning to major in law. She wanted to be a lawyer like her father. I told her I had thought about law, but I was thinking I wanted to write, so I was going for journalism."

"She asked me what my father did, and I told her that he was killed in the war, but that my mother was an airline stewardess. That she had always traveled, and I was raised by my grandmother."

Meredith paused again. "Mary said that her mother had entertained the idea of being a stewardess herself and had even gone through the initial training, but then she had met Mary's father and they wanted to marry and have a family. Since the airlines wouldn't hire married girls and people with children, her mom opted out." Meredith held up her hands. "I froze as her words hung in the air. Some other girl spoke up and said her mother always wanted to go to college, but she didn't get the chance. She was the first in her family to ... then I interrupted. I asked, "Wait a moment. What was that you said? The group stopped and stared at me."

"What did you say about the airlines?"

"The airlines?"

"Yes, that they only hire single women with no children? Is that true?"

"Mary said, yes, that's what she understand. She glanced around at the group.

They were all staring at me with a puzzled expression."

"Some other girl spoke up and said her mother was a teacher, and she wanted to be anything but! The group laughed at that, and someone took exception to it and said she had always wanted to teach. And the conversation tumbled on with laughter and confessions of ambition and joy."

"I just sat there frozen in silence as the conversation flowed around me 'No children' was ringing in my ears. Was that true? How could my mother. . .?"

"For days, the questions hung on in my mind. I could hardly think of anything else. And, as fate would have it, Audrey showed up that weekend, out of the blue. She was in town and just wanted to check on me, she said. She was wrapped in her whirl of importance, as usual. In a new car this time, dressed to the nines, charming a swath of people everywhere she went. I hung back and waited for a chance to ask my questions. It was late in the day, over dinner, just the two of us, that I was able to bring it up."

"I said that my roommate told me her mother wanted to be an airline stewardess like her at one time."

"Audrey gave me a smug smile and said, well, lots of girls do. It's a coveted career. But I hope you will choose something else, dear. There are so many more avenues for women now."

"I told her that the girl said her mother dropped out because the airlines wouldn't hire married women with children."

"Audrey straightened her posture and grew serious. She said, yes, yes that was true twenty years ago. She was a widow, so that was not a problem, and that I didn't live with her, so…"

"So, you just told them you had no children?"

"She took some time to answer. Finally, she said, *honey, you have to understand the situation. At the time the only jobs available were factory jobs or lowly office jobs. The pay was terrible. Airline stewardess was a sought-after position. Better pay. I took it so that I could provide better for you.*"

"And in all these years, none of your friends or co-workers have known about me? I said. As far as your life is concerned, the minute you walked out of Grace's house, I didn't exist?"

Meredith shrugged her shoulders. "Of course she tried to justify it all. She said *don't say it like that. Of course you existed. I did what I had to do,* was her excuse."

"I said, had to do for who, Mother?"

"Then she got defensive. Said she wouldn't be browbeaten over this. That she had worked and saved to give me a better life."

"I just sat there staring at her. My mind was whirling."

"I did it for you darling, she said. It was so hard losing your father. I was all alone. I couldn't just crawl back to

Troubadour and take some piddly job. And then the tears started."

"I told her to stop it. I wasn't Grace. The tears wouldn't work. I got up and walked out of the restaurant and back to my dorm. I didn't see her again for three years. I told Grace about the airline when I saw her. She listened silently, and then she simply gathered me into her arms. We never spoke of it again."

They sat in silence for a bit. After a few minutes, Amy spoke. "I'm so sorry, Meredith."

Meredith shrugged. "No problem. That was just the way it was. She didn't need me, and I didn't need her. End of story."

"So, you never had contact again?"

"Oh, she showed up at my graduation, and later when I married the second time." Meredith said. "Same old thing, all show, desperate to impress everyone. After that I didn't see her again until after Grace died, but that's another story. Not for now." She waved her hand. "Moving on?"

Amy nodded. "So, do you have any children?"

Meredith took a deep breath and smiled. "Yes, one, a girl, Rachel. She's great. In fact, she's the only thing I've ever done right in my whole life." Amy laughed, but Meredith just smiled.

"That's great. Kids are great." Amy seemed to skip over the "in my whole life" part. "Any grandchildren?"

"Again, one, Rachel has a girl, Angela. She isn't a child anymore, of course. In fact, she just graduated from college."

"So you are divorced? Widowed?

"Oh honey, I am the poster child for divorce." Meredith laughed. "You have no idea."

"Okay, this is going to be good. I can tell." Amy reached to refill their wine glasses.

Meredith watched her pour. *What should she say?* "Well, let's see. Where was I?"

"College," Amy directed.

"Yes, college. University of Texas. Journalism major; graduated in three years, going year round, then tackled graduate school. The last thing I wanted to do was come back here in the summer. Along the way I fell madly in love with one of my professors. Scandal, scandal, scandal." She made quotation marks in the air, and Amy laughed.

Meredith continued. "I thought he was brilliant, and unfortunately, so did he. We were into the protest scene, you know, the 60's. He got a job offer, he told me, in California and begged me to go with him. So, I threw a plan for graduate school to the winds and hopped into a VW van with Bentley. That was his name, Bentley Morrison, if you can believe it, and three total strangers."

"A VW van?"

"I know, sounds like a bad movie plot." Meredith rolled her eyes. "I was in my rebellious period."

Amy smiled. "So, California in the 60's. What could go wrong, right?"

Meredith nodded, "And it did."

The lights flickered, and they realized the manager was turning off the open sign.

"That's a signal, I do believe," Amy whispered.

They paid and scurried out as he locked the door behind them.

"There's a Jiffy Mart place out on the highway where you can get some breakfast stuff if you want. You said you were out of everything."

"If you don't mind, that would be great."

"No problem. "

They never got back to her story. Meredith collected a few items to stave off hunger for tomorrow, and Amy drove her home.

"I hate to miss the rest of your saga, but I'm volunteering at the hospital in the morning bright and early, so we'll have to continue this at another time."

"And I've got all my projects to tackle again. This has been great fun. Thank you so much for the dinner and for tracking me down."

"You're welcome. Here's my cell number, and you remember where the house is, I'm sure. We'll do this again, real soon. Let's touch base on Friday.

"Most definitely."

Meredith picked her way across the yard and up to the front door by the car headlights. It took a moment to get the key in the lock since she had not thought to leave the front porch light on. She turned to wave once more to Amy and watched her turn her car and drive away. That was the closest she had ever come to telling her story to anyone, she thought, but maybe it was time. All these years she had spent listening to someone else pour out their tales. Maybe she needed to listen to her own.

Chapter 4

Meredith relocked the door behind her and felt her way over to the light string. She would have to remember to bring a flashlight The yard had been pretty dark to navigate, and she was accustomed to streetlights.

She made her way down the hall toward the darkened kitchen and switched on another light, but even then, the overhead bulb dangling from a single wire gave out only a filtered yellow glow. Life out in the country was surely different. She retrieved a bottle of water from the fridge on her way out to her rocker on the back porch and snuggled down in the chair. There was only a quarter moon tonight, and the faint glow lay over the land like a velvet spread. She took a deep breath and gave the old chair a gentle push with her toe. It squeaked a little as it rocked, an old familiar sound.

Her story. She wasn't sure she wanted to tell it, not even to Amy. Compared to her life, her old friend had followed the straight and narrow. She might not be ready for all her adventures. And it was a long time ago, ancient history, fifty years. She was a different person now.

But when she let herself give into it, she could still remember, sharp as a shard of glass.

Audrey turned up like a bad penny for graduation. They had not seen one another in three years. For that occasion, Audrey had her mother in tow, driving a brand new Cadillac, dropping hints about her latest love and how wealthy he was. As usual she charmed everyone she met. Grace had watched her daughter's antics with a stoic gaze, but Meredith hung back in a black rage watching her mother work the room. Her friends were always totally dazzled by Audrey. Then she zoomed away leaving Meredith to listen to how wonderful her mother was, how lucky she was, how much she was like her. It was all or nothing with Audrey. People either bought her bull shit and adored her or stood in awe and judgement of her like the people of Troubadour, Texas, then whispered about her behind her back. Either way, Meredith thought, she was always left in her dust to absorb the aftershock.

Audrey gave hugs and kisses. She was so proud of her, she said. She wanted to make amends. After all, Meredith was an adult now, and that was what she had apparently been waiting for all those years. She was being assigned to Paris for a year, she said, but when she came back, she hoped they could spend some time together. And then, she was gone again, leaving a big void where she had been.

When Bentley sailed in with his California idea, she was ripe for it. No more being left behind, no more waiting.

That miserable trip out west, wedged in with total strangers who, it turned out, were continually mellowed out on marijuana. And crammed into that airless van with all that smoke, lord, after a few hours of that she was as stoned as the rest of them. The driver, Yellow Jade, he called himself. He was wiped out as well, driving along in a blur. It was a wonder they weren't killed, or at least stopped by the highway patrol. The major shock, though, was Bentley. He seemed to instantly fall in with them; smoking weed like a maniac and teasing her because she declined. She should have jumped out at the first stop light, but of course she didn't. From time to time over the years, in a rush of self-pity, she had blamed it all on her mother. She would never have gone if she had not been so angry with her mother. She would never have listened to Bentley. But even, after all these years, she knew it wasn't true. She would have gone no matter what her mother had done. She was so in love, or something she imagined was love. Later she realized that Bentley offered her an anchor in a life where she had always felt alone. And then when he failed her, she felt as if it were her fault. That it was just as she had always suspected. She wasn't worthy of love. Meredith shook her head in disgust, even now. But at the time she grabbed the chance.

"It's a ride to California", Bentley had whispered. "We'll be free of them when we get there. "Just play along, babe."

The heat began to build in the van even with all the windows down. By the time they reached El Paso she was queasy from car sickness and the smell of burned rope. They stopped at a station to fill up, and it was a chance to escape the cramped quarters and breathe in some clean air. Bentley hovered over her whispering in her ear. "Just be cool, babe."

Yellow Jade, it turned out, had only the van and nothing else. He waited, as everyone chipped in for the gas with the station attendant standing there staring at them. The other two passengers, two anemic girls in skimpy hip-huggers and halter tops, came up with two dollars between them, so she and Bentley made up the rest.

Where Bentley had found Jade and the others he never explained, but as soon as the girls sobered up and started talking it was clear they were not college students, not even college material. She and Bentley were more like ancient senior citizens to them. *Then their stash of marijuana ran low, and the trip went downhill from there.*

Meredith took a sip of water and smiled. *But Lordy, Bentley was a hunk. With dark expressive eyes and black curly hair that was just a little too long, he looked like an 18th century poet. She was head over heels in love, and he could do no wrong in the beginning. The fact that he was an anarchist totally escaped her. He could see the hypocrisy of it all, he said, the chase after the almighty dollar, the greed of the ruling class. The future would be different, he declared, and she believed him. She believed every socialist platitude out of his mouth. Meredith always pictured her mother when he talked about the greed. Audrey was all about the money. That was all that mattered. The best of everything; clothes, jewelry, name dropping about all the places she had been, all the places she was going, all the wealthy people she knew. And all delivered in that phony southern drawl she adopted when she was center stage.*

On the rest of the California trip, she and Bentley bought the gas. At first the others apologized and thanked them profusely, but by the time they reached LA their payment was expected and forgotten, and they were even demanding food money. To say that she had soured on the adventure would be way understated, but Bentley, bless his heart, was all in. Jade and his minions hovered around him listening to Bentley prattle on about breaking free of the chains that society had forced on them, and the eternal search for self, blah, blah, blah. If Bentley were just playing along, he should have gotten an Oscar, she was thinking.

By the time they reached San Francisco she was firmly planted on the outside of the little party, just anxious to break free of them and hoping that Bentley would come to his senses. And he seemed to at first. They parted ways with Yellow Jade and his merry band and waded off into the Bay City.

Bentley, it turned out, did not have a job offer as he had said, but he did have a job interview, and she went knocking on doors for a journalist position. They found a small apartment with way too many steps to climb. Bentley was himself again; sober. She found work with a local community magazine, so they at least had an income, a small one. Bentley was sure he had the professorship at Berkeley locked in. There was just a long screening process he explained. They settled into domestic life, and she had never been happier.

It was 1965 and San Francisco was exploding with energy. Flower Power, street marches, rock bands, lazy days by the bay on weekends. They got married on a whim, in one of those mass weddings in Lincoln Park. Bentley was totally depressed over being turned down by Berkeley. He was lost, he said; he needed her so. He was floating on a cloud of marijuana along with the rest of the crowd, and she was also, due to the second-hand smoke. Anyway, that was her excuse later. And the fuzzy headed guru who performed the ceremony probably wasn't even legal, but she counted it as marriage. Those were the days before the dark times began.

Meredith took in a deep breath and glanced around the porch. Something caught her eye at the screen door. A yellow tabby tom cat was peeking in from the back step. Meredith got up slowly so as not to scare it away. The cat dodged back just enough to allow the screen to open, but he didn't leave the porch. He stared at Meredith as if he was sizing her up.

"Hello, there" Meredith whispered.

The cat sniffed at the opening, then tiptoed through and surveyed the porch. Meredith backed up slowly and sat down in the rocker, as the cat took a cautious tour around the area.

"You want a drink?" Meredith whispered. She slipped off to the kitchen and returned with a saucer. The cat was waiting on her when she returned, craning his head toward the kitchen. She poured some of her water in the saucer and set it down. The cat inched over to sniff it, then drank, his tiny pink tongue flicking in and out of his mouth. Meredith retreated to the rocker and curled her feet up again. She loved cats, their independence and dignity.

"So where do you live, fella?" But the cat took no notice. He finished his drinking and lay down, his paws curled under. Meredith watched for a bit, expecting, she wasn't sure what, but unconcerned with her, the cat stared out the back screen and his eyelids fluttered slightly as he dozed off, contented as could be.

And so did Meredith for a short time before her back started to ache and her foot fell asleep. She started, causing the chair to squeak and the cat stirred, but only slightly. A breeze had come up on the night air that made her hug her arms to her chest. She rose and stretched her back. Time to turn in; she had been out here for hours now. She opened the screen door to let her visitor leave, but he just stared at her. Then when she gave up and headed to the kitchen, he rose and followed. Meredith turned, and the cat stopped and gazed up at her with an expectant look.

"So, you are moving in?"

Meredith went down the hall and up the stairs, glancing back now and then, and the cat followed at a discrete distance. She changed into her gown as the cat explored the room, nosing into the corners. Then she snuggled under the covers and switched off the light, and after a moment she felt the cat leap lightly on the foot of the bed and lay down. In moments, they were both asleep.

Chapter 5

Meredith awoke early the next morning with the help of the sun and looked first at the foot of the bed, but her visitor was gone, and a niggle of disappointment flashed through her mind. She took a quick look around the room and under the bed, but he was nowhere. The room felt slightly chilly, she noted. Maybe Fall was finally here. She pulled on some light sweats and went down to search the first floor. Unless the little guy had grown opposable thumbs he was still in the house somewhere. However, it was a short search. The cat was lounging gracefully on the kitchen floor soaking up a patch of sunshine from the window. He rose when she walked in and sauntered slowly to the back door as though he had been patiently waiting for her.

"So, this is it? You're leaving now?" Meredith opened the door and then the screen off the porch, and without a glance back, the cat slipped out. She watched him disappear around the corner of the house. *The truth is out. I'm just a one night stand, I guess.* She smiled and went searching for breakfast.

Okay, day three. She took a deep breath. So, what to tackle today, paint? That might be a good place to start. Fix up the furniture before she unpacked anything else. Then she thought of the car, and a trickle of dread fell over her shoulders. That noisy junker sat out front as a sort of statement about her whole situation, but maybe the poor thing has rested now, her positive side argued. It will be fine. She retrieved her purse from the bedroom and went out to confront the beast.

The car started right up, just as it had at that shabby car lot when she purchased it. Little miracles. She backed away from the yard fence in a half circle with the steering whining all the way and headed down the lane. By one of the mobile homes a tall young man was bending over under the hood of a pick-up. He straightened when he heard her pass and waved. She waved back.

By the time she reached the town square, however, the engine was knocking badly. She found a parking place in front of the First National Bank building and turned off the key.

Yep, there it was again; rattle, clatter, cough, and this time there were people around. Embarrassing. She shoved her door open to its familiar groan and marched into the bank with all the dignity she could muster as the car clattered on behind her.

The girl at the teller window glanced up at her, then did a double take at an unfamiliar face.

Meredith smiled. "Good morning."

"Good morning."

"I would like to open a new account, please."

The girl blinked her eyes in surprise, but then her professional training kicked in. "Certainly. Welcome to the First National." She pushed a paper through the teller window. "You can just fill out this form. There's a pen on the table there." She pointed behind Meredith. "Then, when you are finished, you can take it to Mr. Higgins in that first office there." She pointed again.

"Thank you."

As she walked to the table, Meredith glanced around to see what seemed like every pair of eyes in the place trained on her. Stranger alert. She concentrated on filling out the form and gradually the hushed noise of normal activity returned. Form in hand, she looked up to locate the Mr. Higgins that the girl had mentioned. A young man in a crisp white shirt and conservative tie sat at a desk in a glass fronted cubicle with a Mr. Higgins sign on display. He was working at something, but he looked up when she walked in.

New account?" He rose and extended his hand.

Meredith nodded.

"I heard you across the way." He gestured toward the teller. "Small room." He explained and smiled. "So, have you just moved to Troubadour?"

"Yes," Meredith sat down "Well, I've moved back, I should say. I grew up here."

"Oh, welcome back." He glanced down at the form. " Meredith Grace Bannon. I'm not familiar with this address."

"It's the old Durham house, just west of town."

The man's eyebrows went up. "Yes. That's a grand old place, but it's been vacant for years."

"Well, not anymore." Meredith smiled. "I'm back."

"I see. Is it your family home?"

She nodded. "My grandmother's house, Grace Durham"

A shake of his head. "I'm a newcomer here so I don't know everyone." He explained. "About ten years now, but I think it takes a few more years than that to be considered a local."

"About forty probably." They laughed together.

"Is Lucas Carter still with the bank?"

"Yes. He's the President. Do you know him?"

"He is the executor of my grandmother's estate. I think I need to talk to him.

"Yes, of course. But I'm afraid he's not here right now. He's on vacation for the next two weeks."

"Oh, I see. Well, that makes a difference, I guess."

"All right, we can get you fixed up here. He started typing at his computer. "Are there any other names to be added to this account?"

She shook her head.

"Any direct deposits?"

Meredith placed her social security card, driver's license, and retirement account info on his desk. He began typing the information in. "Any automatic drafts against the account?"

She shook her head again. After a bit the printer hummed to life and he turned to retrieve the sheets. "Now if you'll just read over this and check the numbers at the spots I've marked."

She compared the numbers and signed.

"That's about it. Your checks will be here in about ten days. You can drop by and pick them up. What sort of deposit do you want to make today?"

She pulled out her manila envelope, took out some hundred dollars bills and slide the rest across to him. "There should be seven hundred dollars there."

He counted the money out between them, then typed the amount into the computer and hit the print button again. "Very good. Welcome to the First National family. You're in good company. Here are a few blank drafts you can use until your checks arrive. You might check back on the days you expect any deposits to be made in the beginning just to be sure that everything is working properly." He rose to shake her hand.

"Thank you." As she walked out, no one turned to stare. She relaxed and took a deep breath. It was going to be fine. Step one accomplished. Now, paint.

The True Value store was just next door. Her entrance got the same reaction as the bank. The scattered customers were friendly but curious at encountering a strange face. Meredith studied the color charts a while, endless choices. Then she decided what the heck, *'it's only paint'*. She settled on three colors, several brushes and paint pans, a drop cloth, paint thinner; quite a pile by the time she was through.

The girl at the checkout met her with a smile, a little shy perhaps, wary of a stranger. "Looks like an interesting project," she offered.

"Either that or a disaster," Meredith confided, and they laughed together.

Step two completed. Step three was the grocery store. She locked her purchases in the trunk of the beast and walked down the street past several empty store fronts. She remembered this square as buzzing with life. Now the empty buildings stood out like missing teeth. The grocery was something familiar, but inside the bustle of customers that she remembered was gone. No familiar faces greeted her, but of course not. That was over fifty years ago! She collected some cleaning products and a stack of frozen dinners. Cooking could come later. Back at the beast she climbed in with the same silent prayer as before and gloriously, it started right up. Of course, the engine knock was worse, but it was moving.

The young man was still working on his truck when she passed his trailer. He raised his head and waved again when he heard her car sputtering by. She waved back, a sort of an apologetic wave. *The car noise must be bothering him.* She stopped at the front gate with the usual complaints from the car and carried her groceries in, then came back for the paint supplies. As she stepped off the porch, she realized the young man from down the lane was walking up to her gate.

"Sounds like you have a problem, ma'am." He nodded toward the car.

"More than one, I'm guessing"

He smiled. "If you'll start it up, I'll take a look at it for you?"

"Oh, sure, certainly." She fished the keys out of her pocket and cranked the engine. After a few gasps and gurgles it started.

The hood gave out a groan when he raised it and propped it up. "Sounds like your carburetor or your fuel pump." He leaned over the engine and wiggled a few hoses.

"How serious is that?"

"Not so much." He straightened and pulled a grease rag out of his back pocket to wipe his hands.

"Not so much as in cheap to fix?"

He laughed. "You can cut it off now."

She followed his directions, and when she was out of the car, they shook hands.

"I'm Daniel Porter." He had an open friendly smile.

"Meredith Bannon."

"I wanted to meet you, and this car seemed a good excuse." He gestured toward the car. "Looks like you are moving in here."

"Yes, I am. This was my grandmother's place." She glanced at the house. "I grew up here."

"Lucky you." He smiled again. "I'm in that mobile home down there." He pointed over his shoulder.

"Yes, I saw you there."

"So, if this is your house, I guess you're the one I need to talk to"

Meredith frowned, puzzled at where the conversation was going.

"If you've been out to your barn, you've seen my 4wheeler."

"Oh! Yes. I wondered who that belong to."

"Well, I'm trespassing. No one was around to ask, so I just took a chance. I wanted to get it in out of the weather."

"No problem at all. I'm not using the space."

"So, when I heard your car, I was thinking I'd trade you some engine work to pay my rent."

"No, no that's not necessary, I. . . ."

"I'd feel a lot better if you'd say yes. Ease my guilty conscience for trespassing. You buy the parts, and I'll do the work."

Meredith hesitated. "Well, that would be awfully nice of you."

He smiled broadly. "My pleasure. I love old cars. How long have you had it?"

"Four days." Meredith smiled at the look that appeared on his face. She did love surprising people. "It's a long story."

"Ah." He looked back at the car sitting there covered with nicked paint, but he was too polite to ask any more questions.

Meredith liked that. "I just opened an account here, and I don't have much in it yet. Could we do this after my next deposit comes in?"

"Sure. Whenever. Or, I could go get the parts and get started, and then you could pay me back. How does that sound?"

"I suppose so, if you trust me."

"Well, I'll have your car, and I know where you live, so I think you're a safe bet." He gave her a sideways smile.

"Okay then. You will really be helping me out. Every time I drive it, I think it is the last."

"Okay. I've got the make and model, so I'll go get a few parts. Probably can't go wrong on most anything." He raised his eyebrows in fake surprise.

Meredith laughed. "Yes, I'm sure you are right about that."

"If you could move it down to my place, I've got my tools down there."

"I've got some things in the trunk. I'll come down in a bit if that's okay."

Daniel nodded and started to walk away.

"Are you truly a mechanic?"

"Shade tree variety." He looked back and smiled

"So, you don't have to be at work anywhere?"

"Self-employed."

"Ah."

She watched him depart down the lane. Self-employed. Yes, she had heard that one before. Self-employed just meant he had figured out a way to get out of working for a living.

Warning bells were going off in her head. Still, if he could get this thing running better.

She carried in her painting supplies and drove the car down to his trailer. He was still out front by his truck. He motioned where he wanted her to park the car, and she pulled in near a tall mesquite.

"See, I told you." He pointed up. "Shade tree."

Meredith handed him the keys. "How long do you think this will take?"

Daniel laughed. "Well, ..."

"You're right. I shouldn't ask yet." She took a deep breath. "Well, good luck."

"I won't tackle anything too expensive, I promise; just the basics to see if I can get it running better for you. I'll let you know."

Meredith walked back toward the house with mixed emotions. Either she had stumbled on to a wonderful streak of luck, or she had just placed herself in the hands of a charming loser one more time. Probably in his twenties, he could be her grandson, and all the time she was talking to him she kept thinking he reminded her of Bentley Morrison. Same jet-black hair and expressive eyes, and probably just as full of himself. She smiled at that thought. Her daughter would have all sorts of warning remarks to make if she were here. She was the cautious one, her rock, more like her great-grandmother Grace in many ways. After watching her fumble her life away all these years, Rachel had, thankfully, taken the opposite path. But what could it hurt? The young man seemed nice enough, and if he could keep that old car running for a little longer it would certainly help.

Chapter 6

When Meredith got back to the house her intention was to change clothes and tackle the painting project, but as she stopped in the front hall to gather up her paint supplies, Grace's trunk caught her eye. She had left it sitting in the corner of the parlor, bungee cords and all. Now it stared up at her with a silent rebuke.

The trunk was one thing. Meredith remembered many happy hours as a child carefully going through its contents, listening to Grace explain what things were, where she had gotten them, why she had saved them. As a little girl she had never tired of the stories. In a life with so few anchors and a mother that appeared and disappeared without warning, those objects and stories and old photographs were a comfort. It gave her connections to the people stored away there and provided her with family beyond her grandmother. The trunk revived fond memories. It was the letter from her mother that had kept her from lifting that lid. Reading that letter was going to tear open some very old wounds, she was sure.

"Not today," she said out loud as though the trunk itself could understand her. She scooped up her painting supplies and carried them out to the front porch. She would tackle the chairs first. She had picked a royal blue color for them. She turned the chairs upside down on the drop cloth, and got to work.

It had been a long time since she had done any painting. Actually, since she had helped Grace with a project in this very house. Yes, it was the summer of her twelfth birthday. She had wanted to redecorate her bedroom, and Grace had made that her birthday present. They repainted all her bedroom furniture and her grandmother had sewn a new bedspread and curtains. Meredith smiled to herself. That was a good time. Good until her mother showed up. Audrey always brought a crisis with her.

It was 1955, she remembered.

Audrey was driving a new Buick when she rolled to a stop at the gate. She and her grandmother both looked up when they heard the car. Audrey in all her fashionable glory popped out and waved. "Hello there!"

Grace laid her brush down and straightened up slowly. "Hello."

Audrey rushed through the gate and gathered hugs and kisses. "My goodness, Meredith, you have grown!" She held her out at arm's length. "Have you put on more weight? I hope these outfits I brought you will fit."

Meredith made no response.

"My, I'm about to perish from thirst. Do you have any cold water in there, Mama?"

Audrey disappeared into the house, and Meredith and Grace exchanged a look. She's back, they were thinking. Grace followed her daughter in, but reluctant to be drawn into her mother's drama, Meredith stayed on the porch. From a distance she could not make out the conversation. It was just mumbled voices at first, but as the argument began, she could hear her mother loud and clear.

"Well, I didn't mean anything by it, Mama. For heaven's sake, you are so touchy."

Mumbled voice.

"Of course, she's fine. I just don't want her to get too heavy like a lot of these girls around here. She'll be stuck here for the rest of her life if ..."

Grace's voice grew stronger, but still unclear.

Audrey drowned her out, "Fine! Let's just drop it. I came down to spend some time with you. Let's don't spend it fighting."

Grace spoke again, but it was still too low to understand.

"Till Saturday. I can't stay long. I just wanted to be here for Meredith's birthday...... Well, I can't just drop everything and come all the time. I'm sorry about last year, but ..... "

"And the year before." You could hear her grandmother just fine now.

"Don't start with me, Mama! I do what I can. You never seemed to appreciate that. I buy her clothes. I'll send money when I'm able.... "

"She needs your time, Audrey, not your money."

"So what am I supposed to do? Quit my job and come sit out here in this dumpy little town?"

Grace's voice was again too low to make out.

"You'd just love that wouldn't you, Mama! You'd like me to come crawling back down here and take some piddly little job."

Meredith eased closer to the screen door.

"Life doesn't always have to be so exciting, Audrey. I was hoping you would see that by now. Your daughter is twelve. Soon

she'll be twenty, and you will have missed out on an amazing child."

"That's not fair, Mama!" Audrey's voice drowned Grace's out. "Not fair at all. I grew up in this place. I know what it's like. People trapped in boring little lives. I couldn't stand that, and I don't want it for Meredith. My job makes it possible to give her nice things, and it will send her to college one of these days. Watching you and Papa tiptoe around one another, I swore I would never settle for your life. Did you and Papa even like one another? Answer me that, Mama! I swear, I can't remember a time when you ever laughed together; ever did anything together; ever even celebrated anything!

"That's very unkind, Audrey."

"Unkind? That's what you call it. My God, Mama, unkind doesn't begin to describe the way you were treated! Papa always off with his dogs, or his gamecocks, or his hunting trips, and you stuck here making do, pinching pennies. Papa had all this land, all this, and we lived like poor white trash!"

"Times were hard for everyone before the war."

"No Mama, not everyone. Just you! Because you never expected more. That's not for me! I swore I wouldn't let anyone treat me the way Papa did you!"

Meredith leaned on the screen door frame and listened for Grace's reply.'

"You're too harsh, Audrey."

"Harsh! Is that all you can come up with?" Audrey was almost shrieking now. It was always the same. Every visit was always the same.

"I don't know how we hurt you so, Audrey." Grace's voice was just loud enough for Meredith to hear. She quietly opened the screen door and stepped into the entry. Both her mother and grandmother were out of sight in the kitchen, but she could hear every word now. She ducked into the parlor and stood by the hall to listen. "We loved you, both of us. We did the best we could for you. Your father. . . . ."

"See what I mean! You don't even call him by name. Your father. Like you barely knew one another. I spent my whole childhood sitting between two people who hated one another. And you don't know what you did to me?"

"I'm sorry, Audrey. I'm sorry if we hurt you, but that does not excuse you from the way you've treated your own daughter."

"I treat Meredith like a princess! I buy her the best of everything. I'll pay for her college and get her out of this town."

"She doesn't need to be a princess, Audrey. She needs to be your child. You need to have her with you more."

"And how would that work, Mama? Do you think the airline is just going to let her fly with me? Or do I leave her sitting alone in Dallas or New York while I'm gone? Answer me that."

"No." Grace's voice was very soft again. "And I don't want to lose her. Meredith makes my life worth living. I would never want her living anywhere else. It's just that. . . . "

"Ok, I'm sorry, Mama! I'm sorry Meredith's father died in the war. I'm sorry I didn't marry some boring little shopkeeper here in Troubadour and settle down. I'm sorry I can't haul Meredith around the country with me all the time.! Audrey's voice dissolved into tears.

Meredith stood stone-still, her fists clinched, her heart pounding. It always ended the same.

"Audrey, Audrey." She could hear the pity in Grace's voice. "My darling, I'm so sorry. Please don't cry."

It always ended the same. The tears always won.

Smothered in memories, Meredith was hardly aware of the chairs. The paint went on easily, and it seemed as if little time had passed when she realized that all the legs and bottoms of the four chairs were finished. She stood back to study her work. It was pretty good. She would just let them dry until tomorrow and then finish the tops. She cleaned her brush and scrubbed her hands and closed up the paint can. The blue was a good idea. It would put a little color back into the old place. Up the lane she could see that Daniel had the hood up on her car. Hopefully he was making progress. It was late she guessed, maybe six. Time to think about food. Time to choose one of those frozen dinners she had bought and fire up the stove. Hopefully it worked, or it would be cold cereal tonight.

Later, after she had successfully operated the oven and eaten her "Chicken Delux", Meredith returned to the back-porch rocker to enjoy the sunset. The cat was not there waiting for her, she noted, and she was a little disappointed. She had always had a cat when she was little. Her grandmother loved them, also. There were always several around the barn, and a special one who insinuated itself into their lives and took over the house. Douglas was their favorite. Her grandmother named him for Douglas Fairbanks, her favorite movie star. Grace talked to that cat as if it were human. Meredith smiled at the memory. The funny thing was, the cat responded as if he understood every word she said. He was company for Grace, she supposed. Her grandmother was sort of a loner, *"no time for gossipy women,"* she used to say. Grace kept her own council, and she was always busy with some project or other, or a book. Not unlike myself, Meredith thought with a wry smile.

And what her mother had accused Grace of that day? That Grace and her husband did not really like one another?. Was that true? She did not remember Grace talking about her husband much. He had been deceased for several years when she was born, and as she grew up, he wasn't mentioned that often. Rarely in any funny stories or happy memories, now that she thought about it. All that was left were a couple of dog show trophies from his hunting hounds, his picture in the parlor looking all so stiff and formal, and his old saddle hanging in the barn. And, she remembered now, there had been a tall hospital bed in the dining room when she was very young. Grace referred to is a Martin's bed. She told her that her husband had slept there after he came home from the hospital. Little other explanation, but she surmised that that meant that Grace had cared for her husband in his last years. Sometime during her grade school years, Grace had sold the bed, and she had not thought of it again until now.

In fact, she knew very little about any of Grace's early life. A few old tintypes of her as a young woman, a few photographs with her husband and Audrey when she was small. She knew Grace had been a teacher in a one room school in her teens, and that she had gone to secretarial school in her twenties. Something fairly rare for a young woman in the early 1900s, she realized now. There had to be some stories there, but she had found few pictures. Her grandmother had not volunteered much, and she had not been interested enough to ask. What a waste. If she were only here now, she would be wise enough to take the time. And, of course, she didn't know her grandfather at all.

Meredith sat there until the darkness had fully fallen, and the cat had never appeared. She took her tea glass back to the kitchen and called it a night. There was a book waiting for her upstairs.

Grace

1915

Chapter 7

Grace Wilson caught the Texas Pacific in Weatherford, in a boil of steam whipped around by a sandstorm; her hat brim flapping against her arm and her skirts bellowing around her ankles. She fought back her fear of the sound of the powerful locomotive and the bustle of life around her on the platform, but at the same time she was excited, also. Only Papa had ever boarded a train, but only once to go to Fort Worth on business. She and her mother had stood on that same platform at the time and waved as he stared back from a coach window, too nervous to wave, too stoic to show his reservations, Mama had said. Grace was only ten years old then and watching him disappear in the distance on that wobblily train in a swarm of dust had made a deep impression on her. At the time, she would never have dreamed she would be boarding the train herself, would be leaving the world she had always known for an uncertain future.

But all was different now, because suddenly in her sixteenth year, her father had died, trying to turn a stampede, they were told. It was a not so uncommon way for a cattleman to go in those open range days. Grace and her mother had lost everything in the aftermath.

Grace had applied to the county for a teaching certificate and had taken a teaching position in the Tankersly community that included room and board. However, her pay was not enough to support both herself and her mother, so her mother had moved back to family in East Texas. It was as though a great earthquake had engulfed them, and their world had rolled and tilted beneath their feet, leaving each of them standing alone in a broken landscape to face the future. For eight years she had taught in the one room schoolhouse and stared into bleak possibilities. She had to act. She had no choice.

Now twenty-four, she was well aware that she was opening herself up to gossip. Young ladies from the tiny communities like Rice Corners or Tankersley did not do what she was doing. Did not strike out into the world alone, did not pursue education beyond reading and writing, did not spurn marriage, or abandon their family. It was well known that Dalton McKinney had proposed marriage three times, and McKinney owned his own farm. He was of good stock and would be a good provider, but his knowledge did not stretch beyond the farm fields, and Grace yearned for more horizons in her life. She had turned him down flat every time. And that Ames boy from over at Bomerton, he had come courting, also. But Grace wanted more than the life of a farmer's wife, so she saved her meager salary and after eight years she had given up her teaching position and applied to the new secretarial school for young women in Fort Worth.

Grace was a pleasant looking girl, quite pretty, the gossips said, religious and strong. She could bear many children. She should make some man a good wife, the ladies of the church whispered, except for that stubborn streak.

She hurried down the platform to the waiting car, rushing to get settled as the train gathered steam. The words and warnings of the community swirled around her like the dust in the air, but she was not discouraged. Her mother understood. She had encouraged her studies, read her stories of far-away places with strange names and amazing possibilities. She herself knew the hunger for learning and being needed more than as a cook or a housekeeper. So her mother had arranged for Grace to stay with her older brother and his family in Fort Worth while she attended school.

Grace watched until there was no more of Weatherford to see. Then she settled back in her seat and turned her attention toward the future. After all it was 1915. Times were changing. Women could do more than be a wife, or more than teach in those tiny one room schools she had occupied. Rumor was that women might win the vote soon. She and her mother had read about it in the paper and heard it talked about among the women after church.

Out the window the land rolled away at breath-taking speed. Grace gripped her pocketbook in both hands and studied the car. There were only six other people. Four men, three in Sunday suits, drummers probably, and one who had the look of a cattleman wearing a leather vest and a wide-brimmed hat. The other passengers were a middle-aged woman with a small boy. The child was begging to hang his head out the window, and the woman was arguing against it with a definite tone. Grace smiled. She couldn't blame the boy. She would have loved to do the same thing, but decorum and common sense kept her in her seat. But, oh the train ride! She was going! After so many dreams and plans, and in spite of her fears, she was going! Patterson Business Academy, the letter had announced. We are pleased to accept Miss Grace Wilson as a student in our school. Please report the 12th day of September, 1915, at our campus, 270 Houston Avenue, Fort Worth, Texas.

Uncle Klyce was to meet her, his letter had promised. Grace stood on the station platform, frozen in indecision. She had never seen so much movement, heard so much noise. People rushing past, talking and laughing, glad to be united with arriving passengers. The woman and boy from her car were scooped up in a crowd of family, all talking at once. The drummers hefted their sample cases and disappeared into the station, and the cattleman swung a saddle up to his shoulder and did the same. In the midst of all the movement and talk combined with the clatter and steam from the engine, no one noticed Grace at all. She turned her head slowly to view the scene, drinking in the atmosphere, and her old feelings of uncertainty flooded back. It struck her that it was the first time in her whole life that she was truly alone.

"Dora Grace?"

Grace looked around quickly and her uncle, Mama's older brother, smiled down at her.

"My goodness, you have changed!" He removed his hat and looked over his spectacles at her. "Do you remember me?"

"Yes. Hello Uncle Klyce. I remember you well." She smiled. "You carried peppermints in your vest pocket"

"I still do" he said as he produced a candy from his pocket and winked his eye. "And I haven't changed so much I would think, but you! You were only a little girl with pigtails when we last met. Thirteen years ago, I think. Now here you are, all grown up."

He reached back to place his hand on the shoulder of a young man standing just behind him. "And this my son, Tanner. Do you remember him?"

"Yes," Grace smiled as Tanner reached out to take her hand.

"You dared me to climb the cliff by the spring, if I remember correctly," Tanner offered.

"And I remember that you were very brave."

"And reckless, I think." They both laughed.

"Is this your trunk?" Her uncle asked. "Are you ready to go?"

Grace nodded.

Tanner picked up the trunk with ease, and her uncle took Grace's valise. The three of them made their way through the jumble of people on the platform.

"Ada is looking forward to having you stay. She has a room all ready for you," Uncle Klyce offered.

"It is so kind of you to take me in."

"Family is family," he pronounced. "We are so glad to do it." He shifted her valise to his other hand and reached for her arm to guide her off the curb. "Here we are. The second motor machine there."

Motor machine! An automobile! Grace's eyebrows raised. She had seen them in Weatherford, however she had never ridden in one. Uncle Klyce cupped her elbow and helped her step up on the running board. Grace followed his instructions and settle in the passenger's seat. Tanner loaded her luggage and came around front to crank the engine while her uncle prepared to drive. Two cranks and the engine came to life. Tanner hurried to jump in, and then they were off! Careening through the streets, dodging wagons and lorries and pedestrians, bumping over iron rail tracks curving through the roadway. Grace realized she was holding her breath. They were going so fast! Faster than a horse could trot! Uncle Klyce wrestled the big steering wheel and, from time to time, squeezed a rubber ball that gave out a sharp warning honk to the wagons and automobiles around them. Grace grasped the side bar of the vehicle with one hand.

"Hold on now!" Uncle Klyce shouted over the engine. "Hold on!"

The car bumped across the tracks behind the train and crossed the river on a wide bridge crowded with wagons and horses and vehicles swarming around in no particular lane or order that Grace could decern. She could feel her hat beginning to lift from the rushing air under the brim, but she felt helpless to stop it. She was too riveted on holding on and gripping her pocketbook.

From the back seat, Tanned reached up and pressed her hat down on her head, and, like his father, he cautioned, "Hold on!"

The traffic thinned after they crossed the bridge, and roads dispersed in several directions, narrower now and less congested. Scattered houses appeared, painted white, or pink, or blue and trimmed in every color. Down a side lane lined with trees and garden plots, they pulled up before a white wood-framed house with soft green lattice trim along the porch awning and a smiling woman waving from the front step, Aunt Ada. Grace smiled, but she was too nervous to let go of her grip and wave.

Uncle Klyce brought the car to a shuddering stop, and Aunt Ada rushed up to reach for Grace's hand. "Oh, my dear. You're the mirror image of your mother!" She helped Grace down from the car and gave her an enthusiastic hug. "I'm so glad you are here!"

"Thank you so much for inviting me to stay with you."

"Family, my dear. We are all together." Ada guided her toward the house. "Come on in, and we'll let the men handle the luggage.

She paused and motioned toward the room. "This is the parlor."

The room was bright with sunshine from big windows on the front of the house. It was furnished with store-bought furniture, a highbacked sofa and chairs. Like something out of Collier's magazine, Grace thought. There was a floral-patterned rug on the floor and pretty things sitting on little tables with crochet dollies under them. Much different from the simple three-room ranch house she and her parents lived in.

Ada motioned again. "Your room is this way."

Tanner and Uncle Klyce bumped into the house carrying her trunk and valise and followed them. The room was just off the parlor. Grace peeked in the door as the men went past her and sat her bags down. A white iron bedstead was made up with a colorful quilt. A desk by the window, a washbasin and stand in the corner. Flowered paper on the walls. Grace was speechless.

"This is Tanner's old room. I hope it will be comfortable." Ada said softly.

Grace recovered her voice. "It's lovely. I . . . . I don't know what to say."

Three eager faces smiled back at her.

"But I don't want to take Tanner's room!" Grace managed to get out.

"No, no, it's fine. I've moved to the back room off the kitchen. Fine for me. I come and go. This way I won't disturb everyone. Don't want to get tangled in all these flowers that Mother put up for you."

"Tanner is engaged to marry next year." Ada put in.

"I'll be gone before you know it. Don't worry about me."

"He and Amelia are buying their own place." Uncle Klyce offered, a ring of pride in his voice.

"Oh, congratulations. I'm so happy for you."

Tanner grinned broadly. "You'll meet Amelia tonight. She's coming for dinner."

"Wonderful." Grace took a deep breath and looked around.'

"Now come have some tea, dear." Ada touched her arm. "Take a break before you settle in."

Grace followed her aunt back to the parlor. Her head was spinning. Parlor? Tea in the Parlor? Automobiles? Dinner rather than supper? Her lovely room? It was all too much, too different. This city life would be more of an adventure than she had ever imagined.

The afternoon went quickly. Grace answered all the questions about her mother and her school. Uncle Klyce and Aunt Ada expressed their sympathy over the death of her father. "He was a fine man," Uncle Klyce said, and Aunt Ada nodded.

"I know your mother is concerned about you, but I'll just write her a note reassuring her. I'm so happy you are here, and I think you will just love the city." She patted Grace's hand. "And it is so exciting that you are enrolling in the school. There are ever so many things for young ladies to do these days."

"Amelia was going to enroll in school before we got engaged," Tanner offered.

"It's good for a young lady to pursue education while she is still single, I think," Uncle Klyce joined in.

Grace smiled, but she kept her thoughts to herself. Uncle Klyce was probably just like her Papa; reluctant to embrace all this independence in women, but even more reluctant to speak out against it. Aunt Ada and Mother were of one mind, she guessed. A career outside the home for women, voting rights; times were changing. She caught a glimpse of Aunt Ada out of the corner of her eye. Was that a warning glance she gave the men? Were plans for school a point of contention?

Tanner left to collect his fiancée, and Uncle Klyce retired to his paper. Grace followed her aunt out to the kitchen to help with supper, or dinner as it seemed to be called here. Working side by side fell easily into place for the two of them. Aunt Ada chatted away about this and that. Grace felt welcome and comfortable with her. This was going to work out fine.

As the day progressed and evening fell, Aunt Ada reached up and pulled a cord hanging from the center of the kitchen, and the room flooded with light. Grace looked up quickly to the source. Electric light! She quickly glanced around the room. No oil lamps insight. Of course, in the city the homes would have Mr. Edison's new lights. She stared mesmerized for a few moments by the glow of a glass globe hanging from a cord. Aunt Ada, busy with the final dinner chores, never noticed her reaction. *Yes, the city would surely be different!*

Within the hour, sounds of a flurry from the front room caught their attention. Tanner was back with his young lady. Grace and Ada went out to meet them. Tanner was helping her with her wrap when they walked in, a small, pretty girl dressed in a pearl white dress with tiny pleats in the bodice and skirt. Even the glimpse of shoes and stockings below her skirt matched. By far the loveliest and grandest dress Grace had ever seen.

Tanner introduced them. "Grace, this is Amelia Cambell, soon to be Freeman."

The girl giggled and rolled her eyes at Grace.

Amelia, this my cousin, Grace Wilson."

"I'm so happy to meet you," Grace said.

"Yes," Amelia offered her hand. "My! You are so big! Why, you are almost as tall as Tanner!"

Grace looked down at the girl. *How to respond to that?* The girl was right. Compared to her, Grace felt like a giant. That Amelia was hardly five feet tall, would be a good guess.

Aunt Ada interrupted quickly. "Here, come to the table everyone. I'll just get Tanner to help me bring everything in. No, no, Grace, you are the guest of honor. Just sit here on Klyce's left, and you girls can visit."

Amelia chose the place across from Grace and glanced around for Tanner. He had started to the kitchen with his mother but stopped short and raced back to Amelia's side to help her with her chair. Amelia smiled sweetly and arranged herself at the table. "So, how do you like Fort Worth so far, Grace?" Her voice was high and fragile sounding, and her gaze was judgmental.

"Well, what I've seen of the city so far is the train station, so I can't give a good opinion, but it all seems very exciting."

Amelia's laugh was high-pitched and insincere. "Well, I imagine it is quite different than, where was it, Rice Corners?"

"Grace has been a teacher these last few years." Uncle Klyce put in. "You've been away from Rice Corners, haven't you?"

"Yes. In the Tankersley Community. No larger than Rice Corners really, but different."

"A one room school." Amalia said. "How quaint. You'll have to share some of your stories with us."

Aunt Ada and Tanner appeared with steaming bowls of vegetables and roast beef. The conversation changed to comments on the food and saying the blessing, so Grace was spared from further conversation for the moment. But not for long.

"So," Amelia leaned forward across the table as she spoke. "Grace, I understand you plan to enroll in the Business School."

"Yes, I'm already enrolled, actually. I start next week, I believe."

"Well, I think that is wonderful. If a woman has no prospects to marry, I mean. I might have pursued education if Tanner hadn't come along and stolen my heart." She cut her eyes around at Tanner and patted his arm.

"Grace has plenty of time to make those decisions. She just has chosen to remain single for now." Ada's voice was shaky.

"Well, I'm sure so." Amelia agreed. "You would look to make a very sturdy farm wife, I would think, Grace."

And just in a blink the comforting spell of her Uncle's house was broken. It would not be easy here. Tiny Amelia was making that quite clear. The lines were drawn. Grace was a country girl as far as Amelia was concerned, and somehow, in some way, that made Grace inferior, or maybe ever an enemy.

"So how are the plans for the wedding coming, Amelia?" Uncle Klyce's voice was louder than necessary, but it did the trick and got everyone's attention.

Amelia, especially, took the bait and launched into a detailed description of all the plans and indecision about the coming event. "Mother is doing a wonderful job. I have my first dressmaker fitting in January. She has ordered the lace from New York ..."

Grace tuned out the shrill child-like voice and effected giggle and studied Tanner instead. Her cousin was staring transfixed at his fiancée, hanging on her every word. She glanced at Aunt Ada, whose face was a complete blank, no expression to give her thoughts away. Uncle Klyce was the same. He was staring at Amelia with a serious expression; perhaps listening, perhaps not.

Amelia prattled on. "Daddy says it is my choice about the wedding dinner, but I just don't know. It seems so expensive to me, but ..."

The word 'insipid' sprang to mind. Grace had never had occasion to use that word before. She only knew it from the spelling bees in school, but watching this child across the table from her, it suddenly fit perfectly. Also shallow, privileged, self-absorbed. She smiled to herself. This word play could go on and on. Yes, there was more story to this scene, she was quite sure.

The rest of the evening's conversation centered completely around Amelia, which was, of course, fine with Grace, and fine with Amelia too, apparently. It seemed she never noticed that she was doing all the talking.

Finally, Tanner interrupted with a suggestion that it was time to go.

"Amelia, at first, shot him an irritated glance, but then smiled sweetly. "Yes, you are right, dear. And Ada, I want to say that your dinner was just lovely. I just don't know how you manage it without help. My mother would be lost in the kitchen without our cook."

"We really need to go, dear," Tanner offered. "I have to be at work early tomorrow, you know."

Amelia giggled and patted his arm. "Yes, did Tanner tell you?" Daddy is promoting him to Head Cashier. Isn't that wonderful? Daddy says the best way to learn the banking business is from the ground up, and Tanner is climbing already."

Tanner beamed at his parents, and the congratulations that were offered. Good-byes were said. Promises to call again soon were made.

"Mother is counting on you now, Ada. She wants you to help plan the bridal tea." She turned to her attention back to Grace, "And I wish you the very best next week. I truly do."

The element of pity was thinly veiled. To Amelia, she was not only a country girl, but a working girl, Grace considered. In a flurry of hugs, the couple was gone, and in their wake, the silence and embarrassed looks from her aunt and uncle spoke louder than any words they might have offered.

"Let me help you with clearing the table, Aunt Ada." Grace turned back and began gathering plates and glasses.

"My, they are all excited about the wedding, aren't they?" Ada voice was shaky. There was a long pause where neither Grace nor her uncle answered. He had gone back to his pipe and paper. "And I just think the wedding is going to be lovely," her aunt continued as she followed Grace out to the kitchen. "This is just such a wonderful opportunity for our Tanner. Amelia's father is President of First National Bank where Tanner is employed."

"Yes, that is what I gathered."

"Of course, Amelia is young. She has a lot of maturing to do, but she just adores Tanner, it seems." Ada tied on her apron and tackled the dishes.

Grace kept her thoughts to herself, but from her observation, Amelia Campbell only adored Amelia Campbell. Tanner looked like "a lamb to the slaughter."

While they washed and dried the dishes, Aunt Ada prattled on, apparently still trying to patch over the evening confrontation. "The Campbells have been so kind to us. Of course, we are not in their social circle. Klyce's store is doing very well, but not to their level. However, they do seem to love our Tanner and have great plans for him."

"How old is Amelia?" Grace asked.

"Nineteen, I believe. That makes her eight years younger than Tanner. She had her 'coming out season last year. That is how the two of them met. Tanner had just taken the position at the bank, and her father asked Tanner to escort her to one of the balls."

"And when is the wedding?"

Aunt Ada blinked her eyes and hesitated a moment. "Next Fall. She paused again. "Apparently long engagements are necessary in the Campbell's social circle.'

Grace smiled. "Well, I'm very happy for him. For them both." It was a dismissive remark, and Grace meant it to be. She had devoted as much time to Amelia Campbell as she intended.

Aunt Ada took the hint and switched topics. Did Grace need anything before her school started, clothes, school supplies? The offer was made to take her shopping, but Grace declined. She was not spending any of the money she had saved until she was sure of her expenses.

"Well, your uncle and I are so pleased that you are here and proud of your plans for schooling."

She reached out with a hug which Grace returned. Then Grace made her excuses and went off to her new room to get settled.

Chapter 8

Uncle Klyce helped her catch the trolley on Monday and made the trip to the school with her, "Just to be sure", he said. Grace was nervous at stepping on the clattering trolley and anxious not to appear too timid, but it all went well. Her eyes darted everywhere as she carefully noted where and how much to pay the conductor and counted the streets, taking notice of the surroundings. The traffic and people seemed a confusing blur to her, but she was determined.

Patterson Business Academy was a square two-story building on a busy downtown street. Uncle Klyce showed her where to get off, warning all the way in a low voice in her ear to watch her step and watch the traffic and watch the curb. Finally, they were there, standing at the front door looking up at the sign.

"So." Her uncle took a deep satisfying breath and squared his shoulders. "Now you know the way."

"Yes," Grace managed to say. She was frozen in place, awed by the size of the building. They stood in silence as Grace took it all in, and her uncle waited patiently.

"They'll be expecting you," he offered after a bit.

Grace glanced at him quickly.

"Will you be okay?" he added. "Can you make the trip home? Because I can come back this afternoon if . . . ."

"No, no, I'll be fine. Thank you for accompanying me. I'll be fine."

"Well, if you have any doubts about which trolley, just show our address to the conductor. He will set you straight."

"I will." Grace held up the paper with the address on it.

"Well, then." And he smiled and walked away to the trolley stop.

Grace took a long deep breath, squared her shoulders, and walked up the steps. She could feel her mother giving her a little pat on the back as she went in the door.

The lady at the front desk smiled sweetly. "Welcome to Patterson." She checked Grace's name off a list and directed her down the hall to the second room on the left.

Grace felt to make sure her hair pins were secure and that her hair was in place as she walked. She noted gratefully that the other girls she passed in the hall were dressed much as she was. Plain black or brown skirts that ended just above the ankle with shirt-waist blouses in different colors and designs. Her mother had been right when she ordered her three new blouses and a new skirt from the Sears catalog. Grace had intended to just wear the clothes she had worn to teach school. Her skirt and blouse and extra dress were still serviceable, and she did not want to squander her money from her teaching position. However, her mother insisted, and even ordered her a store-bought suit, a lovely soft beige linen with brown piping around the collar and sleeves. With her winter coat and her Sunday dress, Grace had a wardrobe she had never expected. Now here in this new place, she whispered a thank you to her mother. She could fit in.

The classroom was full, with only standing room along the walls. Expectant faces turned toward her when Grace stepped in the door. The expressions of the girls mirrored her own feelings of excitement and nervousness. There was a buzz over the room. Grace hesitated at the door and took a deep breath. Then she squeezed into an offered spot between two girls, standing along the back wall.

"Hello," one girl spoke softly, and Grace smiled in return. "So, here we go! Right?" The girl whispered.

Before Grace could respond, a stern-looking woman entered the room and took her place at the front. And suddenly, *'you can hear a pin drop'*, Grace was thinking.

"Welcome to Patterson Business Academy. I am Mrs. Olivia Thurman. I am the director here. I will be handing out schedules and other important information today to each of you. If you have any questions or concerns, you can see me in my office at the times shown on the schedule." She paused for effect. "We are very proud of our program here at Patterson. This is the first and only business school for young ladies in Fort Worth. We have worked hard to develop a strong program for you, and we expect you to prove our value with your hard work and success in your future profession. We hold a high standard academically as well as in moral character for our chosen students. Please read our handbooks so that you are aware of our rules. And please note that any failure to follow our standards will result in immediate dismissal." The woman fixed the girls with a stern glare and paused to allow her words to sink in. "Please come forward as I call your name and receive your packets. Read your schedules, and when I dismiss you, go to your appointed rooms."

Then a slightly elevated voice, she announced, "Ava Abbot."

A girl in the second row stood quickly and went forward to accept her envelope.

"Lucia Aldacott."

"Maud Allen."

The girl next to Grace flinched slightly when her name was called and then quickly stepped forward. Grace watched as she accepted her envelope and returned to her spot along the wall.

"I feel as if I just joined the army," she whispered.

Grace returned her smile, but she remained attentive to the woman passing out the schedules. Under the circumstances, she certainly did not want to miss her name!

The roll call went on, slowly progressing toward the Ws. Whispers started between the girls who had opened their envelopes, and the woman paused to give everyone her stern stare again.

"Grace Wilson."

Finally! Grace made her way to the front. The Thurman woman offered a tight curt smile with the envelope and called out the next name.

Grace went back to her spot along the wall. The girl next to her glanced over at her schedule when Grace pulled it out a little way to 'take a peek.'

"We have the same first class," she whispered.

Miss Thurman's voice rang out over the group. "I believe everyone is accounted for. Please look over your schedule and find your first class. I will be in my office for the next hour if you have questions." And without another word, the woman, skirt and petticoat swishing, swept from the room.

"Well, isn't she charming!" the girl whispered, and Grace fought back a laugh.

The girl offered her hand. "I'm Maud Allen."

"Grace Wilson."

"Let me see your schedule. Maybe we have some other classes together." They ran down the list and found that they were identical.

"Room 204," Grace glanced toward the hall.

"Well, we better get moving. We don't want to let those Patterson standards slip." Maud rolled her eyes.

"So, are you from Fort Worth?" Maud asked in a breathless voice as they climbed the stairs.

"No, I'm from out West."

"Me, too. Well, north actually. Gainesville. Where are you staying?"

"With my aunt and uncle."

"Oh, that's nice to have family here. I'm on my own. I'm in a boarding house with several other girls. They are students here, also."

They reached the landing and looked down the hallway. "There it is, second door." They hurried along.

"It's rather nice, though," Maud continued. "You know, on my own, no family around." She smiled.

Grace nodded. She knew exactly what she meant. *On her own was a double-edged sword, in her own case.*

The rest of the day was a whirlwind of activity. Many introductions, long lists of responsibilities. Grace listened intently and wrote copious notes as the thrill of learning something new washed over her.

After the last class, the girl named Maud introduced her to her housemates in a flurry of names to keep straight. The girls were somewhat younger than Grace, but friendly. Maud seemed to take pride in claiming her as a newfound friend.

"Well, we survived the first day!" Maud announced.

"Yes, we did. Now for the future!" Grace added, and the other girls giggled.

"Which way are you?"

"I catch the trolley."

"Oh, we are close enough to walk. It's back this way; so, see you tomorrow."

"Tomorrow." Grace watched the group as they scurried away, talking and laughing. *A spirited group, to say the least. And not a single "Amelia" among them. It was a good start.* She pulled her directions out of her pocket and went to wait for the trolley. One more challenge to go.

Meredith

2015

Chapter 9

The sun woke Meredith again. *She definitely needed to invest in those blinds.* She raised her head and glanced around the room to find that her reading lamp was still on from last night. Next, she became aware that her book was lying open near her hand, (she had surely lost her place), and she was still propped up on two pillows. Well, she would probably pay for that with a major crick in her neck. But the truth was, she loved reading until she fell asleep. It was a luxury that said she was retired. She didn't have to obey an alarm clock any longer. She could have read all night if she had wanted or lasted, actually. She smiled and stretched. What time was it, anyway?

The floor felt a little chilly to her bare feet. She shuffled into her slippers and headed for the kitchen. What should she tackle today? Finish the chairs, and then the breakfast table, maybe. Tear off that old checkered oil cloth and see what was underneath.

The phone rang while she was buttering some toast.

"Hey Lady, what are you up to?" It was Amy.

"Hello. Just thinking about doing a little painting. What's up with you?" Meredith licked a smear of butter from her fingers.

"Well, I was thinking ahead. Tomorrow is Friday. Are you free for the weekend?"

"As a bird." They both laughed.

"Well then, why don't you plan on coming over on Saturday, and we'll see what trouble we can get into. I'll fix lunch."

"Wonderful! But I have a little problem. My car is being worked on, and I'm not sure when I'll get it back."

"That's no problem at all. I'll just pick you up. Just bring your toothbrush, and we'll make a slumber party out of it. How about that?"

"Well, I believe I can do that, if you don't mind putting up with me for that long. Do you want me to bring anything else. Wine maybe?"

"No, I've got that covered. No need to bring anything except yourself. I'll come pick you up about eleven, and you can just spend the night. It will be like old times."

"Sounds great. See you then."

Meredith was still smiling when she finished breakfast. Beautiful day. Projects to tackle. Saturday to look forward to. What could be better?

But she didn't tackle the painting just yet, because when she reached the parlor, the trunk caught her eye again. There it sat, and it wasn't going away. Maybe some of her questions about her grandmother could be answered there. She retrieved the key from her purse and opened the lid.

Of course, the first thing she saw was her mother's letter. The fresh white envelope stood out from all the age-tinged things around it. But she ignored it. Not now. Not yet.

The top tray held a treasure of tiny items. She remembered them well from when Grace would open the trunk for her when she was little and let her touch each one. There was a story with every item. Meredith's eyes moved to the back left corner cubicle. Yes, they were still there. The delicate braided hair fashioned into an intricate design. The blond one, she remembered, was Grace's baby brother who had died at age four. She picked it up carefully and placed it on her outstretched palm.

My mother cut one of his curls and fashioned this, she could hear her grandmother saying in a reverent whisper. *We had no camera in those days. No pictures to remember.*

Tears came to Meredith's eyes with the memory, as it always did for her grandmother. "He was so very young," she would say. "He had a fever", she would always add.

As a child, with no knowledge of love or loss or death, she had viewed the braid as a curiosity. Now as an adult, she could appreciate the pain of that death for Grace and her parents. The horror of a sick child without penicillin or antibiotics. The weight of that death on his sister, barely older that he. How had that tragedy influenced Grace's life? She replaced the braid carefully.

Another lock of hair was a longer looping black curl tied with a small red ribbon bow. It was her mother's, she remembered. Her grandmother made this one from Audrey's first haircut, the story went. Grace had told her about her mother crying when they started to cut her hair, because she thought it was going to hurt. Her father gave her a peppermint stick to distract her, the story went, which she promptly got tangled in her curls. Meredith remembered laughing and laughing at the story. One, because she couldn't imagine her mother all messy with candy in her hair, and two, because the story made Grace happy, and she loved to hear her laugh. And now, after recalling her mother's accusation that Grace and her husband never shared a happy moment, this did not fit. She placed the curl carefully back in the cubicle.

Another square held an assortment of pins. Intricate patterns etched into metal. One read Woodmen of the World Ladies Auxiliary, another, her grandfather's Masonic pin on a tie tack. Also, the Methodists Women's Club and another gold pin that said, President, Ladies Aid Society, 1920. Grace had led a busy life, it seemed, although most of that was behind her by the time she had come into the picture, Meredith realized. On the bottom of the collection was a cartoonish campaign button with the word BULLY written at the top and VOTE For Teddy Roosevelt, underneath. She smiled with the memory that Grace always vowed Theodore Roosevelt was the greatest President this country had ever had.

In the cubicle next to the pins was a chunk of twisted metal, wrapped in a bit of cloth. An odd sort of memorabilia, Meredith thought, out of place with the smaller trinkets, but underneath it was a newspaper clipping. She unfolded the brittle paper carefully and read the headline.

The Crash at Crush

Waco, Texas – September 15, 1896
A widely advertised attraction became the scene of tragedy
on Saturday afternoon. The Texas-Missouri-Kansas Railroad

Company had planned a collision of two trains as an advertising stunt, but it went terribly wrong when the boilers of the two locomotives exploded showering the crowd of spectators and dignitaries with shards of metal. Two men were killed and many more injured in the aftermath. An estimated 40,000 people had purchased a two dollar ticket to attend the spectacle.

Yes, she remembered this now. Her grandfather had attended this bazaar attraction as a young man in his teens. Grace had described it to her as she had heard it from her husband, and Meredith had been both horrified and fascinated by the story of two big locomotive engines crashing into one another just for sport. Grace had related that her husband said he had found the chunk of twisted metal on the ground several hundred yards away from the collision, and that the metal was still so hot to the touch that he had to use his handkerchief to pick it up. She refolded the clipping and carefully replaced it with the chunk of metal. This was another clue to her grandfather's personality, maybe his adventurous streak. Certainly not the serious man she had always studied in his picture in the parlor.

The next square held bits of tatted lace and a tatting shuttle. She remembered Grace demonstrating making the delicate lace to her. As a child she had tried her hand at the process, but given up in frustration. Now that art was lost to her along with other things she hadn't appreciated at the time. Another space held two tiny tintype photographs, no larger than postage stamps. She picked them up, noting how clear and sharp the images still were. There was a young girl which she recognized as Grace, probably in her twenties. Her smile was the same as she remembered, a pretty, dignified face. Another was her grandfather. She recognized him from the formal picture she had seen. A handsome young man with kind eyes, in a stiff white collar and tie. It was hard to imagine these two people hating one another as Audrey had accused.

A knock at the front door interrupted the silence, and she looked up to see Daniel watching her through the front door glass. He waved as she moved to open the door.

"Hello!"

"Don't want to interrupt you."

She shook her head. "Not at all. You aren't interrupting anything. Just going through this old trunk." She motioned him to come in.

"Just wanted to update you on the car."

So, do I have any hope of driving my junker again?" They both laughed softly.

"Most certainly. I've got it broken down, and I think I've found your problem."

"Wonderful! How about some refreshment. Come on back to the kitchen." She led the way. "So, am I going to be able to afford this?"

Daniel laughed softly again. "No, now, actually the parts aren't that bad."

"I have some iced tea made." She opened the fridge. "Would you like a glass?"

Daniel nodded.

She filled a glass and handed to him. "I'm sorry I can't offer you a place to sit. All my chairs are out there on the porch."

"No problem." He leaned casually against the countertop and continued "I've been cleaning the engine and checking everything as I go. Most of your hoses still are good, but the fuel pump is about shot, and the water pump is iffy. You need a new carburetor, also. After that it's just a matter of replacing the oil and transmission fluid and tuning the engine."

"Oh dear, that sounds like a lot."

"Not really. Only problem is, I can't get the parts until at least Monday. That's going to leave you without a ride for a couple of days."

"Oh, that will be fine. I'm going to be staying with a friend over the weekend."

"Well, that's great. That takes care of that, then. I'll just leave the car as is and put it back together for you next week. Will that be satisfactory?"

She nodded.

"And if you need anything, need to go anywhere, you can use my truck, or I'll drive you, if you prefer."

"You are so kind. Just keep a careful tally of what I owe you, now."

Daniel smiled and looked around the room. "So, this is the old place, then."

"Yes, I'm afraid so." They laughed together. "Not fancy, but as the saying goes, it's paid for."

"And lots of potential. I love these old houses. It must have been spectacular in its day."

"I suppose so." Meredith looked around. "Of course, when I lived here in the forties and fifties, it was already an old house that needed updating. My grandmother was a great one for "making do" as they said during the Depression and then later the war. Nothing fancy, no frills."

So, you and your family lived here with your grandparents?"

"No, my grandmother and I. She was a widow by then, and my mother traveled with her job. My father was killed in the war."

"I'm sorry. I didn't mean to pry."

"No, don't be. It was just the way it was. My grandmother was all the family I needed." She smiled. "How about you. Where are you from? Around here?"

"No, I'm not. He sat his empty glass down on the counter, and Grace refilled it. "I'm originally from the Houston area, but I've been in school in Lubbock for the last few years. I'm a paleontologist, actually, and I'm here for a year working a dig a few miles out of town."

"Really! How interesting! I knew there were fossils to be found. You've noticed my grandmother's front walk, I guess.

"Yes, I have." He smiled. "Ammonites."

"Yes. She was very interested in them. We used to find them in the creek bank after a big rain came through."

"Well, there is a world recognized location that is very rich with fossils just northwest of here. There have been some major finds there over the years. I have a university grant to work here for a year. I'm down right now, waiting for better conditions at the site, but I'll be back out there soon."

"What a wonderful opportunity! And you say it is a world recognized site?"

"Yes, the fossils of animals that were the origins of mammals, in fact."

"Really!"

"Yes, it's a well-kept secret I guess." He smiled. "Outside of the academic world, at least."

Meredith followed him back toward the front door. "Now I feel bad that I'm taking you away from your work, fiddling with my old car."

"No, it's a nice diversion. Gives me a chance to do something different for a while. Like I said, I love old cars. Don't worry about it. As for now, do you need anything from the store? I'll be glad to take you anywhere you need to go."

"Thank you, but no. I'm fine. I've got everything I need for now, and my friend is picking me up Saturday morning."

"Well then, I'll talk to you Monday and let you know if the parts come in."

"That will work, but no rush.

"Absolutely."

Meredith watched as he went down the steps and out the front gate. *So, you should never judge too quickly, my dear. Self-employed indeed. A scientist of some merit apparently.* She went back to the trunk.

There was a collection of old postcards. She remembered those. Heavens, they were probably valuable by now to some collector. And another square held a pair of high button baby shoes. Her mother's, she remembered Grace telling her. A pair of white kid gloves rounded out the tray's collection. She thought of her grandmother carefully storing all these items away so many years ago. It brought a smile to her lips. What a treasure.

Meredith lifted the tray a little. Underneath there were larger items. A quilt top that had never gotten completed, pieced by Grace, probably, and a stack of embroidered scarves that she remembered Grace making. Underneath that layer there appeared to be several articles of clothing. She replaced the tray and closed the trunk. That was enough for today. She wasn't getting anywhere with her painting project. She would save the rest of the trunk for later. She went back to the kitchen to tackle the table, thinking that Grace would probably be pleased that she was here and improving the old place.

It was no easy job to get the oilcloth off. She struggled with a hammer, a screwdriver and pliers to remove the tacks. But when the cloth finally came off, she was pleased to see that the table was in fairly good condition. A new coat of paint, and it would be fine. She would just paint the tops of the chairs and then the table to match. The sun was shining, perfect painting weather. She could be finished in no time.

Grace

1915

Chapter 10

As the days went by, Grace became more secure in her new life. The rhythm of the city suited her, she decided, as she rode the trolley back and forth to school and marveled at the variety of items available in the shops. There were musical reviews in the park, and speakers at the library. An entirely new world opened up to her, and the friends she made at school lifted her spirits every day. No more isolation for her. Her classes were challenging, and she took pride in her ability to learn new things quickly. The stress she had felt with meeting Tanner's Amelia was a mere memory. However, she was reminded almost daily of the upcoming wedding. Aunt Ada was in a constant dither over one thing or another. What to wear to this or that tea or shower being given for Amelia, and the endless planning of the bridal tea to be hosted by Aunt Ada and Amelia's mother.

"I don't want to embarrass my son," Ada kept saying.

And no matter how ardently Grace tried to reassure her that that could never happen, it would come up again. Thankfully for Grace, the young couple was terribly busy with their own social whirl that did not include her. Thank heavens, she was not expected to attend those events.

Fall turned to winter and Christmas and family gatherings. Grace's aunt and uncle were no different from her parents in their traditions. Christmas was a quiet religious observance with a candlelight service on Christmas Eve and a more formal service on the actual day. On the other hand, Tanner and Amelia were swept up in a round of parties and gaiety that seemed to be the traditions of the city social set. That her aunt and uncle disapproved was made clear by their silence. Grace and her mother exchanged letters, but the cost and distance of a visit was out of the question.

January, and new term brought new challenges. The anticipation of learning the type writing machine hung over all the students. Grace looked forward to it more than any other class she would be having. A machine that could write! What a marvel!

"There's a speaker this weekend at the courthouse," Maud whispered as they settled into their seats for the first day of class.

"Speaker?"

"We were all thinking of going. Would you like to come?"

Grace looked up from her books at the tone of her friend's voice. *Was it caution, hesitancy she detected? Not like out-going Maud.* "What kind of speaker."

"Suffrage," Maud whispered and glanced about at the other students around then with a furtive look. "Women's suffrage."

"Ah," Grace followed her quick survey of their surroundings. "Where did you say it is?"

Just then Mr. Thurman's voice boomed out over the class. "Good morning, ladies. Please take your seats. Welcome to type writing instruction."

"Later," Maud whispered.

"First of all, ladies, I want to address posture," Mr. Thurman's voice thundered. "It is very important to this process. So sit straight, both feet firmly on the floor."

He paused for a moment. "Now take a sheet of the paper there on your table and insert it into the roller, as I am doing now." He held up his right hand. "Next, turn the knob on the end of the carriage roller, here." He pointed at the picture high on the wall behind him. "This will feed your paper into position, thus."

He surveyed the room. "Now, please locate the letters on the buttons of the machine. We will, from this point forward, refer to the buttons as keys. Using your index finger, press the key that shows the first letter of your Christian name and then continue to find the correct keys to spell out your name."

Grace positioned the paper as he instructed and studied the buttons before her, or the keys as he had said. Her name? She pushed the key marked with a "g". The machine hardly responded. She glanced at Maud to see if she might be doing something wrong. *More forceful,* she counseled herself. She tried again.

This time a tiny metal arm swung up and struck the paper on the roller and a "g" appeared on the paper. Grace smiled and looked for the "r" key. Around her she could hear the efforts of the other girls. Now the "a", "c", "e". She looked at the paper in triumph. There it was, 'grace' in glaring black ink. A murmur of wonder filled the room mixed with whispers and shy laughter.

Mr. Thurman smiled. "Now, locate this button on your machine." He tapped the large chart behind him. "This button is called the carriage return. With your left hand, please press this button and push the carriage to the right." The clatter of machines responded, followed by a murmur of amazement from the class. "This moves the paper to the right. Now roll the wheel at the end of the carriage to move down to the next line." Mr. Thurman paused for the girls' voices to settle. "Now, locate the blank keys on each end of the bottom row." He pointed again to the chart. "Hold either blank key down. and strike the first letter of your name."

The class responded with a clatter of keys.

"The blank key will create a capital letter," Mr. Thurman's voice rose over the noise. "Release the blank key, and you will type lower case letters. Now, type the rest of your name."

The clatter started again, and then subsided.

"Next, press the long bar at the bottom of the keyboard. This will skip a space."

"Now your last name. Hold down the blank key for your first letter and release it for the rest of your name."

The clatter started again, and then subsided. As the machines quieted, he announced in a proud voice. "Welcome to the age of the typing machine, ladies."

The class erupted in applause.

After a few minutes, Mr. Thurman raised his hand for quiet. "Now ladies, I am going to direct you to page four of your text." A shuffling of paper. "There you will find a chart like the one on the wall behind me. Please refer to it for answers to any questions of operation as they come up for you. Next, turn to page six, and you will find the first writing exercise. Please type the passages carefully, three times each. Experimentation is the best teacher. Trial and error will be your friend as you learn your machine. When you have finished the first two exercises, you can bring your paper to my desk. If you have questions you cannot solve on your own, please raise your hand."

Maud and Grace exchanged smiles and went right to work. *What a wonder!* Grace's index fingers found their way across the keys.

The quick brown fox ran across the field.

The quick brown fox ran across the field.

The quick brown fox ...

It was exhilarating! She hurried to the next sentence, and from time to time she referred to the chart.

It came as a surprise when Mr. Thurman announced the class was over. Grace looked over her paper carefully before she took it to the front desk. It was satisfactory for a first attempt, she thought, not too many errors. She gathered her books and papers and prepared to leave.

"Now, that is what I came to school for!" Maud was waiting for her at the door, her arms full of books.

"Yes!" Grace agreed. She could still hear the click of the keys. "This was great fun!"

"So, as I was saying before," Maud lowered her voice slightly. The speaker is...Millie Fisher Cunningham. She is the

President of the Galveston Equal Suffrage Association, and she is touring the state to promote Women's Right to Vote. Do you want to go hear her?"

Grace hesitated only a moment. After conquering the typewriting machine, she felt ready for anything. "Yes, I would love to hear the speaker. I'm strongly for women's suffrage."

Maud grinned broadly. "Well, good then. Both girls scanned the people around quickly and then nodded. "Tomorrow as soon as classes are dismissed."

Minnie Fisher Cunningham and several other women were inspirational in their speeches. They spoke of the sacred pledge of the Constitution to provide the freedoms outlined there to all citizens, men and women. They spoke of the importance of the contributions made by women for their nation. "It is time that women step forward to accept full citizenship in our nation. And the power to vote, to elect our governing officials, is essential to those rights."

A band struck up a tune.

"Ladies," the speaker called out. "Turn to the back of the flyer you received and join us in the singing of the Suffrage Hymn."

Grace turned her sheet over and listened to the music for a few minutes. Then she joined the voices around her.

Freedom's daughter, hail to thee
Guardian of heroic past
Thine a mighty task shall be
Face it with a courage vast.

By the heralds gone before
By the millions yet to be
Never let thy zeal give o'er
Till earth's mother shall be free.

The crowd sang all the verses several times.

"We will not be silenced!" Minnie Fisher Cunningham cried. "We will be heard. Our cause is just. Write your congressman. Let them hear your voice!"

The band struck up again with the hymn as the crowd surged toward the stage. Grace and Maud and the other girls signed the petition, and all were presented a ribbon badge with **VOTES FOR WOMEN** printed at its center. The girls left the area in high exhilaration. They locked arms and sang the song, again and again.

By the heralds gone before
By the millions yet to be,
Never let they zeal give o'er

Till earth's mothers shall be free.

They were still singing when they boarded the trolley, and still when Maud and the others reached their stop. Grace hummed the melody to herself as she rode the rest of the way home.

"It was glorious, Aunt Ada. So many voices together"

"That is wonderful, dear." Ada clasped her hands in a prayer motion. "But let's not mention your adventure to your uncle."

Grace stopped short in disbelief. Her mother and father had talked about women winning the vote openly and favored it. Surely her aunt and uncle must agree.

"Your uncle supports women's suffrage. He truly does," Ada hastened to explain. "It's the public display and the marches he questions."

"But he will vote for women's suffrage?"

"Oh yes, I'm sure he will. However, the public display is unseemly." Then seeing the reaction to her words on Grace's face. "I mean, he feels it is unladylike to ..."

Grace drew herself up to her full height, prepared to disagree, but Ada hurried on.

"My dear, you are young and feel things deeply, I'm sure. And I do not intend to say you are wrong to join the movement." She spread her hands in a motion of pleading. "However, please do not distress your uncle with this. It will be our secret." She paused for a moment, her eyes flashing with emotion. "And I will join you in your letter writing endeavor. We will reach out in a quiet way."

Grace considered her words. She had never seen such a reaction from her aunt before. "Aunt Ada, I would never do anything to offend you or Uncle Klyce. You have been so kind to me. I'll keep my thinking to myself."

Ada took a deep breath of relief.

"But I will write the letters, and I will attend the meetings." She raised her hand to stop Ada from interrupting. "However, I will not bring this subject up with Uncle Klyce. I promise. Will that alleviate your concerns?"

"Yes, my dear, yes." Ada rushed to give Grace a great hug. "I'm glad you understand."

Grace went to her room. Yes, she understood. She understood all too well, and that made her resolve all the stronger.

Chapter 11

With the new year, rumors of war in Europe began to appear in the papers. Some Duke in Austria had been killed, apparently and now war was beginning to raise its head. Grace heard the story talked about on the street and by her uncle over dinner. Apparently, a number of countries in Europe were caught up in some disagreement. Uncle Klyce speculated about its effect on the United States, but to Grace it all seemed so distant. Not something she understood or care about.

Meanwhile, her classes continued. Typing class was her favorite, but all other endeavors excited her, also. Up early to go over her notes. Catch the trolley to school. Work her way through a busy schedule of classes. Take the trolley home and do her lessons in the evening after supper, (ah) dinner. Then there was her letter writing. First, a letter to her mother each week, telling of her classes and activities, and then, of course, her letters to the state representatives to voice her interest in women's suffrage. She tried to cover all the government officials, and from time to time she would see an article in the paper referring to suffrage. It seemed in Fort Worth, the major opinion was that of Uncle Klyce. General support for women's suffrage but only if the ladies supporting it were "unoffensive" in their approach. And the leading ladies of the city seemed to see that. Their resolve was no less ardent than the marchers in other cities, just more directed toward winning over their husbands and government officials with charm and reason.

She visited with Aunt Ada and Uncle Klyce while they ate, and afterward while she helped with cleanup, but of course, her political views were never brought up. Aunt Ada was as good as her word, however, and she joined her in the letter writing. Tanner seldom was there, off busy with his bride to be, which Grace could only view as a blessing. Her opinion of tiny Amelia was already formed.

Meanwhile, the interaction with Maud and her friends made the days pleasant. The girls were full of life and outspoken. A little shocking in their demeanor, really, but refreshing as well. Grace had always been so serious and proper, she'd been told. But the greatest fear of her young life was that she might somehow disappoint her parents and bring them pain in some way. It had broken her heart to see how the death of her little brother had crushed their spirit, and she had vowed at that young age to never cause her parents any disappointment or despair, if she could avoid it. The people back home had whispered behind her back at her serious nature and her efforts always to excel, she knew. She was a curiosity to them she supposed. So, they should see her now with these new friends. Secretly, Grace hoped to shed her "school ma'rm" reserve, and these girls were welcome in her life.

She asked her aunt and uncle if she could invite Maud Allen to dinner, and they were delighted with the prospect of meeting one of Grace's friends. As she expected, Maud and her aunt and uncle got along very well. Tanner had not left for the evening before Maud arrived, so he came in to meet her, also. Watching the easy conversation between her friend and Tanner and his parents, Grace could not help but think that the four of them seemed much more compatible than with Tanner's fianceé. The conversation was relaxed and shared between the group. No Amelia dominating the topics while everyone else listened. Maud shared stories about her family. The group was a good fit, Grace thought. Too bad Tanner hadn't met

Maud first. Then she cautioned herself to keep her opinions to herself.

As the weather warmed, the promise of summer was everywhere. And with the good weather, Maud kept insisting that Grace come to her boarding house for a visit. "We have such fun on Saturdays," she said. "Mrs. Archer, the owner, plans parties for us and invites guests. She is having one this weekend, and you just must come."

"I'll see. I never know what my aunt might need me for on the weekend."

But Aunt Ada brought up the same subject that very evening. "You are working so hard, Grace. You need to relax a little."

"Actually, I've been invited to a party this Saturday," Grace offered. "It is at Maud Allen's boarding house."

"Well then, you must go! You need to get out some and meet new people."

So, Grace accepted, and Maud was delighted. "Here's the address. Just continue past the school on your regular trolley. When it turns at Runnels Street, we are the third house from the corner."

Grace wrote down the directions. "What should I bring?"

Maud laughed at the idea. "Just yourself. This isn't one of our mother's affairs. Come about one and we can visit. The other guests will come later in the afternoon."

The days flew by, and Saturday came. Grace wore one of her new blouses, the one with lace on the high collar, a little dressier than her regular clothes. She studied herself in the mirror. It was still an amazing idea to her that she had so many wardrobe choices.

Aunt Ada complimented her looks and cautioned her about the trolley and guarding her pocketbook before kissing her on the cheek and sending her off. Grace accepted all the fussing with good nature. Her aunt and uncle viewed her as helpless and sheltered, and that was fine. However, they had no idea of her life as a one-room schoolteacher for the past 8 years. No idea of her independence and the challenges she had faced. Sheltered childhood was far behind her.

The Becker boys flashed into her mind. Two to six years older than her, and as wild and uncivilized as coyotes, the three brothers had burst into her classroom and demanded to be taught to read and write. She could not turn them away, of course, so every day was a challenge between teaching her younger students and fending off their clumsy advances on a young "school ma'rm". Courting her seemed their main objective, and they constantly competed for her attention. Mr. Morris, the rancher who sponsored her as teacher, would escort her to and from school each day, but the rest of the work fell to Grace to keep the brothers in line. Thank heavens, they grew restless with the confines of the school and her lack of interest and wandered off to join the next cattle drive after a month. The people she encountered on the trolley? No match for the Beckers. She smiled to herself as she swung aboard and paid the conductor. No match at all.

Maud's boarding house was a pleasant looking frame building with a wide front porch and many rocking chairs. It was similar to Uncle Klyce's house, but larger. Maud was watching for her and welcomed her into the front parlor, again a larger version of her uncle's house, with a large dining room behind it holding a dining table that could easily serve twelve people. Agnes Archer, the proprietor, was a short well-rounded woman with a jolly smile. Maud introduced Grace, and Agnes jumped forward to give Grace an enthusiastic hug.

"Welcome, my dear. We are so glad to have you here!"

Grace accepted the hug with her usual reserve. "Thank you for inviting me, ma'am."

"Oh no. Agnes or Aggie will do fine. Were we easy enough to find, deary?"

"Yes, just as Maud directed. No problem."

"Well, the other guest will be here before long," Agnes winked her eye. "And I know you will be enjoying that!"

Maud was clutching Grace's arm, eager to speak. She pulled Grace away. "Come on to my room. I want you to see everything."

"What was that about?" Grace asked as Maud practically dragged her down the hall.

"Oh, Aggie fancies herself as quite a match maker." Maud squeezed her arm. "Today some of the flyers from Canada are coming."

"What? Flyers?"

Suddenly they were surrounded by the other girls from school.

"So this is our little home," Maud motioned to the doorway. The room was large with four single beds, four small bureaus and several scattered chairs and desks. Each girl had staked off her private area with different pillows and decorations, and they all wanted to show off her space. Maranda had a quilt she had made on her bed, she said, and Virginia had a basket of her knitting by her chair. Mary had a small bookcase filled with books of every sort as did Maud, and her space was also covered with a collection of framed sketches.

"It's just lovely!" Grace declared, which set off a rash of giggles. "What a comfortable home."

"And the food is good," Mary put in. Aggie is a wonderful cook. Every meal is like a party, really."

Grace surveyed the group. They were so young. She felt as though she was back in the classroom with her students. But it was delightful to be included in their group. Something she had never enjoyed in her isolation on her father's ranch.

"So tell me about this party this afternoon." Grace asked. "What is this about flyers? There are gentlemen invited today?"

"Yes," Maud spoke up. "Aggie wants us to meet lots of 'eligible' young men. Her church group sponsors the gatherings. She has socials on the weekends and invites young men from the community. The men today are here from Canada. They're learning to fly at Taliaferro Field. They will be training for the war in Europe, you know." Maranda said. "They are far from home, and they don't know anyone here. Aggie says it's the patriotic thing to do to make them welcome."

"And they are such gentlemen!" Virginia added. She rolled her eyes. "And handsome." More giggles

Maud caught Grace's arm. "They will be here soon. Let's go back to the parlor."

Grace let Maud lead the way. The other girls were all smiles and whispers, but Grace was struggling a bit with the whole idea. A party of strangers was challenge enough, but a party of men strangers? A church sponsored event at least, but still. Canadians?

The ladies from Aggie's church had arrived and were in full force of helping set out refreshments and arrange the chairs. "It's such a lovely day today. We'll lay out the food here on the veranda, and everyone can find a place to sit here and there," One of the ladies confided in Grace as she worked.

"Can I help in some way?"

"Certainly, help me spread this tablecloth, dear." The women studied Grace as they worked. "Are you one of the student boarders here?"

"Well, I'm a student, but I don't live here. The girls are friends of mine from school."

"Wonderful! I'm so glad you came. "The young men are so lonely for homecooked food and conversation. We like to think we are reaching out to our friendly neighbor countries, you know."

This was sounding worse and worse. Entertaining strange men did not seem to Grace like the delightful idea everyone else envisioned. She was trapped.

Greetings rang out and male voices joined the general noise. Grace glanced around to see a jumble of uniforms coming up the walk. Aggie rushed forward to welcome the newcomers, and everyone fell into conversations. A food line was organized. Introductions. More giggling, laughter.

Grace backed away through the crowd unnoticed, thankfully, and made her way out to the kitchen. She would stay busy and out of sight. Maud and the others would never miss her.

She was helping the ladies from Agnes's church organize the bowls and platters of food when Maud found her.

"Here you are! What are you doing, girly? You are supposed to be out with us." She pulled Grace away to the amusement of the ladies working around her.

"I'm helping the ......"

"Nonsense! You're hiding! This won't do at all! Don't tell me you are afraid to talk to strangers!"

Grace stopped short and Maud stumbled, but she didn't lessen her grip on Grace's arm.

"I'm not comfortable with this Maud, I don't know these people. It's not proper, talking to strange men. I....."

Maud gripped her arm tighter, "Grace, my girl. It's the 20th Century. You went to all the trouble to come to the city and start a new life. Well, you are here! Now what are you going to do about it?"

"But ..."

"But what?"

"It's so forward of a lady to just....."

"Talk to strangers?"

"Yes."

"Nonsense! How will you ever meet anyone? Now come on." She dragged Grace out to the gathering. "See?" Maud held out her hand toward the group. "Isn't this nice?"

People were scattered across the lawn in small groups. The flyers in their khaki uniforms with jodhpur pants and tall brown leather boots to the knee stood out from the local people. Voices and laughter mingled in the air. Local men and women, probably from Agnes's church, had come, also.

Grace could still feel Maud's hand gripping her arm as though she feared that she would scurry away. (And she was right.) She glanced at Maud and then back at the scene before them.

"Well?" Maud paused a moment and repeated her question, "Isn't this nice?"

"Yes, it is," Grace agreed.

"So, what are you afraid of?"

"Afraid!" Grace straightened and pulled away from Maud's grip. "I'm not afraid."

"Maud! Grace!" A call rang out. It was Miranda calling from across the lawn. "Come on, we need two more."

"Wonderful!" Maud took Grace's hand and waved to Marilyn. "Come on, they are starting a game of croquet. Have you played before?" She was pulling Grace along as she spoke.

"Yes, A few times." Grace managed to say before they reached the group.

The four young men introduced themselves. "Wonderful to meet you ladies" one said, and the others nodded.

"Let's team up boy-girl." Miranda suggested as she handed Maud and Grace each a mallet. "Roger and I will be partners, and Virginia and Robert. Reginald, you and Grace, and Maud, you and Arthur." Everyone nodded in agreement. "I'll start off." Miranda chose a blue ball and placed it on the grass. "Everyone ready?"

There was awkward silence from the group at first, some confusion on colors chosen. But they soon sorted it all out, and each person played their turn.

Grace took her shot, and her orange ball rolled directly toward the first wicket hitting Marilyn's ball in the process and knocking it away.

"So, I see we have a professional player here today." One of the men announced, and everyone laughed.

"Well, I fear it may be all downhill from here for me, " Grace replied. Everyone laughed again, and the ice was broken, no more shyness. The game proceeded with hoots of laughter and groans of despair.

It was pleasant afternoon. Grace listened to the conversation back and forth between the others and lost herself in the game. Her partner Reginald seemed too shy to make much conversation. He was young, she thought, probably not yet twenty, like one of her pupils, but the game was fun.

They played a full match and then stopped for refreshments. Mary joined the group, and when a new game was proposed, Grace begged off and let her take her place.

Grace found a chair in the shade and watched. The couples seemed well matched and much closer in age without her, Grace thought.

"Did you win the day?"

Grace turned quickly at the sound of the deep voice. Another flyer was standing there. Grace looked up at him as he bent forward and offered his hand. "William Wallace," he offered. Lt. William Wallace I should say, I suppose. And you?"

"Grace Wilson." Her voice came out as a whisper.

"I see your cup is empty." He nodded toward a near-by table. "May I get you a lemonade?"

Grace quickly glanced at her empty cup and then stuttered a response. "Yes, ah yes, thank you."

He took her cup. "I'll be right back."

Grace watched him go. After a moment, she realized she was holding her breath, and her heart was pounding. She had never experienced such a feeling before. But his voice! She placed her hand to her throat and took a deep breath. And now he was coming towards her again. He was tall, much taller than she, she would guess, and handsome, coal black hair and a small moustache.

He handed her the cup. "May I join you?"

She nodded, made an effort to speak, but failed.

He drew a chair over and sat down beside her. "I've been watching you, and I've decided that you are the prettiest girl here." He smiled.

Grace ducked her head. "That's very nice of you to say so."

"But you doubt me."

She smiled. What was happening here? She had never been at such a loss for words.

"Well, you can take my word for it." William continued. "I'm not in the habit of making rash statements."

Grace recovered her composure. "And you've made a full study of this."

"Yes, I have." And a wide grin spread across his face again.

"Well, then it's useless to argue with you, I suppose."

"Absolutely."

"Then, thank you."

"Tell me about yourself. Are you a teacher?"

Grace smiled. "Yes and no. I was a teacher the last few years, but now I'm a student again at the business school."

"I thought so. The other girls do not have your poise and grace."

Grace raised an eyebrow. "Lt. Wallace, you are extremely forward, I think"

"Yes, I am. I try always to speak the truth."

Grace laughed softly.

He smiled. "It saves time, I've found. Now ask about me."

Grace took a deep breath. "Well, you are one of the flyers, obviously. From Canada, I understand."

"Yes and no. I was a newspaper man for the last few years, but now I will be training to be a flyer. Where are you from, here in the city or somewhere else?"

"No, not the city. From a small farming community west of here, Rice Corners."

"And you came to the city because you wanted more from life than being a farmer's wife."

Grace was a little taken back by this, but she answered. "Yes, I suppose you are right, Lt. Wallace. I wanted something different."

"Same for me. I grew up on the frontier of Alberta, but it wasn't for me. I wanted to live in a city and wear a suit to work each day, so I chose the newspaper trade."

"And did you find it enjoyable?"

"Most definitely. Of course, then the war has intervened, so now I'm a flyer, or I will be soon enough. But one day I'll be back to my news stories. Where do you live?

"With my aunt and uncle, not far from here."

William nodded. "And your school's name?"

"Patterson Business Academy"

"Is it here close by?"

"Yes, on Houston Street. Not far."

"So, if I asked you for your address, would you share it with me?"

Grace bit her lip. Her head was spinning. "Mr. Wallace. ......"

"William," he corrected.

"William, I said you are very forward. I ...."

"Yes, but it is because I'm very sure of what I'm saying. What business is you Uncle in?" He switched conversations again.

"He owns a hardware store. Freeman Hardware."

"Here in the city?"

"Yes"

"And is that you Uncle's name, Freeman?"

"Yes, Klyce Freeman."

William nodded his satisfaction. "Very well. May I see you home this afternoon?"

"Home?" Grace was at a complete loss.

"You took the trolley here I suppose."

She nodded.

"Good. Tell me about you school."

"My years as a teacher, or my school now?"

"Both. I want to know everything about you."

And so the afternoon went. All the others around them fell away and Grace could see only him and hear only his voice. It was as though they had known one another for all time.

"Grace." Maud tapped her on the shoulder, and Grace looked up in surprise at anyone else being nearby.

"Hello, Maud. I want you to meet Lt. Wallace. This is Maud Allen, my classmate."

William stood up. "How do you do."

Maud smiled. "Hello, I hate to interrupt, but the other guests are leaving."

Grace looked around to realize that the evening was fast approaching and most of the guests were gone.

"Yes, we were just leaving, ourselves." William spoke up. "Thank you for a lovely afternoon, Miss Allen."

He took Grace's arm. "I'll see Grace home now." And he gently pulled her away.

Maud beamed in delight and gave Grace a quick wink. "See you in class on Monday."

She came just to his shoulder, Grace realized. It was the first time she had stood next to him. They chatted along as they waited for the trolley and sat silent next to one another among the passengers. All the while it seemed the most natural of situations to Grace. She seemed to be outside herself watching.

Uncle Klyce was sitting on the front porch when they came up the walk, still wearing his business suit. He had probably been home for only minutes.

Grace introduced William. Her uncle was a little taken back at first, but he warmed to William's infectious personality very quickly. She smiled to herself. She wasn't the only one mesmerized by this handsome man.

"Mr. Freeman," William said after a bit more polite conversation, "I came here today because I met your lovely niece at a garden party, and I am very taken with her. I want to court her officially, and I knew she would never agree if I did not have your approval."

"I see." Uncle Klyce seemed to gather himself. "I appreciate your concern, young man." He cleared his throat. "But I believe Grace needs to have the final say on this. Would you agree?"

"Yes, I do, sir." They both looked at Grace and waited for a reply.

Grace took a deep breath. "Yes, I would very much like for you to call, Lt. Wallace. With my uncle's permission, I will look forward to it."

William beamed, and at that moment Grace thought him the most handsome man she had ever seen.

"Then I'll be going, now. I have to report back to the field, but may I call tomorrow?"

Grace nodded and William took her hand. "Tomorrow," she said.

"I'll come at two if that suits you."

Grace and her uncle watched him go down the street and hail the trolley.

"What an extraordinary young man." Uncle Klyce mumbled. And Grace's smile said all that was needed.

Chapter 12

Aunt Ada was delighted with the idea of a young gentleman caller coming to see Grace. Her fussing was a little embarrassing.

"I'll just set out some refreshments, and you can entertain him here in the parlor. Klyce and I will make ourselves scarce."

"Heavens no, Aunt Ada! This is your home. We can sit out front on the veranda or go for a walk. I will certainly not displace you in your own home!"

"Well, we'll see, dear. We'll see. Now tell me about him. How did you meet?"

Grace answered her questions. It was amazing to her also, now thinking about it. The way William found her and charmed her into conversation. Certainly, something new for her.

"And he's Canadian, you say. My, so far from home!"

"I understand there is a whole camp of them. They have been building a new flying field," Uncle Klyce commented. "The men are training for the war in Europe, so I understand."

"My, those flying machines are so frightening!" Aunt Ada said. "I've seen them over the trees, diving and turning in the air."

"Is the field fairly close to here?" She had not asked William where he was located.

"Well, there are several fields," Uncle Klyce explained. "Camp Bowie will be closest to us, I guess, but it is for American flyers. Camp Taliaferro, the Canadian camp, is not far away. They are brave young chaps. No doubt about that."

For some reason Grace felt a tinge of pride at his statement, and at the same time a rush of amazement at herself for feeling that way.

"I'm looking forward to getting to visit a little more tomorrow," Uncle Klyce added.

"Now Klyce, we don't want to intrude, remember," Aunt Ada cautioned.

"No, it will be very nice of you to help entertain Lt. Wallace," Grace said. And she meant it. What an interesting experience this was.

But Lt. Wallace had other plans. He conversed with her aunt and uncle with the same cheerful personality that he had shown to Grace, but when the first introductions and pleasantries were finished, he said. "I noticed a park by the river as I was coming here, and it seems to be a lovely day for a stroll. Grace, would you like to see what is happening there? There seemed to be music and all sort of diversions."

Grace looked at her aunt's expectant face, nodding slightly. "Yes, that sounds very nice."

"And when you get back," Ada announced, "we can have refreshments here on the veranda."

And just like that, William whisked her away.

"I must say," Grace said as they walked, "You are a person with definite plans."

"Is that a bad thing?" William said with a smile.

"No, not at all." She smiled. "I'm very impressed."

"Well, the way I see it, time is of the essence." William took her elbow to guide her off the curb and onto the trolley. "My flight course has just begun. I won't have a great deal of free time, so, if we are going to get to know one another, we cannot waste any of it. How about you? How long is your study course?"

"I have five more months."

He nodded. "So, I am right. We have no time to waste."

Grace smiled. *How could she be this comfortable with someone she had met only yesterday? She was not usually a person who made decisions so quickly.*

They reached the park, and William pulled the cord to signal they wanted to get off. The grounds were fairly crowded, family groups and couples like themselves enjoying the day.

"So, tell me about your home and your family." William interrupted her thoughts as they strolled. "Are you an only child, or do you have a houseful of siblings?"

"Only child, I'm afraid. My little brother died of fever when he was four."

"So, you are your parent's pride and joy?"

Grace smiled slightly. "Yes, I suppose you could say so, but my father died in an accident several years ago. It's just my mother and I now."

"I'm sorry for your loss. Where is your mother now?"

"She lives with family in East Texas. We lost our homestead when my father died. We lost everything."

"So, you decided to come to school here in Fort Worth, and you feel a great responsibility to her?"

Grace frowned slightly. There was truth in his words.

"So, what are your long-range plans?"

Grace blinked. Such honest questions, so aimed at her worries. "Yes. Well, I hope to graduate from my secretarial school and find employment. I want to be able to help my mother."

"Well said," William smiled. "But your leaving is a concern, I think."

And suddenly Grace was telling about Rice Corners, and the ladies at the church clicking their tongues and shaking their heads at her willful behavior. "But I just couldn't stand to think that that would be my life, my whole life. A farm and family, and all that work stretched out before me."

"And you were a teacher for a time."

"I loved school as a child and saw teaching as a way off the farm, but after several years, I could see the same trap awaiting me. I was only sixteen when I got my teaching certificate, and by the time I was twenty, I knew I could not just give in to that life. I had to find a way out."

"And marriage proposals? There must have been some of those."

Grace smiled shyly. "Yes, but none that interested me."

William smiled. "So, the big city and business school."

"Yes."

"It's much the same for me." William motioned toward a park bench they were passing along the river walk. They sat down with scattered groups of people all around them and continued their conversation.

"I wanted no part of farm life, and that seemed to be the only choice. My brothers all became farmers, and my sisters married men doing the same. I have six brothers and sisters by, the way." He smiled. "And I'm a real curiosity to them. I'm bookish for one thing, something highly suspect in my family. I saw the newspaper business as a viable option that was available and grabbed it. I talked my way into a job writing local news stories for a small paper, and it turned out I had a bit of a flair for it. My family all care for me, but they have no idea why I do what I do." He laughed. "Now I've joined the air corps, and they are all sure I've lost my mind."

"What books are your favorites?"

"History, all fields. Ancient, European, Canadian, the United States. My brothers all thought I was balmy." He gave her that crooked smile she was learning to love. "I was forever getting into trouble with them for wasting my time in a book instead of working enough, but my mother protected me from their wrath. She saw to it that I stayed in school as long as possible. I'll always take care of her, also, just as you said. What books do you favor?"

"Everything! Novels, classics, history most especially."

And they laughed in wonder at this miracle that they had found one another.

"So, what is your life plans, as you said?" Grace ventured.

"Well, that has been interrupted a little, hasn't it with the war and all. So first I'll earn my wings." He tapped his collar. "Then I'll do my bit for "King and Country, as they say, and when it's all done, I'll go back to my newspaper writing. Maybe here in Fort Worth. It seems to be a growing place and will be needing good reporters I would think.

"So, you would stay in the United States, then. Not return to Canada?"

William paused and gave her a direct glance. "I would certainly stay if someone were to ask me."

Grace ducked her head, at a loss as to what to say. Her head was spinning. Her heart pounding. "I think that is a lovely idea," she said. She took a deep breath. "I mean, I'm sure there are great opportunities here in Fort Worth."

William squeezed her hand and drew her near. "Grace Wilson, I love you, and I'm never going to let you go." And he kissed her softly. Right there in the park! Grace didn't care. The kiss took her breath away.

William laughed softly at her reaction. "How about a lemonade? I see a stand over there, and I believe I remember that you like lemonade."

Chapter 13

In the days that followed, Grace found that her thoughts were filled with William, no matter where she was, or what she was supposed to be doing. Her fascination was alarming! She had never experienced such an emotion before. At school, a passing word, or action, or something in her lesson would remind her of William, and she would be off in her mind, reliving a moment. Maud and the other girls delighted in her distraction.

William came to see her every weekend that he was free, and every time it was as if he were just supposed to be there, had always been there. She was as silly as a schoolgirl, mooning over a boy, Grace thought in amazement, but then that would bring a smile also because, she certainly was a schoolgirl mooning over, not a boy, but a wonderful man who wanted her time as much as she did his.

By the end of the month, they were talking marriage plans, and their future in Fort Worth, or wherever William's newspaper career took them. She wrote her Mother about him, and she wrote back that she was happy for her, and hoped that William was all that she believed, and she would look forward to meeting him when possible. Aunt Ada, beside herself with delight, wrote to her mother, also, extolling what a fine young man he was, and how happy the young people both were.

Her aunt and uncle invited Tanner and Amelia to dinner to meet William. Grace's encounters with Amelia had been brief and scattered since their first meeting, and if truth be told, she was not looking forward to Amelia's condescending treatment. But the evening went quite differently from their first meeting. Where before Amelia seemed 'honed in' on her, asking questions about her school and hinting at her 'quaint country' origin, this time the girl was totally engrossed in William, but with a very different approach of batting eyelashes and gushing compliments.

"It's such an honor to meet a military man, and an officer as well." Amelia's voice was high and silky. "I do think you are so brave and dashing in your uniform."

William passed her comments off with a slight laugh, but it was only the beginning.

"Tell us about Canada, William. I've heard it is such a lovely country."

"Yes, it is. Much like the United States. Very large."

"And what do you do in Canada when you aren't flying around?" Amelia asked.

Grace watched in shock as Amelia preened and flirted.

"I'm a newspaper man."

"Oh, how exciting! Do you own the paper?"

William laughed and glanced at Grace. "Hardly. I'm a reporter."

"Oh," And a hint of disappointment passed over Amelia's expression. "But I know you must be a wonderful writer. I would love to read some of your stories sometime. My father is a close friend of the owner of our local paper. He handles all their business through his bank. I'm sure he could introduce you to him, if you are interested."

"Well, I'm occupied with other pursuits just now, but maybe in the future." Then leaving no time for Amelia to respond, "Tanner, I understand you are in the banking trade."

"Yes, I'm learning," Tanner responded, seemingly glad to join the conversation.

Amelia slumped back in her chair and waited for a pause, then lost patience and sat forward. "You know, I've done a bit of writing myself," She caught Tanner in midsentence. "I would love it if you would read some of my poetry and tell me your thoughts, William."

"I'm not a poet, I'm afraid. But I'm sure Grace could help you there. She is a teacher."

William continued his conversation with Tanner while Grace watched Amelia sulk back into her chair, arms crossed. It was a classic performance all around.

And that was how the evening progressed. With Amelia fawning over William while he deflected her advances, and the rest of the party sitting in embarrassed silence, watching her performance. Uncle Klyce made an effort at conversation, only to be cut off by Amelia. Grace watched Tanner struggle to maintain his conversation with William, and her heart went out to him. Amelia was a disaster, she concluded. Tanner should make his escape from this child as soon as possible.

Finally, the evening was over, and Tanner and Amelia prepared to leave.

"Now Grace, you must bring William to the wedding," Amelia announced. "I'll tell Mother to add your name." She batted her eyes at William. "It will be such an honor to have an officer from the Canadian military in your wonderful uniform at the ceremony."

"If my schedule permits." William shook Tanner's hand. "Very nice meeting you, sir."

Suddenly Amelia leaned forward and placed her out-stretched palms on William chest. "Oh, you just must come. Promise me you will!"

As a group, everyone froze in place. Aunt Ada did not say a word, but her raised eyebrows showed her reaction. No lady would perform such an overt action! Grace glanced at Tanner, whose face was ashen with embarrassment. William ignored the gesture and stepped back to thank Klyce and Ada for a lovely dinner, as Tanner pulled Amelia out the door. Disaster averted. Grace smiled up at William as he reached for her hand.

The weeks flew past. Summer term continued, and Grace stayed busy with her courses. William was occupied at the new field learning to fly, studying airplane design and maintenance. Only on some weekends he was able to get leave, but he still managed to write her wonderful letters describing his job at the field and planning for their future.

He invited Grace and her aunt and uncle out to the airfield to see a flying demonstration that the squadron was holding for visiting dignitaries. Grace watched in amazement as the tiny airplanes rumbled down the hard-packed runway and lift-ed into the air. Then she held her breath in terror as the planes circled and rolled and chased one another in the sky. Finally, one by one, they landed with a bounce as she covered her eyes, then peeked between her finders to see the fragile machines rumble to a stop, and the flyers emerge.

William waved as he stepped down from his plane and motioned for them to come out to him. They held their hats and approached the machines with caution. He was smiling broadly, his head thrown back in pride. "So, what do you think," He shouted over the din of the engines.

"Looks like quite a busy job up there!" Uncle Klyce shouted back.

William laughed. "Come take a closer look." He reached to touch the wing, and Klyce followed his lead.

My goodness! This is cloth! It's made of cloth!"

"Cloth and glue and mostly wood, I think. It's a JN-4983, the training aircraft. We'll be flying Sopwith Pugs in Europe."

He looked wonderful, Grace thought. Wind tousled and tan, a wide smile on his face.

"How did you ever learn to steer it?" Aunt Ada asked, and the men laughed at her choice of words.

"It has taken some time," William answered, "But it comes easier after a while."

"So, is your training over?" Klyce asked.

Grace flinched at the question. She feared it was, and that meant ...

"We have three more weeks of training, working on battle tactics," William said. "Then we wait for our orders to come through." He glanced at Grace. "Who knows how long that will take."

"Pardon me, sir." A photographer rushed up. "Can I get a picture of you with your plane?"

"Certainly!" William reached out and pulled Grace to him. She shied away for a second. This man probably did not want a picture of her! But William rested his arm around her shoulder and ignored her reluctance. "How's this, governor!"

"Splendid!" The man positioned the clumsy camera stand and lifted off the lens cover. "Smile, please!"

"I'm going to want one of those!" William called after him as the man rushed away to capture other flyers and planes."

Grace gazed up at him in wonder. His arm around her shoulders felt like the safest place in the world.

William smiled down at her, but his voice grew serious now. "I'm afraid there is more news," he said. "We've just been restricted to the base for the next three weeks. Starting Monday, the air tactics training will be every day, no leave." He hugged her shoulders when he saw the expression on her face. "I hadn't had a chance to tell you. We only learned about it this morning."

"But you have today and tomorrow?"

"Yes, I do, and I think we need to make the most of it." He winked at her and then turned his attention to Klyce and Ada. "Thank you so much for coming today."

"It's been very enlightening," Klyce said, and Ada added, "Most enjoyable."

"If I have your permission, I want to steal Grace away from you. I have plans for a special dinner in the city this evening." He glanced at Grace. "I thought she might wait for me in the common room, and we could go straight from here. Is that possible?"

Grace nodded.

"Of course. Ada and I will be going. Grace, we will see you later this evening." And they were gone.

William and Grace watched them walk out to their automobile and waved. "So, I have you all to myself," William whispered in her ear. And before she could respond. "Come on, I want to introduce you to some of the squadron. They have been bashing me pretty good for keeping you a secret."

Chapter 14

The restaurant William had chosen was in the Worth Hotel, the finest in the city. Grace had never been inside such a building before. The windows glowed with the new electric lights. She was speechless for a moment when they stepped down from the trolley. But William took her arm with his usual confidence and guided her up the steps.

"William, should we be here?" she whispered.

He laughed softly and patted her hand. "My darling girl, we should be here or anywhere we choose."

"But can you afford this?"

"I've been saving my money for just this moment."

"Am I dressed properly?" Grace touched her hair, I ..."

"You are the loveliest person in this place. Trust me.'

She smiled. His confidence covered her like a shield. And at least she had worn her Sunday suit today.

"Good evening, sir," the man at the door offered.

Inside, the walls and floor glowed with beautiful sheets of marble. The most beautiful room Grace had ever entered. William guided her toward the restaurant and spoke with a man waiting at the door. "I have a table reserved for Lt. Wallace."

"Certainly sir. Right this way."

William winked at her and whispered, "It's the uniform."

Seated at the table, she gazed around the room, awe struck by the appointments. White tablecloths, fine crystal, fine china, and silver. The other diners seemed to take little notice of them, except an approving nod to William's uniform. Her heart was pounding, and she fought to stay still and calm; to appear as though she belonged here.

William ordered for them, which was very good, since Grace had never eaten in so fine a restaurant and had no idea what to expect. William sat very relaxed in his chair and appeared to be right at home. Grace took a deep breath and tried to do the same.

"See," he whispered. "It's just a restaurant. Just food." He smiled. "And if we are going to live in the city all our lives, we need to learn how this is done. Right?" He sat a small box on the table between them. Grace looked down at it, and her heart almost stopped. "This is something from my mother," he said.

He opened the box, and Grace leaned in to look. A small necklace charm shaped like a rose met her eye. It was sculpted in gold and had a tiny ruby at its center. "This is my mother's," William repeated. It was a gift from her parents when she was a girl. Her dearest possession, I think. When I wrote her about you and that you are the love of my life, she sent it to me to give to you." He lifted the tiny gold chain out of the box and held the necklace up. I cannot afford to buy you a ring just yet, but if you would accept this as a promise token, you would make me very happy."

He paused a moment, and Grace struggled to speak. No words came, just a smile that lit up her entire face.

"I love you, Grace Wilson, and I want you to be my wife."

"Yes," she whispered. "Yes."

"I know our future is unsure right now, but this war will be over soon. And I will be home to you. I want you to have this necklace to remember me and be waiting for me." And as she watched he dropped to one knee and attached the necklace round her neck. Suddenly the people in the room around

them were applauding and calling out best wishes, but Grace
could barely hear them. She could see and hear only William.

Uncle Klyce and Aunt Ada were still up when they returned that evening. "Of course I have my flying bit to do, but
the rumor is that you Yanks are coming in on the fight soon. I
don't think all this will take too much longer. I'll be back as
soon as I can, and we will be wed."

Her aunt and uncle were thrilled at the news, and also at
the plan to settle in Fort Worth. "It will be a good future for
you two young people here," her uncle declared.

"Grace and I plan to write a letter to her mother tomorrow," William continued. He squeezed Grace's hand as he
spoke and glanced around at her for her conformation. Then
he said his goodnight.

Grace walked him out to the front veranda, and he took
her into his arms and kissed her. It was their first true kiss, and
Grace felt faintly dizzy from its effect. She returned it in full
as she felt the wonderful warm strength of his arms. And the
earth beneath her feet spun again.

"I love you Grace," he whispered.

"And I you," she answered.

"We are going to have a wonderful life together." And he
walked away into the streetlight. Grace watched him to the
trolley stop and waved as he boarded. She felt as though she
were floating on air.

She awoke the next morning to sunlight streaming into the windows. She thought of William and rush of happiness washed over her. He would be here soon. The thought got her out of bed and eager to start the day. There would be church, then after lunch they would write the letter to her mother. No time to waste. However, at midmorning a messenger boy brough a note. William's leave had been cancelled.

"Some special training orders for today," his note said. *"I do not know when I will have leave again, but I will write to your mother today. You do the same, and our letters can arrive together. You have made me the happiest man in the world, Grace Wilson. Love William."*

Grace was disappointed, but she understood. She sat down to write her own letter. It would be good for her mother to get letters from each of them. Somehow that seemed to place an emphasis on them. It was pleasant putting her feelings into words, an affirmation of sorts. She worked on the letter, getting the wording just right, for the better part of the afternoon. And as she finished and signed it, she heard voices in the front room. Her first thought was that maybe Wiliam had been able to get leave after all, but then she realized it was Tanner who had come. She went out to greet him with a tiny niggle of dread that she would have to visit with Amelia. However, Amelia was not in sight. Tanner had come alone.

"Amelia and I have decided to cancel the wedding, Tanner was saying. "No, that's not quite true. I have decided to cancel the wedding. I'm the one." He glanced up when Grace entered the room.

"What happened, son?" Uncle Klyce asked.

"It was all a mistake, sir. She is too young. Too scattered. You saw her the other night when Grace's William was here."

There was total silence from her aunt and uncle and Grace. No one saw fit to disagree.

"That was disgraceful the way she threw herself at William." He looked at Grace. "I'm very sorry about that."

"It was not of your doing," Grace whispered.

"Yes, but that was not the only time for something like that." Tanner ran his hand through his hair in a frustrated motion. "She did it at every turn, somehow desperate to get the attention of every man she found attractive. I've tried to talk to her about it. Hoped that it was a silly schoolgirl affectation, but she would not see the position it placed me in. She seemed to relish that I was jealous or something. And that's not the only thing." He slumped in a chair. "I've tried to overlook her selfish ways, pouting at the slightest thing that doesn't go her way. And her demands for constant signs of my devotion, as she called it. Angry for hours if she isn't the center of attention. And her parents seem to support her moods. Always have, I suspect." He ran his hands through his hair again. "Everything about her family is appearances. They flaunt their money and privilege constantly. The lavish lifestyle they live, the hints at how lucky I am to be chosen. The constant reminders from her father in front of everyone and anyone that he is setting me up for success. I can't stand about any longer. Job or no job, I can see what my life would be. Always in debt to him and to her. Always the 'lucky one'. So, I ended it." He took a deep breath and waited for their response.

"Son" Uncle Klyce glanced at his wife. "Your mother and I are very proud of you. You have made a man's decision, and I must say I fully agree." Aunt Ada nodded as her husband spoke.

"What did her father have to say?" Aunt Ada asked.

"Oh, he fired me on the spot!" Tanner began to laugh. "And I have to say, it felt wonderful."

Grace and her aunt and uncle joined his laughter. Ada rushed to hug her son. Klyce shook his hand, and so did Grace.

As the laughter died away, Tanner's face took on a serious expression. "Now, I'm out of a job, so, I decided to enlist in the army." He raised a hand to stop his parents from speaking. "You've read about the 18 Americans that were taken off a train and murdered by Pancho Villa down in Mexico in January. And then not long after, the attack on Columbus, New Mexico. We can't just let Villa get away with this."

"But you have no training, son. You can't just walk into that fight. You..."

"The world is going to war, father. It will reach here soon enough. I don't want to sit here and wait." And then before his father could speak again. "Besides, it's done. I joined last night."

The silence was sudden, looks of anguish on his parent's faces, and a tight jaw on Tanner's. "I'm a grown man. I must make my own decisions. "Right? Well, this is mine."

Grace gave her cousin a hug and left the family to a quiet moment. It was with mixed emotion, it seemed. Tanner had escaped one danger and now was destined for another.

Grace posted her letter on Monday on her way to school. It was exciting to be able to tell Maud and the others of her betrothal. She fingered the rose necklace.

The girls were thrilled at her news. "It's so romantic!" Miranda gushed, and the other girls nodded enthusiastically. The news spread through the classes, and Grace spent all day acknowledging congratulations from the other students and showing them her necklace.

But school business intervened when Mrs. Thurman gave her now famous stern look. "Only three more months left in the term,' she reminded everyone.

William never got another leave. He sent notes almost daily, but the squadron was restricted to barracks. Grace answered all his messages and buried herself in her classes. William hinted that he might get leave before they were shipped out, but it seemed to Grace he was already hundreds of miles away.

When the knock came at the front door, she rushed to answer because it was the usual time that William's messages came. It was the same young soldier, but this time his manner was different. Grace took the letter, but it was not from William. She glanced up at the young messenger.

"I'm sorry, miss," he whispered.

Dear Miss Wilson, the note said. It is with deepest regret that I write this letter to you. Lt. William Wallace was involved in a tragic air collision at the field this morning. I must tell you that he was killed instantly and suffered no pain. I was his commanding officer, and felt I needed to send you this personal notification, although the official report will not be published until tomorrow. Please accept my deepest condolences, and know that Lt. Wallace was a fine officer and a credit to his country.

Col. Forest Simpson
Canadian Air Corp.

Grace looked up at the young messenger.

"I'm sorry, Miss," he repeated. He took her arm and guided her to a chair. "Is there someone here with you?"

At that moment Aunt Ada came out of the kitchen. "Grace?" She saw the young soldier standing there. Grace was sitting with her head bowed, holding the letter. "Is something wrong? Grace?" But Grace gave no response.

The look of sadness on the soldier's face spoke volumes. Ada gently took the letter from Grace's hands and read it. A gasp of despair was her first response. "Oh, my dear." She reached to take Grace into her arms. "Oh, my dear."

Grace awoke in her own bed. She had no recollection of how she had gotten there, or how much time had passed. Hours? Days? She remembered awakening in the night, crying, sobbing, and she could not stop. William. Gone. It couldn't be true. William. She cried herself to sleep only to awaken to tears again. She felt as if part of her had been torn away. William.

Aunt Ada was in and out of the room, and Grace was vaguely aware of her. By morning light, Grace awoke and looked around her. The familiar things she saw brought her back to the present. Her tears had all left her, and she felt numb, frozen, as if all time had stopped. William was gone. Their brief happiness was gone.

Aunt Ada's face appeared around the edge of the door. "Are you awake, dear? I've brought you some soup." She carried a tray to the bed. "You need to eat something." She lifted a spoon toward her.

"What day is this?"

"It's Wednesday, dear. Klyce went by your school and explained that you couldn't be there."

Grace made an effort to get up.

"No, dear, no." Aunt Ada placed her hand on her shoulder. "You've had a terrible shock. You need to rest."

"No, I have to face this. I have to..." And the tears began again. Aunt Ada held her as they cried together."

"I knew that his flying was dangerous. I knew the danger." Grace's eyes were vacant with the pain. "But..."

Aunt Ada stroked her hair. "I know, dear. I know."

"I didn't ask anything." Grace's voice trembled. "Can I go to the field? Can I see him?"

"Klyce contacted the colonel. It was a midair crash, and there was a fire. Another flyer was killed, also."

The reality of her aunt's words washed over her. "No, no."

There will be a memorial this Saturday, we are told. There's nothing more you can do. I'm sorry, dear."

"Then I have to prepare. I'll get up now." Ada started to protest, but Grace stopped her with a hand motion. "I have to face this. I must."

And she did. Through the rest of the week. Through the memorial. Through the kind words of his fellow squadron members and his commanding officers. Grace faced it all with stoic resolve. As they left the ceremony, one of William's squad members pressed something into her hand. "I know William would want you to have this."

Grace looked down at the photograph the man had taken that day at the airfield. William was smiling with his chin up in pride. She stood beside him, held fast by his strong arm, her head resting slightly against his shoulder, a look of pride and delight on her face. The camera had captured their joy that day. "Thank you," she whispered. The flyer nodded and walked away.

And she never cried again when anyone was present. Only in the dark of night would she awaken in tears. William was gone.

In the following weeks, Grace returned to school. Her friends were considerate, and after their first words of sympathy, they left her alone. Even Mrs. Thurman showed a soft gentleness as she talked to her. Grace threw herself into her work, but her days as a carefree schoolgirl were over. The gold rose pendant around her neck was her touchstone when the days threatened to overwhelm her. Her world had again shifted beneath her feet.

One evening Grace sat at her desk with her hand clasped around the golden rose William had given her. Before her was the photograph of them at the airfield. The emptiness that she felt was complete, and even movement seem impossible. *William*, she thought. *And his mother, his family. How must they feel? So far away, helpless to react. Mourning with no closure. She reached for paper and began to write.*

To William's mother,

William talked of you and his brothers and sister and their families. I wish we could have met. He told me he had written to you and shared our plans for the future, and our intent to marry. My grief at losing him has been overwhelming, and I can only imagine how great your sorrow is. William came into my life and brought me joy and hope for a bright future. I loved him deeply and will always do so. Please know that he was the same wonderful man here in Texas as I am sure he was with you. I will never forget him, and if there is any way I can help you in the future, please contact me through my uncle, Klyce Freeman at Freeman Hardware here in Fort Worth. He will know how to contact me.

Yours sincerely,
Grace Wilson

The Patterson Business School was not a place for frills. Graduation was a solemn occasion presided over by Mrs. Thurman and her husband. Very dignified, of course, but hardly a celebration. The director reminded the young ladies that they carried great responsibility to the school to go forth and be successful in their endeavors. Grace listened with half her attention, as did the girls around her, but for different reasons. Pride in what they had accomplished filled the girls' thoughts and eagerness to find work flowed over it all, but Maud Allen and her roommates could hardly wait to escape the ceremony to begin their celebration, Grace was sure. She, on the either hand, could only hope to escape the crowd and go home. She was still numb with sadness, still empty, still stunned by her loss.

However, Maud and the others would have none of her excuses. They dragged her away to a luncheon celebration, and Grace was too kind to refuse. Likewise, her aunt and uncle planned a special dinner for her, which she did appreciate.

"So, what are your plans, dear? Do you have a job in mind, or did you think you might go to your mother for a visit first?" Uncle Klyce asked.

Grace hesitated. Her plans? Her plans were all bashed, she thought. Her plans would never be. Tears filled her eyes.

"Maybe she isn't ready for this now," Aunt Ada whispered, but uncle Klyce ignored the warning.

"I understand your school offers to help its graduates find posts. Is that true?"

"Ah, yes it does." Grace regained her composure. "However, the offers are very thin right now. Most businesses are still inclined to hire men, I'm afraid." She took a deep breath. "The girls who have family businesses are going home, but for the rest of us..."

"Well, that's going to change, I would wager," her uncle offered. With all this trouble along the Mexican border and the war talk in Europe, there will be many young men leaving. A great number of men are joining up. That will leave businesses here with openings that fit your qualifications, I would think."

"That might possibly be true, but..."

"You are welcome to stay with us for as long as it takes." Aunt Ada reached out to touch her hand.

"You certainly are," Uncle Klyce confirmed. "It will all work out, I am sure."

However, it didn't. Grace checked faithfully with her school, but no acceptable offer appeared. She took several temporary positions in the months that ensued, but nothing that would support her independently.

Meanwhile, the country continued the march toward war. Tanner shipped out for El Paso, and he wrote of the preparation for an invasion of Mexico to capture Pancho Villa. He quoted General "Black Jack" Pershing with pride and reported that the general had brought modern weapons and automobiles, even two wheeled motorcycles to the fight. His letters were filled with a young man's enthusiasm, but Grace knew her aunt and uncle worried. In Fort Worth the paper was filled with stories of the war in Europe. President Wilson had pledged to keep America out of the European conflict, but the flood of world events was pushing against that tide, it seemed.

By the end of summer, no positions had materialized, and the weight of living on the kindness of her aunt and uncle was becoming hard to bear. Her mother had written often to encourage her to come for a visit, but the thought pushed her even closer to despair. The truth was she had no home to return to. Visiting her mother would only be adding to her relatives list of house guests. That would be failure, and she could not give in to that. It would be wonderful to see her, but the trip would be expensive, money she could not afford, and she was too proud to borrow. She would visit when her future was more secure.

Then suddenly Patterson Business School sent out a notice to her. An insurance company in Troubadour, Texas had contacted the school looking for a young lady to employ at their firm. Mrs. Thurman had recommended Grace.

Troubadour, Texas? Grace and Aunt Ada got out the atlas and looked the town up, and there it was, population 743, ninety miles west of Fort Worth, along a rail line.

"Not so very far," Ada observed, and not so terribly far from your mother"

Grace took a deep breath. Yes, she would accept. The salary was adequate, if she watched her pennies.

Meredith

2015

Chapter 15

Meredith was watching for Amy and went out as she drove up. "Thank you so much for coming to get me. I would be stranded without you."

"No problem. So, your car is in the shop?"

"Well, under a shade tree, actually. Right down here on the right." Meredith pointed at the car as they passed. Daniel was nowhere in sight, but his tools were evident. "This nice young man took pity on me and offered to try and get the thing running better."

"Oh really. Who is he?"

"He is a scientist, interestingly enough. A paleontologist, would you believe. He's out here on a grant from a university working a dig site not far away."

"Wow! That's interesting."

"Yes, I was quite surprised to learn about it."

"Hmm," Amy gave her a side-long glance. "How young?"

Meredith smiled. "Very! Young enough to be my grandson, so take that smirk off your face."

"Darn the luck!" And they laughed together.

"It's for the best, believe me. If I were younger, I would be very interested. He looks alarmingly like my first husband."

"Really! Well, I'll have to check him out. Put a visual with your description of Bentley the other night."

Meredith smiled. *Yes, Bentley,* she thought. *My original mistake.*

Amy's house looked much the same from the street. New paint and some new landscaping, but Meredith would have recognized the place on her own. Its gabled roof and inviting front porch were just as welcoming as they had always been. Inside Amy had made a few changes, upgraded the kitchen, and the furniture and decorations were new. Meredith had always loved this house, or maybe it was just the feel of the connection and peaceful love between Amy's parents. A type of partnership foreign to her. Meredith felt safe and loved in her grandmother's home, but it was different from the joy and security so present with Amy's parents.

"I've set you up in the guest room, just off the kitchen here," Amy was saying as Meredith followed her in. "I've got some lunch fixed when you are ready. I'll let you get settled in while I put it on the table."

Meredith sat her small bag down on the bed and looked around. This had been Amy's room as a girl, and she remembered many nights of laughter and tears and long talks as they shored one another up through the delights and tragedies of their teen years.

"You know where the bathroom is," Amy was saying over her shoulder as she headed back to the kitchen. "This is like old times, isn't it?" she added.

Meredith smiled. *Old times.* She glanced at her image in the mirror and brushed her windblown hair down with her fingers. "Can I help with lunch?"

"No, it will just take a minute. Do you want tea or water?"

"Tea please." Meredith said as she came back to the kitchen.

"I've got a roast in the slow cooker for tonight, so I thought just a sandwich would carry us for now."

"Looks great."

"Chicken salad. My secret recipe." Amy raised her eyebrows in a show of mock pride."

"Mmm, very good," Meredith said after her first bite."

Amy smiled. "My kids love this. I have a secret sauce in there that I have never divulged." She laughed. "It will be in my will."

"Do you like to cook?" Meredith asked.

"It's more like I like to eat, I think. How about you?"

"Same thing, I guess. I've never made much of a chef. Just the basics. I've never found the time."

"Did you have help when your daughter was small?"

"Well, in the beginning in Dallas, but later? Heavens no! Couldn't afford that. I guess Rachel and I survived on box dinners and takeout."

There was a long pause in the conversation while they polished off the lunch, and all the while Meredith was thinking. *So now she expects details. My life story. What should I say?* She could feel the tension crawling across her shoulders as her defenses went up.

However, Amy tossed her another option. "I don't know if you are ready to join in quite yet, but just so you know, there are plenty of programs and groups and such to get into here in Troubadour, if you are interested."

Oh really. I haven't checked into anything yet, even thought about it, actually. That's good to know." Meredith caught her breath and relaxed. *No pressure, not from Amy. She should know that.*

"I know you need to get settled first. Not trying to pressure you." Amy refilled their glasses. "I started out with volunteering at the library. Still do, but I've branched out some over the years."

"The library sounds good. I still can't find enough books." They chuckled softly remembering.

"Yes, I figured you are like me and still reading everything you can get your hands on. They have a nice little library here. Sort of the command center for social action, if you know what I mean. Good place to make friends and learn the latest. Pretty well stocked and up to date.

"Good to know. I'll go get a card as soon as I have all my stuff unpacked. What else do you do?"

"Well, let's see. I volunteer at the hospital once a week, helping incoming patients and their families. This little hospital here has quite a large client area. You'd be surprised. We're blessed with a good team of young doctors who moved here to practice."

"That's wonderful."

"And there's a tutoring program at the school, both elementary and secondary. They are always needing another someone. There's a women's club that does book reviews and such. They are always looking for someone to do a review. There's a food pantry and a used clothing place that need people to sort the donations. And there's a travel club, in case we want to go see the world."

"Wow! I'm impressed." They laughed together.

"Well anyway, just so you know. You may have something else planned entirely."

Meredith smiled. "Of course, I don't have a great track record with the social set in this town, you know. I don't think that's changed."

"Those were children, Meredith. Stupid little pathetic children. You..."

"Who probably grew up to be stupid little pathetic adults."

Amy didn't disagree. Instead, she offered, "You still carry those scars?"

Meredith laughed softly. "Sort of hard to forget. I know it was a long time ago. Lord, I can hardly remember the faces, but their intent? I remember that quite clearly."

"Have you ever figured out what set them off?"

Meredith shook her head. "Not really. My clothes apparently. That's what they kept yelling at me when they jumped me."

"What was it, four or five little girls?"

"It felt like a dozen. I was too busy to count them. And they weren't so little. Several of them were older."

"I wish I had been there that day. I could have helped, maybe."

"No, you would have just gotten beaten up, also. There was no stopping them. It was a mob mentality. I realize that now."

"I remember that my mother picked me up early for a dentist appointment that day. What was that, fourth or fifth grade?"

"Fifth. Miss Olson's class. I stayed late to work on sets for the school play and missed my bus. When I realized that I just struck out walking, angry at life for having to walk the mile and a half home. Of course, two blocks from the school it started raining. Torrents!" Meredith took a deep breath. "I was so busy stomping along feeling sorry for myself, I didn't even hear them coming after me.! First thing I knew, someone slammed me so hard in the back that I fell forward in the mud and dropped all my books. Some knotty little girl was standing over me screaming at me that my fancy dress didn't look so good now, did it? Then the other girls caught up with us, yelling that I thought I was so special in my store-bought dresses. That the teachers all thought I was so perfect. That I always got a part in the play. Something about living in that big old house. That I was stuck up. I don't know what else. All that time they were ripping my dress to shreds and pulling my hair out. Kicking me in the ribs. If a car hadn't happened by, I think they would have kicked me to death." She paused for breath and laughed softly. "They all ran off when they saw the car, and the driver didn't even stop." Meredith fell silent, the memory too vivid once again. "You know, it's been sixty years, and I still can feel the horror and the shame of that long walk home. Gathering up my ruined books and papers, trying to hold the scraps of my dress over my body, praying no one would see me the rest of the way."

"Did you figure out who they were exactly"

"Oh, those faces stayed with me for a long time. I would see them around school. Remember that girl in our class. Nancy Crownover, or Crownmont, something like that? She was one of the leaders of the pack. My grandmother didn't say a word when I stumbled into the kitchen. She just grabbed me in a big hug and started checking my cuts and scratches. After she put me in a hot bath and doctored everything with Mercurochrome, she held me in her lap until I fell asleep.

The only question she asked the next day was who did it. I told her what I could remember, and what the girls were yelling at me, and she just nodded.

"It's ignorance and jealousy, sweetheart. Just ignorance and jealousy. That little Nancy girl. She's just poor white trash. She can't help it. She doesn't know any better."

"I told her that I'd never done anything to that girl, or any of them. Grace just hugged me close and said, "Hatred and ignorance and jealousy don't pay any mind to reason, dear. They just exist. Don't worry over it. I'll take care of this for you. Don't you worry. I think she did talk to the principal and maybe the sheriff. She told me to never walk home alone again, and for me to tell her or a teacher if I ever felt threatened again. And we dropped it."

"Were you ever bothered after that? Amy asked. "I don't remember anything."

"Oh a few snide remarks about some dress I wore, maybe. My mother was forever sending me clothes, usually something too fancy for Troubadour. But I wore what I had. I didn't have much choice."

"I don't remember that your clothes were so different. I mean, they were pretty, but ...""

"And not homemade. That seemed to be the point. Of course, my mother always wanted everything to be a big sensation. She was never around, but when she did show up, she was forever saying that I should be different, show off the latest fashion. I hated that. She was all show. I could see it even as a child."

"And you were nothing like her, Meredith." Amy smiled. "I'm sorry you had to suffer through that. My mother use to say, the best thing that ever happened to you was that your mother left you here to grow up with your grandmother."

"Really? I never knew people felt that way." Meredith was silent for a moment. "I mean it was true. It was best. I see that now, but as a child..."

"And you handled it well. I never saw you react badly to anyone. You had many friends, Meredith."

"But it put me on my guard." Meredith laughed softly. "I never opened myself up to many people after that. If it hadn't been for you, I would have had no close friends at all."

"And we didn't need any, did we?"

"No, we didn't." Meredith smiled. "And we did have fun in high school. Especially after we were old enough to date."

"Weren't those great years? All those dances. Kids don't have that so much now, I suppose."

"Rap music" Meredith offered. "It's sort of hard to dance to, I would think."

Amy got up to clear the table, and Meredith helped. It didn't take long. Amy checked the roast. "Doing fine. It should be perfect by about seven. You up for a drive?"

"Certainly."

"I thought it might be fun to go look up the old haunts and see how things have changed."

"Sounds like fun. Just let me grab my purse."

Chapter 16

They spent the afternoon touring the town. The high school and the new elementary school, the library, the hospital, their favorite hangout spot, Hamberger Heaven, still going strong, the drive-in theater plot, now abandoned. They drove out to old classmates' houses, and Amy filled her in on what had happened to their old friends, some things good and some things not so good. Some of the houses had been remodeled and looked like they now housed young families, and some were badly in need of a redo. There was a lot of 'remember the time we...' and a lot of laughter. It was a good afternoon and gave Meredith a guide to finding her way around the town.

But by 6:30 they were finished with the tour. Back at Amy's house they were met with the smell of the inviting pot roast. Meredith opened the wine and set the table while Amy warmed up some green beans and tossed a salad. Within the hour they sat back, fully sated and sipped at the last of their glasses.

"This was wonderful." Meredith said. "Thank you for inviting me. I haven't had a homecooked roast dinner in quite some time.

"Well, for me, either. Not something you make when you're cooking for one person. Right?"

Meredith took a sip of wine and nodded.

"I got in the habit of cooking when my kids were little." Amy said. "I stayed home until my twins were in school. Did the homemaker thing, you know, sewed our clothes and made macrame plant hangers." She smiled. "I went through a period there where I even bought all our fruits and vegetables at the farmer's market, and made jelly and froze vegetables. I even baked bread, for Pete's sake. My hippy period, I guess." She laughed.

Meredith smiled. "Oh, I remember your mother's home-made bread. Remember how we managed to come to your house after school on bread making day?"

"Yes, I do. I remember that we could polish off an entire loaf with butter and jelly, just the two of us!"

"We could eat like that and never gain a pound!" They laughed together.

Amy got up to clear the table and load the dishwash, and Meredith helped.

"Once my kids were all in school, I went back and finished my degree, like I said the other day. Douglas pitched in on the cooking at that point and after, when I started working at the museum. My cooking became like you said, box dinners and take out, and I saved my recipes for holidays and birthdays." She reached to refill their wine glasses. "Let's move into the living room."

They found their spots on the sofa. "So, you said the other day that you went to California."

Meredith flinched at the question. "Are you sure you are up to hearing my story? I've got to warn you, it is very messed up."

"No, now fair is fair. I told my story. Now it's your turn."

Meredith took a deep breath and let it out slowly. It was time. Her caution barriers went up. "Yes, my own hippy period, as you called it." She patted herself on the chest. It was her turn to talk. "Well, like I said the other night, I followed a man out there, Bentley Morrison, who I was madly in love with at the time. He lured me there by saying he had a professorship lined up, but that wasn't quite true. I found a part-time job writing street news for an alternative newspaper in San Francisco. Not much pay, but it was all we had." She shrugged her shoulders. "There were a lot of things about Bentley that weren't quite true, it turned out."

Amy, sitting silently, took a sip of wine.

There is no way out of this, Meredith thought. *I'm going to have to tell at least something.* "You mentioned your hippy period. Well, I wager mine trumps yours. I was there in 'the belly of the beast', as they say. Haight-Ashbury, Lincoln Park, the whole mess. In it up to my withers before I even realized it. Bentley started out on weed, then graduated to cocaine and LSD. He was very proud of the fact that he knew Timothy Leary personally." Meredith shifted her position on the sofa. "After a while I could hardly recognize the man." She laughed under her breathe. "And he was stoned. He couldn't recognize me either. We were married in one of those mass weddings in Lincoln Park with the flowers and tambourines. The most stupid decision I could have made, I thought almost immediately. But then, at the time I hadn't seen my future choices yet." She smiled.

"What happened to him? Amy's voice was almost a whisper.

"I'm not certain. I heard a few years ago that he died of an overdose around 1985, but I'm not sure. I had left him long before that, as soon as I could save enough money to get back to Texas. Which took a while, since he kept finding my hiding places."

"I'm so sorry."

Meredith waved her hand dismissively. "Self-inflicted wounds, honey. I only have myself to blame. The place was a crazy nightmare. I don't like to remember it."

"So you escaped."

"Yes, and thankfully I had never gotten pregnant. That's a blessing. I got out. Left him shacked up with some new wide-eyed co-ed, both of them stoned out of their minds. Got myself on a bus to Texas and never looked back."

Meredith paused to take a sip of wine. *The worst is over.* "I got a job with an in-house magazine in Dallas, got a new wardrobe. Threw away all my patched-up jeans and flowery tops." They laughed together about that.

"Weren't the styles in the late sixties and early seventies the absolute worst ever?" Amy exclaimed.

"The worst!' Meredith agreed. "Especially where I was. Everyone looked like a labor camp. All the time!"

"How long were you in California?"

Meredith felt a jolt of tension again. "Five years."

The look on Amy's face was the very reaction she had feared. "Why so long, if it was that bad?"

"I'm not sure. Guilt maybe." Her heart was pounding. "I mean I'd gotten myself into this thing. I guess I kept hoping for a better outcome."

The bewildered look on Amy's face didn't go away.

"I'm a slow learner, I guess." She added. This was what Meredith had feared about all this rehash of history. She knew exactly why she stayed five years, but she did not want to admit it, not to Amy. Not to anyone. "Anyway, I survived, right?" And she covered the uncomfortable atmosphere with a smile.

"Yes," Amy agreed. "You know Douglas and I knew a couple that got caught up in that drug culture. More than one, probably. I know it happened. We just never took those steps, I guess. Never made those mistakes."

Meredith studied her friend. *Now she's judging me. No more of that!* She waved her hand. "Anyway, I made the break. Got myself free and back to reality. I'm rather proud of that accomplishment, really."

"As you should be."

Silence again.

"So, Dallas?" Amy asked after a few minutes.

"Yes, Dallas. New job, a real 9 to 5 one. New wardrobe. New outlook on the future."

"Was your mother in Dallas then?"

"No, no, she had been gone to New York or London or somewhere for years. I had Dallas all to myself." Meredith took a deep breath. "Loved my job. Got to travel quite a bit doing interviews, etc. Very involved with the Dallas social scene, rubbing elbows with the rich and famous." She smiled. "Within three years I was named managing editor. I had a personal shopper at Neiman Marcus and an apartment on Greenville Avenue, where the young "Up and Coming" lived. I met husband number two there, Harold Westman, a lawyer. We met at a mixer at the apartment complex. He wined me and dined me and won my heart, just like in the movies, as they say." Meredith laughed softly. "Remember all those sappy movies we grew up watching?"

"Yes I do." Amy toasted her with her wine glass. "Memories of Doris Day!"

"We married after a year. Mother and Grace came to the wedding, and I finally managed to impress my mother. It was at the Statler Hotel. She was floating on a cloud the whole weekend. Talking with a fake British accent for a change, while she dropped names all around about all the famous people she knew. Harold paid for everything. Quite a splash in the papers. We went to Hawaii for our honeymoon, and I got pregnant over there. Just like that!" She snapped her fingers. "It was the fairytale, all the way."

"Doris Day would be so pleased." They laughed together.

"After a while, we built a house in Preston Hollow. Harold's career was flourishing, so I retired to be a mother and homemaker with all the trimmings.'

Amy split the last of the bottle between their glasses, and they paused for a sip.

"That all sounds wonderful."

"Yes, too good to be true, I guess. Harold turned out to be a work-a-holic, gone ninety percent of the time, and when he was around it was a whirl of social life. Good for the career, he kept telling me. Then Rachel started school, and I found myself with no one to mother. Too much time on my hands." Meredith smiled. "I tried aerobics. Turned into the aerobic queen." She made parentheses marks in the air with her fingers, and Amy laughed. "I volunteered at the shelter for the homeless, one day a week, at first, then three. The people looked like the ones I had escaped in San Francisco. Drugged out, confused. I got too involved, if you know what I mean. Partly repelled, partly drawn into the whole scene. Took in a few strays who usually wound up robbing us in some way. Objects disappearing from the house, or missing cash from my wallet. Finally, a young couple I brought home actually came back later with crowbars and literally tore out our appliances and sold them while we were out of town. Harold was furious. I was defensive. It was as stupid dangerous thing to do, I see now, but at the time I believed I was saving the world."

Amy made no comment. It was hard to read how she was taking all of this. Meredith rearranged herself on the sofa and tucked her legs under. "I lost Grace during that time. She had cancer. She was undergoing treatment, and it was hard on her. I came down on weekends and hired a nurse to stay with her. Finally, she went peacefully in her sleep. She was ninety-five and had enjoyed good health until almost the last. Not a bad record, I suppose."

"That was the year before my mother died. She called me about it."

"I'm so sorry. I knew nothing about your mother."

"Heart attack. Just like my father. No warning. They were both too young."

"Grace's death threw me completely for a loop. She was my rock. I always knew no matter how bad it got, Grace would be there for me. I just sort of lost it there for a while."

She paused for another sip of wine and Amy joined her.

"There was a group at the shelter; three women like me. Privileged by marriage and feeling guilty about it, I guess. They told me about a group they had joined that was helping them cope with the realities of life. "Find themselves", was the term they used." I began attending the meetings. The idea was to search your inner self to find your true purpose, some such rot at that."

Amy smiled.

rocked on like that for several years. Now I was in my fifties, and you would think smarter, but no." She took a deep breath. "Raul came along. Latin lover. Swept me off my feet. Think Ricardo Montalban." She stopped for another sip of wine and watched as Amy opened another bottle and refilled her glass before she continued.

"It had been a long time celibate for me. I guess I was menopausal or something. Whatever, I married him. He was supposedly independently wealthy. Sold a company for big bucks or something and was living on his investments. That was his story. Anyway, almost immediately I was doubting my decision. A string of phone calls demanding payment for this or that. Shady characters calling the house asking for him. Strange behavior. Long periods of absolute silence, then nonstop talking, rambling nonsense. Three months later he had a psychotic episode. Woke me up screaming that I was someone named Diego, and I was there to kill him."

"Dear God!"

Meredith nodded. "I had to call the police, and the whole nasty mess came out. He had been under psychiatric care for years. His family had been looking for him. His mother, would you believe. His family stepped in and whisked him off to a posh psychiatric hospital, and I filed for divorce."

Meredith studied the shocked look on Amy's face. "I told you this was a long disastrous story."

"But amazing! I mean who else can you tell all of this to? I'm your best bud, remember?

"You are right, lady, you are so right." Meredith took a deep breath. "So, I was single again. I still had the house in Preston Hollow. I had my job. Rachel was grown, almost out of college."

"And your mother?'

Meredith ducked her head for a second. "Let's just say, she wasn't a problem for me anymore."

"What ...?"

"I don't want to go into it, Amy" Meredith held up her hand. "I'm sorry. It's another story for another time."

Amy studied her a moment. "Okay, I understand."

Meredith smiled slightly. "Thank you." She took another sip of wine. "So, back to my saga." She took another deep breath. "I had my career, my house, a good life with many friends. The symphony concerts, the theater center, neighborhood social life. You would think I was set. That I had learned my lesson, but no, I had not."

"Oh dear," Amy whispered.

"Oh dear is right. He was younger than me. I had been divorced seven years when I hired him is as the advertising director for the magazine. Handsome, very cultured. What can I say? He swept me off my feet. Made me feel young again."

Amy laughed softly. "Sounds like a dream."

"A dream and a nightmare. It took Damon. That was his name Damon Bannon. It took him two years to talk me into trying marriage again. Two years! Then we had about six months before all hell broke loose. He started disappearing for days, then weekends. Work related, he assured me, and of course, friends. I was completely clueless at first, and of course, he was a darn good advertising director. Landed a lot of top clients. However, the truth began to dawn. His friends, his constant companions were all gay. The art world, you know. Artists, film makers, musicians. People we featured in our magazine, people supporting the arts. Wonderful bunch of guys. I loved them all, but my husband? When I finally confronted Damon, he never even blinked. So what, was his response. In his world view I was his perfect cover. Someone to squire around to functions when he was courting the straight crowd. And for my part, he assured me, I was the lucky one. Young, good-looking husband, the perfect escort, as he put it. Old broad with a young guy.'"

Meredith reached out to set her glass on the coffee table before she continued.

"I was in shocked silence for a while. Worrying that everyone, EVERYONE had seen this except me. Feeling the fool. Then I came to my senses and filed for divorce." Meredith shook her head. "You would not believe what went down.

Damon lawyered up, and we tangled over every scrap of furniture I had, every painting, even the house itself, which had gone up greatly in value over the last thirty years. Went at it for two years! Battling back and forth over everything. Mainly he wanted the house, but I was determined not to give it up, even sell and split the money. You would not believe the fight he put up."

Deep breath.

"Meanwhile, I retired. Turned the magazine over to the younger set. Damon finally settled last March. I gave up my 401K and my car. I had a brand new Mercedes, but I kept the house and all its furnishings. The Mercedes clinched it for me. Damon loved that car. He couldn't pass up a big show of luxury."

"And what is your house worth, if you don't mind me asking?"

"I have no idea. With today's market, I'm sure it has got to be up there. Preston Hollow is a good address. I just have to hold out until it sells."

"Good heavens! What a story. You win girl, you win!" They both dissolved into laughter. Amy held up the wine bottle. There was just a splash left. She divided it between them and lifted her glass. "To old friends."

"To old friends," Meredith repeated. "Thanks for listening to my sordid story."

"Thanks for sharing it." Amy smiled. "And your adventures are safe with me. You know that."

"Yes I do." *And the rest of the story will never be heard,* she thought. "So what time is it anyway?"

"Late, I think." Amy looked at her watch. "Heavens, it's two a.m.! Time to call it a night."

They stood and stretched and gave each other a hug. "Let's sleep late," Amy counseled, "No rush. I'll just set the glasses in the kitchen."

Meredith went off to her room. She could hear Amy in the kitchen and then down the hall to her own room. "Goodnight," she called. Then silence.

Meredith climbed into the comfortable bed and switched out the light, but she didn't sleep. Her mind was crowded with all the stories she had never shared before, and all the stories she still had not shared. California. Amy wasn't ready to hear what it was truly like. And she would never be. It had been too easy to slip into the drugs. That was the one constant in that world. Not food, or a safe place to sleep. Just drugs to dull the hunger pains and shut out the reality of all those nights she woke up next to someone she had never seen before. All the shame she felt and self-loathing when she would come out of the fog. The commune where she and Bentley landed after they left San Francisco was little more than a hovel in a camp in a northern California forest. Panhandling, half stoned, always hungry. The place seemed a hazy hell to her now, a distant nightmare. A flash of memory made the night appear again. The blood. That was all she remembered. Her wrist with the cuts gurgling. But she passed out before she could finish the job, and by some miracle, some blessed soul saw her lying there and saved her life. When she came to, the man was hovering over her, pressing a bandage to her wrist and whispering that life was too precious to squander.

When she awoke again, her savior had disappeared. Maybe he was a dream, but his words were echoing in her mind. *"Life is too precious. . .Life is too precious.* And so she lived. And escaped. Lifted Bentley's camera (that she had paid for), and the few dollars she found in his pocket while he slept off another stupor, and hitchhiked to Sacramento. She sold the camera and bought a bus ticket to Dallas. Washed up as best she could in the terminal restroom, dragged a comb through her hair, and spent two dollars on a sandwich in the coffee shop.

When she boarded the bus, she kept glancing over her shoulder, half expecting someone, even Bentley, to be standing there to drag her back. But as the bus pulled away from the terminal, she felt a wave of relief she had not known in way too long. The people around her didn't even glance her way. She had made it. She was free. Seventeen hundred miles and a package of cheesy crackers later, she was in Dallas.

She called Grace from the terminal pay phone. And her voice was the most wonderful sound she had heard in a long time.

"Grace," was all she could get out at first, but she had been recognized instantly.

"Where are you?" Was Grace's only question.

"In Dallas."

"Where in Dallas?"

"The bus station, I. . ."

"I'll be there in three hours. You stay right there" Grace had said. "Right there. Do you understand?"

"I'm sorry. I'm so sorry."

"You don't need to say that, dear. I'm on my way. Stay right there at the bus station." And the line went dead.

Meredith lay still in the dark room and remembered. The sound of Grace's voice. The relief that washed over her. The exhaustion and humiliation. She took a deep breath. Grace had come, just as she promised. Collected her and her pitiful little collection of possessions, placed her in the car and driven straight back to Troubadour.

She slept most of the way. And when she was awake, Grace talked of anything but her condition. No questions. No lectures. She talked about the house, and the town and people Meredith could hardly remember, until she fell asleep again.

She had been home three days, most of that time in bed, burning with fever, or shivering with chills, before Grace asked any details. Meredith answered carefully, side-stepping the sordid truth when she could. Grace watched her as she spoke with a look she long recognized. The one that had always let her know that Grace understood without much explanation. It was like the day the girls had beaten her up. Grace's arms were again around her. She understood. It was going to be fine.

"I know what it is to be broken." Her grandmother whispered. "So sad and low that I didn't think I could go on. But it isn't true. A very wise man once told me that we cannot control the situations that life presents us. We can only control how we respond to them." She stroked her hair. "You can go on. And you will be stronger for all of this. Trust me, my darling. You just need to rest and start again."

Meredith lay in the dark of Amy's house and remembered. And so she did. She stayed six months, suffering from withdrawal, by turns hallucinating or crying. Sleeping to awaken in panic. Or lying awake too weak to move. And all the while Grace was there, holding her hand, and calming her fears.

And slowly, she recovered. First her strength, then her will to face herself in the mirror, and then the future. And then her courage to try again. So, she returned to Dallas, armed with a loan from Grace, to tackle the city and find a job.

"And, I did," she whispered to herself. "Just as Grace said."

Chapter 17

They slept late the next morning. Meredith heard Amy go into the kitchen and willed herself to get up. It was almost eleven o'clock, they discovered to their amazement.

"I guess two bottles of vino are a little excessive for us." Amy smiled.

"Well past my limit, but so very good last night."

"How did you sleep?"

"Very well. And you?"

"Like a log!" Amy said. "How about some quiche?"

"Wonderful! My goodness, you thought of everything."

Over a brunch of quiche and fresh fruit, they discussed their plans.

"There's a farmer's market and a craft sale out at the county pavilion today. Would you like to take that in?"

"Why not. We just might find a treasure out there."

"I like the local jellies and such, and I'm sort of addicted to pickled okra."

"Sounds good."

They cleared the kitchen together and drove out to the site at the edge of town.

"What a neat place. When was this built?"

"Maybe five or six years ago. Before I moved back. Isn't it nice?" Amy parked among the surrounding cars. "I think the ag students at the high school originally built it, and then the county took it over."

Scattered through a large shed were tables of baked goods and jams and jellies, side by side with craft booths. There was a fair crowd of potential customers at the booths, and several people recognized Amy and spoke. Amy provided an introduction for Meredith, and she was greeted with smiles and welcomes. A few people commented that they remembered her and were glad she was back. Meredith responded with smiles and thank yous, but to tell the truth, she saw no familiar faces. Not until Daniel appeared through the crowd.

"Well, hello there!" He called. "I thought you might be here today."

"Hello!" Meredith placed her hand on Amy's shoulder. "This is my friend I told you about. Amy Howard, meet Daniel Porter, my neighbor and automobile savior."

Daniel laughed. "Don't speak too soon. I haven't gotten it running yet." And to Amy. "Glad to meet you," as they shook hands.

"So you are the one who has come to her rescue."

"Well, we'll see. We have a plan, don't we?"

"Yes, we do." Meredith nodded toward Amy. "I was telling her about your work in the prehistoric fossil beds."

"Yes," Amy chimed in. "That sounds so interesting. I had no idea that something like that was near here."

Daniel smiled. "Yes, I was telling Meredith the other day that we are a well- kept secret."

"I don't know about that. It sounds like a very important find."

"Well, it is an honor to be working here. It is a world-renowned location."

"I would love to know more about it. Would you be willing to speak at an event here in town sometime? Let the people know more about your work?"

"Maybe we can work something out." Daniel said. "We try to keep a low profile while we are working a site. You understand, I'm sure."

"Oh, of course. I understand that you don't need trespassers," Amy nodded.

"I was just leaving right now, but we'll talk soon." He turned to Meredith. "I'll talk to you tomorrow when I find out more about the parts for your car."

As he walked away, Amy flashed raised eyebrows at Meredith. "Very good!"

"Don't you start!" And they both turned their backs to hide their smiles.

"Listen girl, if your first husband looked like that, then no wonder you followed him off to California!"

They wandered through the tables occasionally tasting the sample jellies and jams, and buying a few jars. Amy found her pickled okra source and stocked up. Meredith found a set of place mats made from quilt squares that would look nice on her newly painted table. A fun afternoon. It was almost 5 o'clock when they left the pavilion.

"Ok, it's my turn," Meredith announced. "You've been feeding and entertaining me for days now. Let me buy you dinner. You get to name the place."

"You're on," Amy said. "There's a neat little place over in Centerville that is open on Sundays."

"Centerville! They actually have a restaurant there now? I remember that place as nothing more than a cotton gin and a post office."

"Well now it's a restaurant, a post office, and a filling station. In fact, the restaurant is in the old gin building."

"Wow! Well, I need to see that. Sounds fun. How far is that, twenty miles?"

"Something like that. It's not fancy, but they have some mean barbecue."

"Wonderful."

Amy turned the car onto the highway. It was that special part of the day when the light had softened just enough to put a golden glow across the landscape. Again, Meredith marveled at how striking the view was. Maybe not lush and beautiful, but rather grand, she thought.

Her phone rang, and Meredith scrambled to retrieve it from her purse.

"Hello?'

"Mom, it's me, Rachel."

Meredith smiled. *Of course it was. Who else would be calling her Mother.* "How are you sweetheart?"

"Fine. I just wanted to let you know I'm back. Got in this morning.

"Wonderful! Was it a good trip?"

"Good enough. It's over. And after two weeks of twelve hour work days, I'm taking some comp time. How about some company?"

"That would be wonderful, but I don't have any extra beds. Just be warned. Could you bring a sleeping bag or something?"

"Sure. I'll bring a cot. How about that?"

"That would be perfect. I don't have much of a shopping option here to go find anything."

"No problem. I was already planning on bringing something since I know you can't be so settled yet. In fact, I'll bring two cots. Angela is coming with me."

"Wonderful! When?"

"Tuesday. I've got some catching up to do on bills and stuff tomorrow. So, we'll come down Tuesday morning. I've taken the whole week off, so we can stay until Sunday, if that's ok."

"Better than ok!" They laughed together.

"Well, great then. Other than the cots, is there anything else I can bring? Anything you need?"

"No. It won't be fancy, but I have the basics."

"Great. We'll be down on Tuesday, and we can go have lunch somewhere. If you think of anything you need, just give me a call."

"Wonderful! Drive carefully."

"Will do. Love you."

"Love you."

Meredith put her phone away and looked at Amy. "Well, that's a nice surprise. Do you get to see your kids often?"

Amy glanced around at her and then back at the road. "Not as often as I would like. They are pretty scattered. Major holidays mostly. How about you?"

"The same. I talk to Rachel fairly often, but it's hard to fit in many visits. She travels a lot in her job." Meredith laughed softly. "She wants to check on me. She's not sure I haven't lost my mind by moving back here."

"I think my kids thought my coming back was a good idea. Arizona was foreign territory to them, and they never connected with us there very often. Of course, Texas is foreign to them also, but they feel like it's home for me, so. . ."

"I thought it would feel foreign to me after all these years, but now I'm not so sure. It feels pretty good."

Amy just responded with a big smile.

The eating place hardly qualified as a restaurant. More of an antique shop with an eatery, but the food was good, just as Amy said. Big picnic tables with red and white checkered plastic covers. Plastic plates and utensils, paper napkins and huge slabs of some of the best barbecue she had ever eaten. The potato salad was an exact copy of Grace's salad as she remembered it, and the beans were just right. She didn't even want to think about the calories! Just bring it on.

They listened to some 80's rock on the radio on the way home and sang along to "Hotel California". Back at the house they said their good-byes. "Thanks again for a great visit. Next time it needs to be at my place."

"Sounds good. Whenever you are ready. Give me a call next week, and we'll stay in touch."

"Yes, I want you to meet my daughter and granddaughter while they are here."

Meredith waved from the porch after she got the door unlocked. She had remembered to bring a flashlight this time, so the path to the door wasn't so perilous. She spread her new place mats out on the table and admired them. *Looking good.*

Then the back porch beckoned, and she went out to her rocker. This had to be one of the most restful spots anywhere, she thought. The sun was just down and night sounds and silence had settled over everything.

Movement at the back screen door caught her eye. The cat was back. She pushed the door carefully open, and the cat strolled in, as if entering his own private domain. Meredith backed up and sat down in the rocker. This time instead of exploring, the cat walked straight over to her. She reached down and stroked the top of his head. "So we are going to be friends now?" she said softly.

He gave her a few minutes and then lay down with his paws tucked under, and they stared out into the night together. In the far distance sheet lightning danced on the horizon and a soft breeze brought the smell of rain. A night bird's call broke the silence, and the cat stirred. He rose and stretched and then walked to the screen door and stared back at her with a steady gaze. She got up and opened the screen, and again he left without ceremony. *Just a short visit this time.* Meredith watched him disappear around the corner of the house. "Mister Mysterious" she said out loud, and then laughed softly.

She went straight up to bed and tried to read, but she kept dropping the book. Finally, she gave up and turned out the light. She had something to look forward to.

Chapter 18

Meredith awoke early the next morning to the sound of rain, and old memories flooded back. She stretched luxuriously and listened to the rain on the tin roof above her. She had loved that when she was a child. The patter of drops echoing down from through the attic sounded like a muffled version of a marching band she had always thought. She closed her eyes and listened for a while. Yes, there was something to be said for this coming home thing. Then she remembered the girls were coming tomorrow. *Up and at 'em. No time to lose.* She glanced at the clock. Six-thirty! Great! This gave her the whole day to get ready. *First thing, coffee,* she counseled herself on the way down the stairs. She noticed that the rain had stopped, and sunshine was flooding the house.

Two sips of coffee later, Meredith looked around the kitchen. *'Yes, definitely organize all this. Get the boxes out of here and clean the cabinets. That would be doable.'* She set to work.

And Angela is coming. She is back from Europe, and no job yet, apparently. Interesting. Her granddaughter had been the hot topic the last time she and Rachel had had a long talk.

Angela marches to her own drummer, Rachel was given to saying. *I never know what the child will do next.*

Meredith had always thought she was a delightful child, smart as a whip, but none too serious about life. She knew it worried her responsible mother. Rachel had been a grown-up all her life. Probably caused by watching me mess my life up so often.

Rachel carried responsibility around like a precious trophy, never wavering in her march to adulthood. Now she was struggling with a child who seemed to have no plan and no worries. Angela had changed her major 3 times in college. First Archeology, then medicine, then Human Studies, whatever that was. Meredith could only watch from an amused distance.

"When will she ever get focused?" Rachel always fretted. *"Settle down. What can she do with a Human Studies degree, for heaven's sake?"*

Meredith's job? To listen and sympathize. She could offer little else.

Then the trip to Europe. All of a sudden, Angela had decided to *"Take a year off,"* Rachel reported. *"I don't know from what!"*

"How is she paying for it," had been Meredith's question, but Rachel had explained. Angela's father, Rachel's ex-husband, had stashed away money for her college and she hadn't spent all of it, so ......

"I told her she should hang on to that money and invest it. But heavens no, she saw no purpose it that," Rachel just shook her head in disgust.

Meredith had kept her opinion to herself, but it sounded suspicious to her, possibly a boy involved. Whatever, she was certainly no one to make judgements. Anyway. It would be great to have some time with her granddaughter.

She rolled up her sleeves, dragged the chair over to the cabinets, and started the process of scrubbing the shelves and laying down shelf paper. Not her favorite chore!

Once she had wrestled the shelf paper in place, the job went fairly fast. She had only brought the basic spices and dishes and gadgets, so in no time the place looked pretty good. The table and chairs, all freshly painted, looked decorative with her new place mats. She stood back to admire it all.

Next, she made sure the spare room was clean and cobweb free. She brought up two of the crates to act as bedside tables and located the extra bed linen so that they would be ready. The girls could share the room, she was sure.

The phone rang again. It was Daniel. "Hello! How are you this fine day?"

Meredith laughed at the joy in his voice. Happy people make good company, she thought. "I'm great. How about you?"

Well. A little behind schedule on the car, I'm afraid. The dealer tells me the parts won't be here until tomorrow or Wednesday, so that takes care of that, I guess."

"I'm in no rush."

"Good, because it's out of our control. So, since I'm free today and the rain has stopped, I want to take the 4wheeler and go check on the dig site. You seemed interested, so I thought I'd invite you to come along. It will take no more than two or three hours.

"Oh, I would love that." She looked up at the clock. It was just past eleven. "When were you thinking of leaving?"

Any time. I'll come down and load up the 4wheeler."

"Wonderful!

"Are you ready to go now?"

"Yes," she looked down. "I'll just change my shoes."

"And bring a hat. You'll need that. I'll be right down."
And the phone line went dead.

Meredith looked around, then rushed up stairs to change her shoes. *And a long sleeve shirt would probably be good. There would be plenty of time to get the girls' room ready when we get back. .... Maybe some snacks.*

She was putting together some sandwiches when she heard Daniel's truck at the barn. She grabbed her supplies and sunhat and went out the backdoor. Daniel was loading the 4wheeler into his truck bed. He waved and cut the engine on the 4wheeler. "Did you bring something long sleeved." It can get hot out there real quick, so you'll need some protection."

"Yes, got it right here, and some sun screen. I've got some lunch for us too.

"Excellent! Well, hop in and we'll be off.

Meredith settled herself in the truck cab. "How far is it?"

"About twenty miles. It won't take long to get there. I'll unload the 4wheeler there, and we'll go into the red beds on that. It may be a little muddy, but I don't think the rain got out that way. I just want to check the site."

Meredith nodded, and they drove along in silence for a while. Again, she was struck by the starkness of the land. Flat to the horizon scattered with low brush and mesquites. They turned off the highway to a dirt road.

"When was this site discovered?" she asked.

"In the late 1800's."

"Really! That long ago. I'm surprised I haven't heard of it over the years."

Daniel just smiled.

"And you say it's world renowned?"

"Yes, a professor by the name of Edward Drinker Cope worked out here before the turn of the century. He found a fossil bed that turned out to be the best and largest in the world for Paleozoic fossils."

"Drinker? That's an interesting name." She smiled and Daniel did, also. "So how old is this bed of yours?"

"Around 298 million years."

"Wow! So there were creatures out here then?"

Daniel smiled again. "Yes. Creatures, he mimicked.

"What sort?"

Amphibians, fish, insects, ancient plants. This area used to be a string of oxbow lakes. The climate began to change, and creatures called synapsids developed. The creatures that would one day become mammals, vertebrate land animals."

"Wow! So dinosaurs?"

"No. Dinosaurs came along about 40 million years later."

"Really! 40 million?"

"Yes."

"So how old are my ammonites?"

"Some of the oldest. Over 298 million years. Actually, from an earlier time period."

Meredith sat processing the numbers.

"The man who actually did most of the digging in later years was Charles Sternberg. He worked for Edward Cope."

"The Drinker guy?" She smiled.

"Yeah, him."

"I can't believe this is so little well known around here."

"Well, at the turn of the century there were a lot of people who didn't believe any of this was true. There was a strong belief by some religious groups that the world was only six thousand years old, according to someone's interpretation of the Bible. This science flew in the face of religion. So, of course, scientists in the field were kind of low key about exposing their dig sites."

"You are kidding!"

"No, I'm not. "You would be surprised at the pushback we still get." They both laughed softly at the idea.

"Well, I've never been to the red beds before, and I've never seen a dig site, so this should be fun."

They crossed the Salt Fork of the Brazos and dropped off an escarpment into a land like she had never seen before, not in Texas anyway. Rugged deep red cliffs layered occasionally with chalk white strips. The land was broken with cliffs jutting up at odd angles. The low bluffs looked like layer cake slices.

Daniel stopped the truck in an arroyo and set about unloading the 4wheeler.

Meredith studies the situation. She hadn't done anything this crazy since she was riding Mickey. "I've never been on one of these. What do I need to know?"

"Just hang on," Daniel smiled. "I'll take it real slow."

And they were off. Up embankments and down into canyons. The broken land stretched away for miles. And very little rain had fallen, it seemed.

He stopped the 4wheeler and pointed ahead. "Looks good. We had a gully washer out here a few weeks ago, and I haven't been able to work. But it's dried now, so I can get back out here.

"Is this where you are working?"

"Yes, down this canyon. Look around and you can find some fossils here. He reached down and picked up some small rocks, almost pea gravel size. "Here's some." He poured the pebbles into her hand. "Pieces of bone washed down from the cliffs.

"I would love to see some pictures of your finds out here. It would give me an idea of what you do."

"I've got a book I'll show you back at the house."

Daniel busied himself checking several markers along the cliff. There were stretches of plastic sheets laid out down the canyon. Meredith followed him as he walked.

"Here, look at this." Daniel held up one corner of a sheet at one site. Meredith looked down a broken layer of red dirt. Then she realized it was arrangement of bones just barely exposed.

"This is a fossil of a Dimetrodon. I think it's going to be a full skeleton when I get finished. Possibly an important find."

"How long before you can dig it up?"

"It's a long process. I'll expose the top surface and cover it in foil. Then over that I'll lay strips of cloth soaked in thin plaster. That has to dry thoroughly, then I'll add more layers. After that's secure I'll dig around the outer edges and add more plaster. When I've reached the lowest part, I'll flip it over and cover that side in foil and plaster. It can take maybe a year to complete the job."

"Really! That long."

Daniel recovered the site, and they continued down the canyon. Daniel checked on several sites and paused to look around. "Well, it looks good. No damage. Everything is holding up." He turned and began to walk back to the 4wheeler. "How about those snacks you brought?"

They ate their sandwiches in the shade of a cliff overhang. Other than the scream of a hawk now and then, the land was silent.

"So, you can start work again?"

Daniel nodded. "I've been waiting for supplies and to let the land dry some. I'll get back out here in the next few days. It's between terms at the university, so I'm waiting for two new graduate students to work with me. They will be here is a couple of weeks."

"Well, thank you for the tour."

"Glad you enjoyed it. What are your plans for this week?"

"More house sorting." She smiled. "And my daughter and granddaughter are coming tomorrow for a week's visit."

"That sounds nice. I'll get on your car as soon as the parts arrive. Shouldn't take long.

"Well, like I said, I'm in no hurry."

"Are you ready to go?"

"Whenever you are."

Daniel dusted his hands and helped her collect the picnic remains. They drove back to the truck and reloaded the 4wheeler.

"It's certainly rugged country out here." Meredith said.

"Yes," Daniel said, "And just imagine what it was like to work out here a hundred years ago. This is an afternoon's drive for us. Back then twenty miles would be more than a day's travel. They had no refrigeration to keep their food from spoiling, and they had to bring in any water they would have."

"Well, it doesn't look like the land has changed much since then.

Daniel smiled. "Lucky for me."

Chapter 19

On Tuesday, Meredith had just finished sweeping the kitchen when she heard a car out front, and she got to the front door just in time to see her girls coming up the front walk. When they saw her, they were all smiles.

"Hello!"

"Hello, did you have trouble finding me?"

"No, I remembered it easily."

"Besides that, it's the biggest thing on this side of town," Angela chimed in. "You can't miss it, Gram."

First Rachel then Angela wrapped her in their arms.

"This is so wonderful! Meredith said. "A nice long visit to do all our catching up."

"Yes." Rachel looked around. "I hope you didn't go to a lot of trouble, Mom."

"No, no, not at all. It's going to be pretty spartan around here, but I hope you will be comfortable. Did you bring the cots?"

"Yes, we did. We'll bring them in later. Right now, I need to find your bathroom."

"Off the kitchen." Meredith pointed toward the back of the house, and Rachel scurried away.

Meredith reached to hug her granddaughter again. "I'm so glad you came!"

"Me too, Gram. Me too." Angela took a deep breath. "So, this is the old home place."

"Yes, emphasis on the "old" part." They laughed together.

"But it's lovely, Gram."

"Well, maybe it can be. Right now, it needs work." They walked back to the kitchen. "So how was your trip?" Europe, right?"

"Yes, Italy. It was wonderful."

"Did you go with friends?"

"Yes, school mates. We stayed in hostels mostly."

"And took the trains?"

"Yes."

"Great way to get around, I understand."

Rachel rejoined them. "She brought down a phone full of pictures."

"Wonderful! I want to hear all about it."

Angela dashed off to her turn in the bathroom.

"So, your baby is home?" Meredith offered.

Rachel sighed. "Yes, all safe and sound.'

Meredith offered her a bottle of water, but Rachel declined. "I'm fine. We're just about to have lunch. Right?"

"Yes, I'm sure there's a lunch place here somewhere, and if all else fails, I know where we can get a pizza."

"Great." Rachel looked around. "Your kitchen already looks settled."

"After a fashion. I haven't tried cooking yet. Just heating up frozen dinners."

"Well, we'll have to cook something this week, just to see how it all works."

"Yes, maybe so." Meredith replied. *Rachel the responsible strikes again. Nagging me back to a healthy, thrifty life.*

Angel joined them. "Ready for lunch? I'm starved."

"There's my car," Meredith pointed out as they drove down the lane.

"So, you found someone to fix it?"

"Yes, by chance. He's a scientist, actually, not a mechanic. But he heard the dreadful noise my car was making and came over to volunteer."

They laughed softly at the wonder of that.

"We're waiting for parts right now, and he says they should be here today or tomorrow. He just came down to the house to introduce himself. Said he loves old cars and thinks he can get it running better."

"And he's a scientist?" Angela asked.

"Yes, a paleontologist, out here working a dig site. He has a grant from a university. Very impressive, I think."

"That's very interesting."

"Yes, I went with him out to the site yesterday. He obviously knows what he's doing."

Rachel glanced around from her driving, but Meredith didn't notice.

"It's a very ancient site apparently. Some 298 million years. I want you two to meet him. He is a very nice young man."

Rachel glanced again. "So, how young?"

Meredith noted the change in her daughter's voice. "Very! I could be his grandmother, dear, so wipe that suspicious frown off your face."

They all laughed together.

"Turn here at the light. I think I saw a place as I was coming to town the other day that looked like a little sandwich shop. If I'm wrong, we'll try the pizza place."

The sign announced, "Mimi's Place – Sandwiches and more." There were two cars parked out front of an old Victorian house with a welcoming front porch and several tables scattered about. They were greeted with smiles and surveyed the board announcing several sandwiches, salads, and "Mimi's Soup Today." They ordered and found a table to wait.

"So," Meredith announced after they were settled. "Who goes first? I want to hear all about California and Italy."

Rachel and Angela looked at one another.

"Well, my pictures are going to take more time, I'm thinking, so I say Mom goes first. Right?"

Rachel smiled. "Ok, but I doubt my story is as interesting as yours."

"How long were you in California, a week?" Meredith asked.

"It was actually longer, a little over two weeks. The company needed a major upgrade. It is a small moving company still owned by the founders, but it has outgrown their vision. I installed a new accounting and marketing system. We trained a team. It went well, but it took some long hours. The owners should be able to keep up with the new business coming in now. We had to train the employees and introduce our programs and policies. Same old thing."

"I've always thought it sounds like an interesting job you have. Rescuing companies, turning them around." Meredith said.

"It is. Usually, I'm walking into a welcoming situation. Everyone knows we're there to save their jobs. And every company is different. Different products, different problems."

"And Mom gets to save the day," Angela offered, and they all laughed.

"It fits you perfectly," Meredith added. "You've always been the one who could sort out any situation."

Rachell smiled. "OK you guys, don't overdo the praise now."

"So, what's next, then?"

"I have no idea. I'll find out next Monday. I just needed a little break." She looked at Angela. "OK, your turn."

Meredith looked at Angela, also.

Angela laughed. "Ok, I see how this is going."

Meredith and Rachel smiled.

"Well, it was a group of friends from school. Mom, I think you know Evelyn. She was my roommate my freshman year."

Rachel nodded.

"Evelyn was the one who put the trip together. There were six of us, four girls and two boys. I didn't know all of the others before we left, but Evelyn did. It was a good group. We stayed in hostels, mostly. One of the boys had done this before and knew all the tricks."

"So you toured Rome, and what else?"

"Yes, Rome and Tuscany. One of the girls, Anna, was an art major so we got the grand tour."

"How was your weather?"

"Perfect. We caught it just right, apparently. No rain, and it wasn't too hot. We took the train everywhere."

"What was your favorite place?" Rachel asked.

"Without a doubt. Sienna. It's one of the hill towns of Tuscany where they have the horse race in the town center every year."

"Yes, I've seen pictures of that. But the race wasn't on, was it?"

"No! I don't think I would want to be there if it were. The town was crowded enough with just tourists. I'm sure the horse race crowd would be impossible." The best thing there was the church, the Duomo. It is by far the most beautiful building I ever hope to see. I have some great pictures to show you. This tale will be much better with my pictures, but it's sort of awkward here.

"Was Marilyn with you?" Rachel asked.

"No, she didn't come. I was with a group from my art class."

"Marilyn was Rachel's roommate," Rachel explained to Meredith. And then to Angela, "Have I met any of them?"

"Other than Evelyn, I don't think so."

"So, Devin didn't make the trip?"

"Devin is history, Mom. That ended a year ago."

"Really? I didn't know. What happened?"

"Life, Mom. Life happened. Do I have to keep you posted on everyone I date?"

Meredith listened to her daughter and granddaughter tiptoe around the subject. Of course, Rachel wanted to know if there was some boy involved. With Angela there usually was, it seemed. But, of course, Angela was volunteering nothing.

"So, what else did you see?" Meredith asked, as she was thinking to herself, *Why did she feel this need to shield Angela from her Mother's questions?*

Angela took a deep breath as if she were preparing to go underwater. "Well, we started out in Rome, of course. Spent four days there just wandering through the guidebook. Spanish Steps, the Forum, the Colosseum, Trevi Fountain, you know, all that stuff."

"The Vatican?"

"Yes! It was fabulous, but pricey. Colton, one of the guys on the trip, is also an art major, so he and Anna covered everything, and we tagged along."

"That's good to have a guide," Rachel interjected, with a quick glance at Meredith."

"Then we just hopped on a train and headed to Florence. We spent the next week wandering around. The hill towns are so beautiful."

"Did you get over to Venice?"

"Just for a couple of days. Our hotel was a pit! And it was hot there."

"So, you flew home from Venice?"

"No, we went back to Rome and flew home from there. We were gone almost three weeks.

"Well, what a wonderful way to celebrate your graduation." Meredith said.

"So, what now?" Rachel asked.

"Angela brushed her hair back from her face. "I don't know for sure. Graduate school, maybe. Daddy said he would pay for it," she added quickly.

Meredith watched her daughter straighten in her chair and felt the tension level go up.

"And what sort of graduate degree would you be going for?" Rachel asked.

Angela straightened also. "Ah, Counseling maybe? Or Humanities." She studied the look on her mother's face. "It's just an idea. I'm not sure about going. I haven't applied yet."

"Maybe you need to get a job for a while and figure out what you truly want to do," Rachel said. "Then you could make firmer plans."' Rachel cut her eyes toward her daughter and waited for an answer.

"Yeah, maybe." Angela flipped her hand as a sign of dismissal. "Carrie has a job in San Francisco for the summer, and she wants me to come out there. That might be fun."

"Who is Carrie?" Rachel's voice was calm, but very flat.

"A friend," Angela volunteered.

"So, she had a job for you, as well?

"Yeah, she is running a shop on the pier, selling tourist stuff. She says she has a job if I want it."

"Can you live on that?"

Angela fixed a hard glance on her mother. "I'm sure I can, Mother. You don't have to worry about me getting into your pocketbook. Daddy says he'll help me out if I need it. Geez! Why this third degree, all of a sudden?"

"No third degree, sweetheart." Rachel reached out to touch her daughter's arm. "I'm just concerned about you."

"I'm sure you are, Mom. I mean, you've made it abundantly clear how you feel about my Human Studies degree."

"What exactly does a Human Studies degree include?" Meredith broke her silence. "It sounds very interesting."

Both mother and daughter looked at her as if they had just remembered she was there.

"It's part of Humanities Studies. You know, art, culture, civilizations. It touches on a little of everything."

"It sounds very flexible," Meredith said.

"What did you major in, Gram?"

"Ah, journalism, actually."

"Really? So have you used it over the years?"

"Yes, I did."

"Your grandmother was the managing editor of Profile Magazine for many years," Rachel spoke up. "You should remember that. It was just a few years ago.

"Really! " Angela repeated. "Wow, I'm impressed, Gram. How did you get started in that?"

Meredith smiled. "At the very bottom, dear, at the very bottom."

"You know, I took several journalism classes as electives, and I really enjoyed them. I've thought about being a writer."

Rachel sat in shocked silence as she stared, first at her daughter and then at her mother.

Meredith smiled. "Well, you might think about it, then. I loved the business for many years. It's no way to get rich quick, but it's a good job." She glanced at her daughter and started to speak, but Angela called her back.

"How would you go about that?" she asked.

"Well, maybe find a small magazine or newspaper at first. Ease into it and see if you like the work, and it likes you. That's what I did. I was in San Francisco, and I wrote for a tiny little street paper for a couple of years."

Rachel got up to get their food order and drinks. Angela hardly noticed. "That's a good idea," she said. "Something small to get started. Let me think about that."

Rachel came back with the food and gave her mother a smile and a wink.

The lunch was very good.

"Was Carrie on this trip with you?" Rachel asked after a bit.

Angela glanced quickly at her mother. "Yes, she was."

"So, she's going back to San Francisco now to run this shop?"

Angela nodded as she chewed and swallowed. Then added. "Her dad owns several shops there, so she can take her pick."

"Oh, I see." Rachel replied. Her tone was very flat again.

"You see what, Mother?"

"I see how she could take three weeks off for Italy and still have a job waiting for her."

The silence left a hole in the atmosphere.

"So, when were you thinking of going out there?" Rachel asked, after a moment.

"This week, actually, but I put it off to come see Gram. I have an open ticket, so I can go when I'm ready."

"Oh." Then silence again.

"San Francisco is very different now, I understand," Meredith said. "Do you have a place to live?"

"Carrie does. She has her dad's apartment, and she says we can share."

"So, you wouldn't have to pay rent?" Rachel asked.

Angela nodded her head, as if this was the most common of situations. Then she reacted to the look on her mother's face. "What?"

"Angela, you just spent thousands of dollars to get a degree." Rachel's words were a mere whisper. "And you are going to settle for a job as a clerk in a tourist trinket shop on the pier?"

"Mother, you are such a snob!"

"No, my dear, I'm not. I'm a realist. You are twenty-three years old, Angela, not seventeen. You don't need a summer job. You need to be building a career."

"But I'll be in California, Mother. Out of your hair. I would think you would be jumping for joy over this."

Meredith glanced around the porch where they were sitting. Only one other table was still occupied, but the people were obviously listening to the exchange at their table.

"Are you ready to go?" Meredith asked, and Angela and Rachel both turned to her, then glanced around. They gathered their purses and left.

Chapter 20

As they passed through town, Rachel offered. "Do you need anything from the store while we are here?"

"No, I think we are good. I hadn't planned on cooking tonight, so I'll take you two out for dinner."

"It's a deal. Ok, then, we'll save all the pictures until we get back to the house." Rachel said. "Mom it's your turn. What have you been up to since you got here?

Meredith laughed. "Nothing as exciting as what you girls have. But it's been good. My dearest friend from high school, Amy Howard, has moved back here, it seems. We reconnected, and it was like no time had passed. That's the best bonus I could ever hope for."

"Wonderful! I want to meet her."

"Yes, we'll get together while you are here. She wants to meet you, too."

"Sounds good."

Meredith took a deep breath. "Other than that, not much has happened. I've been unpacking and putting away where I can. I'm woefully low on furniture, as you saw, but it will do until the house in Dallas sells. Then I can get organized."

"Any idea when that will be?"

"No, I haven't heard from the realtor, but I'm sure I will."

"The market seems strong right now. And Preston Hollow is a good neighborhood. It shouldn't take long." Rachel said. "I have always loved that house."

"Yes, we have some great memories there, don't we?"

As they passed Daniel's trailer, Meredith saw that he was busy working on her car. "Pull in here, please. I want you two to meet my mechanic."

Daniel straightened up as they came to a stop. "Hello." He wiped his hands on a big cloth from his hip pocket.

"Is it ok if we interrupt you?"

"Sure. Come have a look."

Rachel and Angela followed her out of the car. "This is my daughter and granddaughter, Rachel and Angela Posten. And this is Daniel Potter, my savior and mechanic."

Everyone laughed softly as they shook hands.

"It is so nice of you to do this for mother," Rachel said.

"No problem. I had to repay her someway, and I love messing with cars." Daniel said.

Rachel looked puzzled.

"He says he owes me rent for sheltering his 4wheeler in the barn," Meredith explained.

"I like to pay my debts," Daniel added with a smile.

"So, how's the old girl looking?' Meredith walked toward the car.

"Coming along fine. I'll be ready to road test it as soon as the rest of the parts come in."

"That's wonderful." Then to Rachel, Meredith added. "Daniel heard my car rattling down the road here and took pity on me."

"I tried to warn Mom off buying this thing, but she insisted." Rachel laughed softly.

"Well, I love old cars like this, so this is therapy for me." Daniel patted the fender.

"Gram tells us you are a paleontologist." Angela spoke up.

"Yes. That's my paying gig."

"And you are working a dig site near here?"

Daniel nodded, but before he could respond Angela spoke again.

"I took several archeology and paleontology courses in college. It was very interesting. I would love to see your site."

Meredith and Rachel both looked around at Angela. There was something in her voice. "I would love to see your work site."

"Sure, I'd be glad to show you," Daniel said. "It's the largest site identified in the world for the period; about 298 million years old. There have been some major finds out there."

"The Permian period, then," Angela offered.

Daniel looked surprised at Angela knowing the name. "Right."

"So, amphibians and early land animals?"

"Yes, one of the first examples of the link between amphibians and synapsids was found here, the Seymouria

"Impressive! I would love to see some of your finds."

"I'd love to show them to you."

"Mother says you have several projects in progress right now." Rachel offered.

Daniel and Angela looked around at her.

"Yes,' Daniel said. "I took Meredith out the other day."

They walked back to the car.

"I'll call you tomorrow when the car is ready to go. Or maybe it will be the next day."

"Certainly. Thanks again."

Rachel and Meredith climbed in the car, but Angela took a few moments. "It was wonderful meeting you, Daniel. I hope to see you again soon."

They rode in silence back to the house, then Meredith had one more statement to make. "I had no idea! Want an amazing young man!"

Rachel and Angela just nodded, and the tension from lunch was gone.

"Listen" Rachel said. "We better get these cots, sweet-heart."

"Right. Where do you want them, Gram?"

"Upstairs. I've got everything set up for you across from my room."

The girls wrestled the cots up the stairs as Meredith led the way. They got themselves settled in short order and helped Meredith rig an old sheet over the window. Now they were all ready for the night.

The rest of the afternoon drifted past. Angela showed Meredith all of her pictures and told the tales that went with them. Rachel and Angela helped Meredith unpack some boxes and make decisions on where to put things.

"I'm sorry I don't have more of the place fixed up," Meredith offered. "I need more furniture before I can actually get settled."

"I think you've made real progress, Mom. I mean, it's only been a week, hasn't it?"

As it began to get dark, they set out to find the Italian restaurant where Amy had taken her.

The truce still held, and there were no more arguments between Angela and her mother. Meredith told them about finding Amy after all these years and enjoyed reminiscing about growing up in Troubadour. They set up late on the back porch, and she told them about the cat, but again, he didn't make an appearance. She told them about her grandmother's cat named Douglas since Grace's favorite movie star was Douglas Fairbanks. They liked that story very much. It was a very pleasant evening with the promise of a week's visit laid out before them.

Rachel got up and stretched her back. "Ladies, I'm beat. Time for bed. There's more fun tomorrow, right?"

"Good idea." And Angela and Meredith followed her into the kitchen. They stopped to give hugs.

"Wow!" Angela lifted up a portrait from a cardboard box sitting on the breakfast table. "Who is this?"

"That's your great- great-grandfather, Martin Durham." Meredith pulled the box toward her. "These are some old photographs that my grandmother had up in the house."

"He's a very handsome man!" Angela said. "What did he do?"

"He was a barber. He had a shop here in Troubadour, and for a time he was City Marshal as well."

Meredith took the picture from Angela's hands and studied for a moment. "He died several years before I was born. I never knew him."

The three of them stared silently at the picture for a few minutes.

"He looks so serious and important in the picture," Rachel said.

"Well, he was a fox! I'll tell you that." Angela announced, and Meredith and Rachal laughed softly.

They continued their path to the stairs. Meredith glanced again at the photograph in her hands and then set it down against the wall.

Grace

1917

Chapter 21

Grace was reading a book when the conductor came through the car announcing the next stop, Troubadour, and reminding passengers to secure all their belongings before leaving the train. She closed her book and glanced out the window as she gathered her satchel and pocketbook. Scattered houses at the edge of town with bare dirt front yards and few trees were her first impression. As the train slowed to a stop at the station house, she made her way to the exit along with several other passengers.

"Station stop is 30 minutes." The conductor cautioned. "If you are reboarding listen for the call and whistle."

Grace stepped carefully down to the platform and gazed about. Several people moved past her, carrying nothing, indicating they were getting off for a short break, but planning to reboard. Only two other people carried luggage as she did. Both were drummers carrying sample cases.

"Miss Wilson?"

Grace turned to see an older grey-headed gentleman smiling at her.

"I assume you are Grace Wilson?"

She nodded.

The man removed his hat and offered his hand. "Carlton Hunt, Miss Wilson.

Mr. Hunt, a pleasure to meet you."

"Yes, the pleasure is mine. Let me help you with your luggage." He took her satchel from her hand. "Do you have more?"

"Yes sir, a trunk."

They both looked back toward the baggage car where bags and boxes were being unloaded and then walked together toward the porter.

"How was your trip?"

"Pleasant enough," Grace responded. "Not too crowded. Fine country."

"Yes, Troubadour looks better in the Spring, I think, when everything is green and the flowers are out, but the Fall weather has its points too, I guess"

Grace located her trunk and matched the tags.

"Is this your only piece?"

She nodded and watched as he hoisted the trunk on a trolley and directed a baggage handler toward the street.

"The second automobile there in the line," he directed.

It was a Model T "fliver", Grace noted. Not nearly as fine as Uncle Klyce's car. Grace climbed up, and Mr. Hunt went through the motions of starting the engine, setting the spark, turning the crank. Finally, they were off. "We don't live far," he shouted over the engine. Mrs. Hunt and I want to offer our home to you until you find your own place. She has supper waiting for us."

"That is very kind." Grace held on to the side bar of the car and surveyed the town. A late evening wind was stirring the dust in the street. Grace held on to her hat and gazed about at her new world.

The house reminded her of her uncle's. White frame, but with white trim decoration along the roof line and the veranda instead of color. As they drove up, a woman, flashing a big smile stepped out of the front door as if she had been watching for their arrival.

Mr. Hunt braked the car and cut its wheels sharply to the left as he shut down the engine.

"Hello!" the woman called as she walked out to the car.

"Let me introduce my wife. This is Olivia."

Grace returned the smile. "Hello, I'm Grace Wilson."

"Yes, I'm so glad to meet you." The woman offered her hand. "Did you have a good trip?"

"Yes, very pleasant."

Carlon Hunt wrestled her trunk out of the car and started into the house.

"Can I help with anything?" The lady, Olivia, asked.

"No, thank you. I have just this one extra parcel."

Olivia rushed ahead to get the door for her husband and motioned for Grace to follow.

The front room, like her aunt's house, was comfortably furnished with sofas and tables.

"Your room is here off the parlor." Olivia said as she led the way.

Again, like her room in her Uncle's house, it was simply but tastefully furnished.

"We know you will need time to find your own place," Olivia said. Until then, you are welcome here."

Thank you so much. This is very kind."

Mr. Hunt sat her trunk down by the bed, and Grace followed with her small valise.

"I've got some refreshments ready for us if you like. We'll have supper in about an hour. You can rest a bit before you try to settle in."

Grace smiled. "That would be very nice." *Supper, again,* she thought.

Olivia scurried away followed by her husband. "Come out to the parlor when you are ready then."

The dinner, or supper, Grace corrected herself, went well. Grace answered questions about herself and her family. The Hunts seemed delighted to have her.

"My wife was first to suggest hiring a woman," Mr. Hunt explained. "With all the young men joining up and going to war, she suggested that what we needed was someone more stable." He smiled at his wife. "We have only one child, and he is a doctor in Erath County. We have no one to pass the business on to, and we need help."

"Well, I'm so glad for the opportunity," Grace said. "I will try hard to meet your expectations."

"Your school was very complimentary of your skills and character," Olivia said.

"Well, that's good to know," Grace laughed softly, and the Hunts joined her.

"We'll go in tomorrow and start acquainting you with our systems, but we thought you might want a day or two to learn about the town. Possibly find a place to live that suits you. That may take some time," Mr. Hunt said.

"And I would love to show you around and introduce you to people," Olivia interjected.

"That sounds wonderful," Grace replied.

"There are a number of young people here in Troubadour, and many clubs and activities. Maybe not as many as Fort Worth, but some."

"Well, I'm actually a small town girl, Mr. Hunt," Grace said. "In fact, Troubadour is much larger than my home community, so I'm sure it will be fine."

The Hunts smiled. So far, it seemed, she was being viewed in a positive light, Grace thought. When Mrs. Hunt, or Olivia, as she seemed to want to be called, began to clear the table, Grace joined her.

Olivia protested at first. "Now you must not think you are expected to do these household chores."

"I understand," Grace assured her, "But tonight, let me help you."

After the table and kitchen were put right, she said her goodnights and went off to her new room to get settled.

Before she went to bed, she sat down to write her mother and let her know she had arrived safely, and that the Hunts seemed to be very pleasant people. Her mother had been anxious about her traveling to an unknown town for this job. She would need to arrange for her to visit as soon as possible to set her mind at ease.

The next day was a whirlwind of activity. After breakfast, Olivia suggested that she would take Grace on a tour of the town and help her with finding her own living quarters.

"There are several boarding houses to choose from. Some more inclined toward your needs than others, I would think. We will take a tour and let you see them. No rush, however," she quickly added. You are welcome to stay here as long as you want."

"Thank you for that," Grace assured her, "However, if possible, I would like to establish my own place."

"Yes, I understand. We'll make some inquiries, and in the meantime, I can show you our little community. The churches", (Olivia was delighted to learn that Grace was a Methodist like she and her husband). "We have a number of young people in our congregation," she assured her. She pointed out the different shops in the town, the post office, the courthouse. "Troubadour is the county seat of Thatcher County. We are growing all the time."

They went back to the house for the noon meal and then later to the Hunt agency office, which was on the main street of the town. Olivia gave her a tour of the office and where she would work. And Mr. Hunt added the list of activities they were asking her to take on.

It was a pleasant day, and Grace already had an idea which of the boarding houses she was interested in. It was a block closer to the office than the Hunt's home on the opposite side of main street. Three blocks to walk to and from. She could manage that, and Olivia highly recommended the lady who owned it, a Mrs. Hatcher. Tomorrow, they agreed, they would go to meet with her and see what the possibilities were. Things seemed to be progressing smoothly, Grace thought.

And the next morning, just as she hoped, all went well. Mrs. Stella Hatcher was a tall woman with a friendly smile. Her house was neat and well appointed, and the room she offered Grace was adequate, the price reasonable. She met several of the other boarders, two elderly women and two gentlemen, all who seemed pleasant enough. Arrangements were made for Grace to move in on Saturday.

"Now," Olivia counseled as they left. "I think you should take the next few days to rest. You can start in the office next week after you get settled in your new place. This has been a very busy week for you, and you need to take time for yourself."

"That is very thoughtful of you. I could use the time to gather myself and make some preparations, see to my clothes, some personal shopping."

"Then it's settled," Olivia said. "Let me know if you need anything, now."

Chapter 22

Martin Durham

It was that day again. Martin sat in his shop and stared out across the street toward the courthouse. It was a slow morning for business. With time on his hands, the old memories flooded back. Three years gone, and still his pain was no less. *Irena was dead, and his loss felt as painful and fresh as when she first died,* his life a whirl of anger and sadness and questions. How could it have happened? So quickly? So final? It was only a fever, the doctor had said at first. Bed rest, he had prescribed. But the fever grew worse, and the pain began. Doubled over in pain. Crying in pain. He had been helpless. There was nothing he could do!

Too late, the doctor recognized the signs of appendicitis. Too late! Irena had died in his arms.

Martin looked down at his hands lying useless by his lap. There was no time. There had been nothing he could do. Nothing.

And now? Three years gone by? What was left? He sat there as darkness covered him and stared into the blackness. What now? He pictured Irena's sweet face. Her smile. They had planned a great future. Children, sons. He wanted three sons, he had told her, and they decided on all the names. And a daughter for her. Someone to be her companion. Such plans, so little time.

He had known the moment he first saw Irena that she would be his. It was the Spring of 1911. He had just moved to Troubadour and opened his barber shop. He was standing with some men, watching the workman put up his sign over the front door, in fact. Then, he glanced down the street and saw her alighting from an automobile in front of the ladies' dress shop. She looked up and their eyes met for just a moment. Then she was gone, disappearing into a shop.

"Who's that girl down there that just got out of the motor car?" He asked his friends.

"What girl? Harper Ramsey asked.

"She just went in that store down there. Did you see her?"

"No, no I didn't, but that fancy machine belongs to Judge Tacket, so I'm guessing it was his daughter, Irena."

"Irena," Martin repeated.

"A little out of your league, fella." Someone said, and the group of men around them joined in his laughter.

"Why's that?" Martin straightened and shot a hard look at the group that stopped the laughter.

"Tacket is the wealthiest man in this town, for one thing, and his wife died several years ago, so Irena's his only family and her daddy's pride and joy for another."

Martin looked back down the street where she had disappeared. "So what does her rich old daddy do for all his money?"

He owns the largest ranch in the county. That's what."

"But you called him Judge."

"That's just out of respect. He used to be a judge. He ain't no more."

"Do you know her?"

"Well, I know who she is, if that's what you mean, but I ain't never talked to her."

"I have."

Martin looked around to find Arthur Prentiss smiling at him. "I know her family, and I know her. We went to school together."

Martin studied the man for a moment, and Arthur stared back. "So?" He said finally.

"So what?" Arthur asked.

"So, can you introduce me?"

The group of men laughed again, but it was subdued, reacting to the seriousness of Martin's expression.

"Sure," Arthur glanced around at the others. "When?"

"Now." Martin motioned with his head and turned to walk down the street.

Arthur caught up with him. "You sure about this?"

Martin looked around at him with a tight smile. "Just get her attention. Say something pleasant and then introduce me. I'll take it from there."

"Right." Arthur squared his shoulders and took a deep breath.

They reached the shop and took a quick glance in the window. She was in there, alright. Martin could see her talking to a clerk.

He straightened. "How do I look?" He asked.

"Pretty fair. Brush your hair down a little."

Martin followed his instructions. Time ticked away as they stood waiting. Several people nodded hello as they passed on the sidewalk, and Martin even was starting to be uncomfortable with all the attention when there was rustle at the shop door, and Irena stepped out, carrying several packages.

"Irena!" Arthur spoke up. "How are you?"

Irena looked up, "Well, hello Arthur. I'm fine. How are you?"

"Fine, fine. Been shopping I see." He could feel Martin leaning in.

"Some gifts," Irena smiled. She glanced at Martin.

"This here is my friend Martin Durham. Martin this is Irena Tacket."

Martin stepped forward. "It's a pleasure, Miss Tacket."

Irena blinked her eyes and smiled as she offered her hand. "A pleasure, Mr. Durham.

"I've just moved to town," Martin continued. Opened my barber shop just down the street there." He motioned over his shoulder.

"Well, welcome to Troubadour."

"Thank you. Can I carry those packages for you? You seem to have your hands full."

She paused for only a moment. "Well, thank you, sir."

Martin reached for the packages. "Where do you need to go?"

Irena smiled as she looked up at him. "Just down the street there. I have one more stop to make."

"You lead and I'll follow," Martin said with a nod.

"Good day, Arthur," Irena said with a dismissive tone. Then she turned and walked away, with Martin following. He glanced back at Arthur and winked."

As they turned the corner, Irena looked back and slowed a little to let him catch up. "I appreciate this, Mr. Durham."

"Can't it just be Martin?"

She smiled. "I don't know you that well yet, I'm afraid."

Yet! Martin thought. *Good word.* "Very well, I'll wait," he said with a smile.

That was how it had started. Just like that, he had known she was the one. It took several "chance meetings" before he asked her out on a formal occasion. And there was the meeting with her father to ask his permission to court his daughter. Judge Tacket was just as Martin expected. Rather pompous, accustomed to intimidating Irena's suitors. He didn't let that bother him. He wasn't easy to discourage. No one had ever seen Martin Durham back down.

The courtship had progressed, and they were married with all the finery a year after they met. Judge Fancher had accepted Martin as 'a serious young man with a good head on his shoulders', he confided to his friends. And the town agreed. Martin Durham was not to be taken lightly. His business flourished, and he even hired another barber. Durham's Barber Shop became the unofficial men's club of Troubadour, a place where a man could let his guard down a little, where no ladies were present. Where talk of politics and hunts and hunting dogs were often the topic, and a place where a friendly game of poker could happen on occasion with no one the wiser.

Their lives seemed destined for success, and when in that same year, the judge died suddenly of a heart attack, their fortune was set. Irena was her father's only heir, and she inherited the family home and ranch. The great white house just west of town had become their home, and they settled into a life that Martin could only have dreamed of as a boy. A home almost palatial compared to the house he had known in his early years. Room for the family he wanted, room for his future sons to flourish.

However, then after two years, Irena was gone. Gone.

At first, he went a little crazy. Let his business go and depended on his employee to make decisions. He took to the river with his hounds for days on end, and if he had been a drinking man, he might have lost it all. But Martin Durham was too serious, too responsible, too unbending to be broken.

When the fracas with Pancho Villa erupted on the border, it was an excuse for Martin to take another path. The idea of going into a fight was an escape, and in his despair, he truly did not care if he died. He took the train to El Paso intending to volunteer, but 'Black Jack' Pershing had his forces in place. Martin was turned down. After a week of rambling and confusion in El Paso, he gave up and returned to Troubadour.

His friends and customers welcomed him back, and he stepped back into his shop.

That had been a year ago now. Three without Irena. Martin went through his days with determined purpose, and his friends saw a difference in him. A seriousness that had not been there before. Now, in the spring of 1917, when the troops were called up for the war in Europe, he tried to volunteer again, but at 35, he was too old, he was told.

He watched the young men join up and march away and felt he was missing a chance at glory. So, when the town leaders approached him to become City Marshal, it was as if one last chance was offered to him. One last chance to chase his demons away and risk his life. He could run his shop and Marshal the town at the same time. The job just required a steady hand and a reputation for no nonsense. Martin Durham was that man.

It was the first cold windy Tuesday of the year with few people on the street. A day to keep the folding doors of his shop shut tight. No customers had wandered in yet. Luther was lounged back in his barber chair, catching a short nap while Martin washed up his customer's barber mugs and cleaned the shelves. The shop was doing well. It was satisfying to see how that collection of regular customer mugs had grown. He glanced back out at the street from time to time, but all he could see was a brisk wind swirling dust down the empty brick street. The customers would be few and far between today.

Motion caught his eye. There was someone out there. He walked over to the window and look closer. Huddled in a corner between two shops next door was that colored boy he saw around town with a shoeshine box. Telly, everyone called him. He had noticed him off and on, standing back to the wall, watching the town people go by, or busily popping his rag and polishing men's shoes on a Saturday. Nobody seemed to pay him much mind. He was just a fixture on the street, and about the only black person you ever saw in downtown Troubadour. Martin wondered about that. He knew the black town was down by the river, but the towns didn't mingle much.

It was as miserable morning. He watched the boy huddled against the cold. He was wearing only a tattered cotton shirt and pants, no jacket. Martin opened the door a crack and stuck his head out. The boy reacted to the noises and looked up at him with a wary gaze, posed to run, he guessed.

Martin motioned him over, and the boy rose and hesitantly walked toward him. "Looks a little cold out here." Martin surveyed the street. "You want to come inside out the wind?"

The boy blinked, but he didn't move.

"Come on," Martin motioned. "It's cold out here. I want to shut the door." He backed up as the boy followed. "Here, get over here by the stove." He motioned towards the kerosene stove throwing out a circle of heat in the middle of the room. The boy did as he was told. Martin raised his hands up to the fire.

"Well, I'd say there isn't much business for either of us. Do you think?"

The boy smiled as he stepped into the warm air from the heater. "Naw, sir, there sure ain't today."

Martin backed up and sat down in his barber chair. "You'll get no business today. Nobody's going to stop on the street for a shine."

The boy shrugged. "Maybe so, but I gots to try."

Martin laughed. I know what you mean. I'm down here in an empty shop hoping for the same thing."

The boy nodded agreement.

"I've been watching you," Martin added. "You're a hard worker. Out there in all kinds of weather every day."

"I gots to make a living." The boy shrugged again.

"Yah," Martin agreed. "Yah," he repeated. They both stared at the warm stove.

"You're the Marshal," the boy said after a bit.

"Yeah, I am."

The boy nodded.

"My name's Martin Durham. And they call you Telly, I believe. Is that right?"

The boy nodded again.

Luther stirred a little in his chair, and that got both of their attention for a second.

Martin ran his hand across his chin. The thought that he needed a shave flashed through his mind. *Wouldn't do for the town's barber to look sloppy.* "I've been thinking about you for a while."

The boy, Telly, knitted his brow a little, but he didn't speak.

"I mean, being as how we're kind of in the same business, I was thinking maybe we should go in together."

Telly responded with silence.

Martin continued. "We're both looking for the same customers. What would you think about moving in here to do your shoe shining? You'd be out of the weather, for one thing, and I'm thinking you might do pretty well, shining the shoes of my customers."

Martin paused, but the boy was just stared, dumb struck.

"What do you think?" Martin repeated.

"All the time?" Telly finally responded.

"Yeah. All the time."

"Why would you do such as that?"

Martin smiled. "Cause I don't like looking out at you shivering on the sidewalk. And cause I believe you'll generate more business for me, too."

A slow smile crept across Telly's face. "I believe I could do that, yes sir."

Martin noticed Luther was awake and listening. "Luther, I believe we've got us a new partner."

Luther just smiled and nodded.

Martin left out at noon, saying he had business to attend to. He left Luther and Telly warm by the fire. He stopped off at the Man's Shop down the street and bought two pairs of pants and two shirts that looked like they would fit Telly. One of the shirts was work shirt blue, the other was a kind of rusty red color. He figured Telly would like that. When he got back to the shop, he handed the brown paper wrapped package to the boy. Telly took it hesitantly and opened it.

Martin smiled. "Something to celebrate our new business partnership."

Telly just stared at the clothes in amazement.

"You can get changed out in the back room there, and throw those old clothes of yours out for rags. Let me know if they don't fit. I can fix that."

"Thank you kindly, sir. I'll pay you back."

Hiring Telly caused a bit of a stir in the town. A black working in a white man's shop, right out where customers could see him. Talk in the street and in the churches bantered back and forth. Was it wise to mix those people in? Was it dangerous?

But in the final say, the Marshal could do as he pleased, they concluded. Martin Durham was no man to question.

Chapter 23

Martin could always count on Telly being there early. Telly was always there before him, at the shop door waiting for Martin every day. This morning was no different. Luther was late, he noted. That was not different either. Martin smiled and greeted Telly. Bringing him into the shop had been a good idea. After the initial fuss and feathers, the town folk had settled in, and Telly was keeping the shoes and boots of Troubadour in good condition. On top of that, the novelty of having a shoeshine boy, and a black one at that, had brought in a whole new rank of customers. Martin had added at least ten new shaving mugs to his shelf.

Luther slipped in the door. "Morning boss." They were ready for a new day.

Martin Durham went out to perform his first morning ritual, sweeping the front walk. He was sweeping away when he saw her for the first time, walking toward him from down the street. A stranger, not often met in a small town. A young woman, pleasant in features, tall, dressed nicely with an air of dignity. As she stepped up on the walkway before his shop, Martin stopped his sweeping and nodded a "Good Morning."

She smiled and returned his greeting, then swept on past him down the walk. He watched her until she turned the corner at the end of the block. Then he glanced around quickly to see that no one was watching him. He gave the walk another rash of sweeps and went indoors.

Grace was happy with her new job. The Hunts, Carlton and Olivia, were pleasant people. They welcomed her into their home and business with ease. Grace accepted this with a smile. She was thankful for the position.

And her new home in the boarding house was comfortable, if small. Grace was settled in her new room and routine. The work for the Hunts was interesting, an insurance office. And

Grace was thankful every day for all the training she had received at the hands of the Thurmans and their business school.

Each morning as she walked to work, she encountered a man sweeping the walk in front of a barber shop. At first, he only nodded and thoughtfully stopped his sweeping as she passed. He was a handsome man, she thought. Tall, much taller than she. Older, she guessed, but not too much. He easily fell into her routine each morning. Always with a nod and a smile, as he stopped sweeping when she passed.

Seeing him there became part of her morning ritual on her route to her new job. But after several weeks, the routine changed. As she walked to the office, it began to sprinkle, not heavy but noticeably. Grace didn't own an umbrella. She paused to pull a scarf from her bag and tie it over her hat, and then increased her pace. The rain was coming harder. If she could reach the corner of the main street, she would be under an awning, but that was still over a block away.

Up ahead she saw the man at the door of his shop, and he was watching her. He reached back into his shop and came out the door, running to meet her down the street, busily trying to open an umbrella, which he accomplished just as he reached her.

He was laughing. "May I help you?" he asked. He held the umbrella out over her head.

"Thank you!" She smiled. "You are so thoughtful."

He joined her under the protection of the umbrella, and wiped the rain from his face, as they hurried along passed his shop to the corner.

They reached the awning and stopped to catch their breath.

"Thank you so much." Grace wiped her brow and looked down to see how much damage the rain had done to her skirt and jacket. "I wasn't prepared for this."

"Glad I could help." Martin shook out the umbrella gently. "I'm Martin Durham."

"Grace Wilson."

"I see you every day, but I'm not sure where you come from, or where you are going."

Grace smiled. "I'm on my way to work. I'm secretary in the Hunt's Insurance office. I live in Mrs. Hatcher's boarding house, on Liberty Street."

Martin nodded. "Well, that's my shop you pass each morning."

They stood silently for a moment, having exhausted their conversation.

"Well, thank you for rescuing me. I will endeavor to buy an umbrella today, so I won't disturb your day again."

Martin frowned. "Oh, I hope that isn't the case. I mean it's wise to have an umbrella, but I hope to see you again."

Grace blinked, not knowing quite what to respond. "Yes, well thanks again." She stepped away and continued on to her office. When she reached the door and looked back, he was still standing there watching her. She smiled and waved, and he responded in kind.

All day, when she had a minute to reflect, he would come into her thoughts again. Shortly before closing, she caught a moment when Mr. Hunt was out of the office, and she and Olivia were alone. "I need to buy an umbrella today, if I can," Grace ventured. Would they have those in a shop nearby?"

"Yes, Poston's, I think. Two doors down," Olivia replied. "Did the rain catch you this morning?"

"Yes, a little, but a nice gentleman rescued me. Do you know Martin Durham?"

Olivia smiled. "Yes, I do. Was he the one?"

"Yes, he saw me making a dash up the street and came out with an umbrella."

"Oh!" Olivia took a deep breath. "Yes, Martin would be one to rescue you. He's the town Marshal, as well as the owner of his barber shop. He's a widower." She dropped her voice. "His wife died suddenly three years ago, from appendicitis, I believe. He's a good man, highly thought of. He has some strange ideas but all and all, he's respected.

"What sort of strange ideas?"

"Well, he hired that black boy, Telly, to work in his shop, for one thing. That stirred people up for a while. And he takes all customers in his shop, for another, even the Mexican laborers. Course, it's a barber shop and strictly for the men. So, it's accepted, I guess. And he's a good Marshal. Keeps the town quiet. People look up to him.

Grace nodded, but she did not respond. Martin Durham sounded like a man she might have respect for.

"Well, I believe I'll be going, if it is okay. Everything is completed. I'll just have time to drop in at the shop for the umbrella, I think."

"Yes, wonderful. See you tomorrow."

She found the shop and made her purchase. The new umbrella in hand, and Grace started her walk home. When she turned the corner toward the barber shop, she noted that the man was nowhere in sight. She glanced at the people around her and acknowledged their greeting. It was a pleasant afternoon, and the sun had erased any evidence of the morning shower.

As she neared the barber shop, however, the man, Martin, stepped out and smiled. "Good afternoon! Then spying the umbrella. "So, I'm out of a job, I see."

Grace smiled. Yes, I thought I would plan better and follow your example."

He laughed softly. "Well, I'm always here, if you need me." There was an awkward pause in the conversation. "Listen, I was just locking up." He pointed over his shoulder at his shop door. "If you could wait a moment, could I walk you home?"

"Yes, that would be very nice."

"Fine, just give me a minute." Martin turned to his shop door and then waited as a young black boy scurried out.

"Night boss."

"Good night, Telly. See you in the morning." He shut the door and turned the key and came back to her. Then he gently took her elbow and guided her down the steps to the street.

As they walked, he said. "So, you are new to Troubadour?"

"Yes, I moved here from Ft. Worth to take the position with Hunt Insurance."

"Did you grow up in Ft. Worth?"

"No, I'm from Hood County. My father was a cattleman there."

"Was a cattleman?"

"He died several years ago in an accident."

"I'm sorry to hear that. Where is your mother?"

"She moved back to East Texas to family. I took a teaching position in West Texas for a number of years and then moved to Fort Worth to attend Secretarial School.

Martin nodded. "Like me. I'm from Johnson County. My father is a farmer. I left the farm to attend barber college and then I moved here to open my shop."

They walked in silence for a bit.

"There's a church supper at the Methodist Church tomorrow night. Would you like to attend with me?"

Grace looked up at him and smiled. "That would be very nice. Do I need to bring something?"

Martin hesitated, a moment. "No...no. I'll take care of it. You don't have to worry. I'll bring something."

"That's very nice of you. I don't have access to a kitchen..."

"I understand. Don't worry."

They walked on to the boarding house in silence.

Grace stopped at the front walk. "This is it."

Martin glanced up at the house. "Yes, well." He took a deep breath. "I'll see you in the morning I guess, and I'll come for you at 6:30 tomorrow evening. Will that be satisfactory?"

Grace smiled. "Yes, very. Good evening." She walked to her front door and looked back. He was still standing as before. She waved and he did the same. Then she watched him as he turned and walked away toward town.

Their courtship unfolded in a predictable way. The church supper was a first step. Grace sometimes felt she was watching from a distance. Martin Durham was a gentleman, she surmised from the beginning, guiding her through the social circles of Troubadour, Texas, introducing her to everyone – the old guard, church leaders, and the younger crowd of men and women who had planted their roots in this small Texas town. She felt welcomed by all she met and grateful to Martin for his courtly manner. And she liked the fact that he treated everyone fairly. He had hired that young boy in his shop, and apparently accepted all customers, no matter who they were. It seemed to raise a few eyebrows in the town. In polite asides in her conversations with this and that person, it would come up that Martin had some strange ideas. But apparently no one questioned his actions to his face. She admired that.

She thought back to the way she had felt with William; the instant attraction, the rush of emotion each time she saw him. It was not the same with Martin. However, maybe that could never be again. Maybe that only happens once, she reasoned. And she was older now, late to marry. And she so wanted children. Maybe...

The weeks played out with party invitations from his friends and civic occasions that involved the whole town. He was easy to talk with, she found, and she was glad to find he had a bookish side, loved history, seemed up on politics. Her bookish self was comfortable with him, and she enjoyed their talks. They had been walking out together for several weeks before they ventured into serious conversation. It was walking home from a town festival when they slipped from polite words to serious thoughts.

"I've never asked you your age," Martin said suddenly.

"I'm twenty-eight."

"So, seven years younger than me," he said. They walked in silence for a bit.

"I was married before," Martin said. "I suppose someone has told you that."

Grace nodded.

"Irena and I had only been married two years when she became ill. Appendicitis, I was told at the end, but at first, it was a mystery. By the time the doctor grasped a diagnosis, it was too late." They walked in silence for a few minutes. "She died in my arms," he added. "It has been very hard for me. Very lonely. When I first saw you walking by, was the first time I had taken any interest in a long time. Can you understand what I am saying?"

Grace took a deep breathe, and her answer was but a whisper. "Yes, I can. I have my own experience. And she told him about William and their plan to marry, and his sudden death. "I know what you mean. I have been stunned with grief, and then later just shocked into isolation. You are the first person I have talked with, also." They walked on for a short way.

"It seems life has given us both a turn." Grace said. "I feel sometimes that it is all out of my control, as though the earth shifted beneath me without warning."

"Yes," Martin responded and after a moment he added, "Maybe we can help one another to make a new start."

"Grace looked up into his eyes and saw gentleness. "Yes," she whispered.

They were almost to her boarding house. A soft light burned by the door. Martin touched her arm to stop her. "I hope we can," he said. "I admire you very much, Grace." He pulled her close and kissed her for the first time. "I hope you will allow me to court you formally."

Grace reached up and returned the kiss. "Yes" she whispered.

The events played out quickly, then. Martin and Grace became a couple in the eyes of the town. Grace watched it all in amazement, as though it was preordained somehow. The people of Troubadour, the community, as a whole, rushed their relationship along. Grace felt helpless at its progress at times. Martin was attentive and kind. She had no cause to doubt his feelings or his intent. He was a fine man, as everyone told her. They were a lovely couple, she was assured.

Within weeks, Martin had formally proposed, and as if being drawn along by unseen forces, Grace said yes. She heard herself say yes.

She wrote her mother and invited her to come for the wedding with Martin's approval. However, her mother declined. "I have been a little under the weather. I'll come later when I am stronger. The trip by wagon would be too much, I think and a train trip too expensive and round a bout."

Grace understood.

The wedding was at Martin's house that he had inherited from his late wife. The ladies from the church pitched in to provide refreshments. They were married in the parlor. Grace had only seen the house from a distance until the wedding. It was an imposing two story Victorian not far out of town by about a mile, still furnished as Martin's wife, Irena, had designed. Much finer than any house Grace had ever been inside. A wide veranda across the front, tall columns by the door. A parlor, a dining room, a library, and kitchen on the first floor, and three bedrooms on the second.

Martin gave her a tour as they waited for the wedding guests to arrive. Grace was almost speechless with shock at how fine a place it was.

"I've never seen such a house," she whispered.

Martin laughed softly. "I felt the same way when I first saw it. It's much finer than anything I've ever known, than my parent's house. But ... life brings great surprises at times. Irena grew up here in this place. It was home to her. When her father died suddenly it became hers. And within two years I lost her."

Grace gazed out the window toward the horizon. She could see far out across a prairie toward distant flat-topped mesas. "Is all this land yours as well?"

"Yes." They stood in silence gazing into the distance. "I never thought that I would have anything like this." Martin motioned toward the view. "I never conceived of this. But it's true. It happened to me, and now to you." He took her into his arms. "We can build a wonderful life here, Grace. You will never want for anything, I promise, and we can fill this house with children."

Chapter 24

And so, they were wed. The future shone brightly in front of them; the acceptance and friendship of the town, the beautiful house that Grace could make her own, their plans for a family. Grace began to plan for her mother to come for a visit. It all lay out so clearly, smoothly, except for Grace's job.

They had never discussed it, of course, but Martin was shocked when Grace mentioned getting back to her duties at the insurance office.

"There's no need for that," he said. "I will support this family. You needn't worry."

"But what about the Hunt's agency.? They need my help. I promised to work for them."

"No," Martin said. It's unheard of!" "I am not some loafer who depends on the support of a woman, and I'll not be viewed that way by the town!"

"But what if this happened in your shop? What if your other barber quit without warning? How would you cope?

Martin's eye contact wavered slightly. "Well, I would find a replacement."

"And so will the Hunts, but they need time. So many young men are off at war, and few women have my office skills."

"A woman's place is in the home."

"Well, I, at least, have to tell them. I need to help them until a replacement can be found."

Martin frowned. "I'll discuss with Carlton. He's a reasonable man." And he walked away.

Grace watched him disappear out the door and knew deep down that he would not change. Mr. Hunt would probably agree. Heavens, his wife would agree. She was working herself only until a proper replacement could be found, meaning, of course, a man.

Carlton Hunt was reasonable, just as Martin suggested. Grace should be at home now that she was married, but he added that Grace's office skills were not widely known in

Troubadour. A replacement would be hard to find at this time. So, Martin agreed, reluctantly, to a short time when Grace would continue.

The answer came in the next mail. Aunt Ada wrote congratulations on their wedding and, also sent news that Tanner had come home. He had been injured slightly, she said, and the army had released him. Now he was home and looking for employment. Grace imagined the relief that her aunt and uncle felt. Tanner would survive.

When she told Martin about her cousin, he quickly caught the connection. Tanner needed a job, and his experience in banking and the business world should flow easily into the insurance business. Carlton Hunt agreed, and the necessary communications were made. In record time, really, Tanner arrived in Troubadour.

Grace watched her career decisions being made without her interaction in silence. It was no use to protest. However, a wonderful surprise did come her way. Tanner did not come alone. Maud Allen was with him. It seemed that Tanner had kept in touch with Maud since Grace first introduced them. Now, wonder of wonders, Maud was his wife and Graces's dear friend from Fort Worth was here in Troubadour.

There were many things to be thankful for. Carlton Hunt had his new employee. Her aunt and uncle suggested that it would be good for Tanner to start new somewhere away from

Amelia and her banking father. Grace was delighted to have her close friend nearby. Martin was delighted to have Grace at home, in her place. Everyone was settled, except Grace missed the challenge of her office job, and now she knew that no one would take her side. She had loved her work, and in her darkest moments she could see her future quite clearly. Not life on an isolated ranch, at least, but a housewife in a small town, no more than that. The very job she had wanted to escape.

However, the sadness didn't last. Within the month she realized she was with child. Martin was overjoyed. The family he had so dearly wanted was to be. Grace was thrilled, also. She wanted a family. All thoughts of work outside the home were put on hold. Maud also reported she was expecting, and Grace and her friend shared the planning and anticipation of motherhood. It was a gift to have Maud there.

Her pregnancy went well for the first months. There seemed to be no problems. Martin was attentive and caring and delighted. His first son would be named Martin James, Jr., he declared.

"But what if it's a girl?" Grace cautioned.

Martin kissed her forehead. "Then you can choose the name."

However, in the final weeks of her pregnancy, Grace's pain became apparent. The old doctor sensed that something was not right, but it was guess work for him. When the time finally came, the doctor was summoned in due time, but he was worried. Her pain was great and her labor long. In the final minutes the doctor announced the baby appeared to be breech. There was little he could do except try to comfort Grace and let nature take its course. Finally, the child was born, and Audrey Marie Durham backed into the world. Grace had chosen the name Audrey for Martin's mother and Marie for Grace's.

The baby was fine, the doctor announced, but it had been a struggle to get her clear of the birth channel and breathing. "Breech births are very hard on the mother and baby both", he explained to Martin. We were lucky today. But the doctor had more to say. "Your wife suffered internal damage, I fear. I had so little time to get the baby out and secure her breathing. I was able to stop the bleeding, but the damage is still done. Only time will tell as Grace heals, but in my experience, she will not be safe to have more children. And another pregnancy would be fatal for her."

Martin stared at him as he spoke, trying to take in his words. He had feared he would lose both Grace and the baby during the birth, and was relieved beyond measure that they both survived, but no more children? No sons? The blow was too much, and the doctor's words too definite. The horror of again losing his wife was too great.

Grace regained her strength slowly, and the baby flourished. Martin doted on the child. She was the light of both of their lives, but behind his loving gaze, Grace could see Martin's disappointment. A girl. No sons. He would have no sons. The warning of the doctor was too real. A line was drawn between them in many ways that neither Grace nor Martin could reach across.

Gradually, Martin drifted back toward his separate life at his shop and his hunting friends. Grace's world was the baby and their home. Society dictated that they would not divorce. Martin would never abandon his family, but he would not include his wife and child in the life he lived. It was not proper for a lady, nor a proper life for a tiny wisp of a girl. In turn, Grace could see no way to mend their marriage. She certainly had no interest in cock fights or hunting hounds. Their marriage was based on a pledge to create a family, not love. Their fate was reserved respect for one another, not closeness.

Still, Grace was grateful to Martin. He was the one who suggested that her mother come to live with them. *"We have this big house for just the three of us,"* he reasoned. "I know you worry about your mother. Why not bring her here? You could enjoy her company and know that she is cared for in her old age."

Grace's mother responded quickly to the offer, and Grace looked forward to being able to have her mother close again.

So it was arranged. Grace's mother arrived by train on a ticket that Martin purchased for her. It had been years since they had seen one another, and their only contact had been through letters, but their bond was strong, Grace knew. Her mother had always been her best friend, company for one another on the isolated ranch. Bright light filled Grace's world when her mother arrived. Marie Wilson quickly took in the relationship between Grace and Martin and understood.

In turn, Martin warmed quickly to his mother-in-law. He regarded both his wife and her mother with great respect, but in their place, in the home.

Marie encouraged Grace to get involved more in the community. However, the other women of the town busied themselves with church work and sewing crafts. Maud seemed to have no trouble fitting into the community, but Grace could not so easily give up her dreams. Her home and her child were wonderful in many ways, except that Grace missed an intellectual outlet. She felt diminished by the flurry of club meetings and bored with the routine of housework and childcare, and the endless prattle and gossip the social occasions offered.

Martin never heard the comments or felt the exclusion Grace encountered because of his interaction with the minority communities of Troubadour. No one would have dared question him to his face, but his wife? Grace sensed the reserve of the other women in town and caught the thinly veiled remarks that came up from time to time. So, as time went by, she withdrew from most social contact, and in the future she foresaw only housework and isolation. She thought of William and the life she might have had as his wife, in a city with the libraries and plays and the intellectual challenges of a newspaper man's wife. She was frustrated with herself for such daydreaming and longing, but still. The boredom of her days, the void of an intellectual challenge; it wore on her.

Audrey presented another kind of challenge. Not an easy child, Grace thought. She remembered her gentle connection with her own mother. There were never arguments and cross words between them. But with Audrey, life was one continuous battle. The child was contentious, Grace thought. Always wanting a different food than what was offered, or the other toy, usually the one some other child had. Grace tried to smooth it over with the other children and their mothers, but it became painfully clear as the years went by that Audrey had few friends. Maud and Tanner's first child was a girl, also. It would have been a blessing if the children could have been friends. But that was not to be. Audrey seemed to make a point of not fitting in, whether it was Sunday school or a birthday party, or even the dinner table. Because of this, Grace and Maud drifted apart over time. At home with her, Audrey adopted a silent disapproving attitude. Bored with the books Grace read to her and reluctant to join in any activity with her.

It was only slightly better with her father. She seemed to want his attention, but Martin almost totally ignored the child. He loved her, even hovered over her in pride when she was small, but he did not include her in his life anymore than he did Grace. *Grace* observed the child stand at the window and watch as her father left, off to hunt, or off to work, or to some other pursuit he deemed unsuitable for girls or women. However, she could not fill that void for her child.

Audrey grew to resent her father, who never had time for her. She struck out at her mother with silence and mini disagreements. Grace was frustrated with the child. No matter how hard she tried, Audrey was never quite happy, always complaining.

But, amazingly, Audrey warmed slightly to her grandmother. Maybe to the fact that she shared her name. At any rate, Grace could see that Audrey responded differently to Marie than to her and or Martin. Less argument, less dissatisfaction, less conflict for Grace. Marie delighted in her granddaughter, and that eased the tension between Grace and Audrey. In fact, she was the same calming influence of the Durham household she had been to Grace's childhood home. But with Audrey, Grace watched the child grow more and more hostile to her and her father, and any attempt to reach out to her fell on deaf ears.

Meredith

2015

Chapter 25

On Wednesday, Rachel insisted they cook at least one meal together. Meredith knew her daughter was just worrying over her, wanting to make sure the kitchen worked. So, Angela was sent off to the store with a shopping list, and Rachel set to work in the kitchen. They invited Amy over, and it was a wonderful evening. Rachel and Amy hit it off immediately, and her daughter and Angela seemed to enjoy listening to all their tall tales about growing up in Troubadour. Especially all the dances.

"We need more of that now," Angela said. "What a great way to meet people, I would think."

They all agreed.

"It's different now, isn't it?" Amy nodded toward Angela. "With your generation, it's all cell phones and internet, I guess."

"Or bars, or maybe work," Angela said. She shrugged her shoulders. "Slim pickin's. Of course, there is the chance encounter," she added. "Daniel has asked me out for tomorrow night. Dinner and some dance place he knows about."

"That's wonderful!" Meredith exclaimed.

"When have you seen him?" Rachel's voice was flat with a slight accusing tone.

"This morning, I went for a run early, and he was out working on Gram's car." Angela smiled at her mother's reaction. "We got to talking and then he asked me out."

Amy clapped her hands together. "Oh, girl, he is so good looking!"

"And nice," Meredith added with a look toward her daughter. "He's such a nice young man."

"Well, good for you, sweetheart," Rachel said.

"I also have some more good news." Angela sat forward propping her arms on the table. "I've been thinking about what you said, Gram, about journalism. Starting small. I went by the local newspaper office today after my trip to the grocery. Talked to the owner, a nice lady named Emma Frazier. There's an opening there for a local news correspondent. Not a lot of money, but some. I'm thinking of taking the job and staying down here with you if you will have me."

"That would be wonderful, darling. I would love the company."

So, no flight to California? No job on the pier?"

Everyone looked at Rachel.

Angela smiled. "As you pointed out, a trinket shop is not a career move, Mom. At least I'll be using my degree, right?"

Rachel didn't respond, but the silence was covered by Amy. "I knew they were looking for someone. Mattie French has been their correspondent for years, but she retired last year."

"Yes, Emma mentioned that. I think it will be fun to do this. Learn the town and the county. Get a little experience under my belt."

Meredith glanced at Rachel's silent stare toward her daughter, and Daniel Potter's face popped into her mind. She knew that was what Rachel was thinking. *A boy again, always a boy.*

They didn't see much of Angela for the next couple of days. No surprise there. Angela left early for her run, then spent time with Daniel as he worked on the car and came home late. Daniel sent word that Meredith's car would be ready on Friday.

Meredith and Rachel slept late each morning and then unpacked boxes and ratted through all the "stuff" taking up the dining room. They were busy sorting through the buffet when Angela turned up at noon on Friday. "I just brought your car down. Daniel says it's ready to go."

"Wonderful!" Meredith looked out the front door. Daniel was climbing out of his truck. They all walked out to meet him. "So, is it all new again?"

Daniel smiled. "I think you are going to be pleased. It sounds and drives a lot better."

"Wonderful!" She gave Daniel a hug. "Now what do I owe you?"

"I've got all the records at the trailer. We'll worry about that later. He opened the driver's door with a grand gesture, and the awful grinding screech was gone! "I fixed your door also."

Meredith hugged him again. "Thank you so much! Come on in."

Daniel shook his head. "I've promised to take Angela out to the dig site this afternoon. Can we settle up and celebrate later?"

"Certainly! I'll take it for a test drive."

Daniel turned to Angela. "I'll go get the 4wheeler."

"When are you thinking of leaving, Mom?" Angela asked

"How about say one or two o'clock on Sunday? We can have lunch first." Rachel offered.

"So, did you take the job?" Meredith asked.

"Yes, it will be part time, really, at the newspaper, and that way I can help Daniel out at the dig site." I'll go back with Mom and bring my stuff down."

Just then, Daniel pulled up in the truck with the 4wheeler loaded in the back.

"Great then. I'll plan on noon, and we can have some lunch somewhere." Angela said. "Ah. Here we go. I'll see you this evening." And she was gone again.

Rachel and Meredith watched them drive away down the lane.

"You know, a very wise person once told me that we can't dictate another person's journey in life," Meredith offered.

Rachel looked around and smiled slightly. "I'm sure that is true."

"So what are you thinking of tackling next?" Rachel asked as they walked back into the house.

Meredith took a deep breath. "I'm not sure. Let's don't worry about it now. Let's just enjoy the rest of your visit." She held the door open for her daughter.

"Mom, I'm here now. I don't know when I'll get back. Let me help you while I can."

Meredith smiled, "You are a sweetheart, baby. And a good motivator. You keep me focused." They laughed and shared a hug.

"How about that room?" Rachel pointed toward the library. Have you been in there yet?"

"No. Something is blocking the hall door, and I haven't tried the parlor door."

They both looked into the parlor. Rachel walked over and turned the knob on the door. She pushed on it, and it moved slightly.

"That's a little better," Meredith said. She helped Rachel push on the door and gradually they got it open enough to squeeze through.

The place was still filled with furniture, just like the parlor and dining room, but there was something covering the windows, so it was hard to make anything out. A desk in the center of the room was stacked with boxes and the floor was covered, also. Meredith found a light switch and as she moved over to it, her foot hit one of the boxes that gave out a clinking sound like glass hitting glass.

They both reacted to the noise and then surveyed the room. The place was covered in stacks of boxes, several large canvas bags and even a bushel basket or two. Bottles. Liquor bottles, wine bottles.

"What on earth is this? Rachel asked

Meredith took a minute to answer. "My mother," she said. "She lived here for her last years." Meredith reached into one of the baskets and came up with an empty quart whiskey bottle. "She had quite a collection here, I guess."

"My heavens! She must have been a raving alcoholic!" Rachel said.

Meredith shrugged her shoulders. "Apparently."

"You didn't know? Or was this the reason you stayed away from her?"

"My mother had a number of problems. Maybe all this was her final solution."

They worked their way toward the center of the room. Everything was filled with bottles.

"Well, we need to get all of this out of here," Rachel said. "What do we do with it all?"

Meredith shook her head. "I don't know. We can't just set them out on the street for the trash man to find."

They stared at the mess for a while. "Do they have a town dump here? Rachel asked. "They have to have one somewhere."

"I believe they do. They had at one time."

"Do you know where it might be?"

Meredith smiled. "Yes, I do, actually."

"Well let's drive out there and see if we can get rid of this."

Meredith nodded. "Dry run first, to see if it's still in use."

"Right." They worked their way out of the room.

"It's out of town to the north about five miles." Meredith directed. "I think I can still find it. We'll try out my car."

It started right up. No rattle at all. Meredith backed the car around without its usual whine and turned down the lane. As they passed Daniel's trailer, she noted that his truck was gone and she noticed that Rachel was looking, also.

"Heavens, this is almost like a new car!" Meredith said as a diversion.

Rachel laughed softly, "It may not look new, but it sounds new."

"Maybe I don't need to worry about getting a new car after all."

Rachel just rolled her eyes. "Maybe."

"I would rather get this cleaned up without alerting anyone else. You know how small towns are." Meredith said. And the thought crossed her mind that no, Rachel had no idea about small towns.

"Gossips?" Rachel ventured.

"Yes."

"Same as big towns." Rachel smiled. "Don't worry Mom. We'll get this done ourselves."

Grace found the spot that was the turnoff. Almost covered over with high grass was a sign announcing, "City Dump".

This looks encouraging," Rachel said.

They bumped down a dirt road and around a curve. Spread out before them were mounds of dirt and scattered earthen pits with a lacing of tire tracks circling the area.

"It looks like it's still working. There's a huge earth moving thing over there." Rachel said.

"Great! Let's go back and load up what we can. We'll cover the seats and everything."

"Right."

An hour later they had wrestled 10 boxes of bottles out to the car to fill every available space and driven back to the dump. They picked an out-of-the way spot and unloaded. Then went back to the house for another load. Meredith pulled the old sheet down from the windows, revealing plenty more boxes to move. They went to work without comment. After shifting boxes around, they reached a wide table in the center of the room. Sitting on the middle of the surface was an antique typing machine.

"Wow! Look at this." Rachel exclaimed. "You still have this? I remember it from when I was little."

"Yes," Meredith brushed dust off the keys. This was Grace's.

"I remember visiting here, and you letting me type on it." Rachal said.

"Yes, me also. Grace would let me type on it when I was little."

"It's huge!" They both laughed at that.

"It took some strength to press the keys, I remember. Grace could fly on it though. I remember that she only used her index fingers." Meredith held up her fingers.

"Really!"

"Yes. They apparently had not designed the typing method that we learned in school. Her school didn't teach it, and Grace just never changed. She could type very well with just these two fingers. When I was little, she worked as the church secretary. Typed all the bulletins and newsletters on this thing.

"Amazing!" Rachel touched the keys. "This is an antique. Probably worth something to a museum."

"Probably." They looked at it for a few more minutes, and then Rachel announced. "OK, back to work!"

It was after six when they emptied the car the last time. Meredith had lost count of the number of trips. On the way back to town Rachel suggested they just grab some burgers and fries for dinner and go home and put their feet up.

"Good idea."

Tired and dirty, they got back to the house and ate their burgers on the back porch watching the sun drop into the West.

"Thank you, sweetheart. But I'm sorry you had to see that."

"No problem, Mom." She smiled. "But I believe this entitles me to some back story here. I've never understood the situation between you and your mother. I would like to know."

Meredith took a deep breath. "I guess you deserve an explanation." She smiled slightly. *"Where to start"* Meredith paused for a few minutes more. "I was born here at my grandmother's house. I don't remember anywhere else until college. I lived with my grandmother, as you know, and my mother showed up on rare occasions." Meredith stared out across the back acreage into a beautiful sunset.

"When I was little and got old enough to realize other children had mothers and fathers, I began to worry about it. Everyone else had parents, you know. I was different. I wasn't short on attention or anything. Grace gave me all the love and attention I needed, but other kids would ask me where my parents were. I felt ...I felt as though maybe it was my fault. Something I had done. My mother turned up at odd times, just enough to keep me confused, I guess. Anyway, as the years went by, I absorbed the story. My father was killed in World War II, I was told, and my mother worked in the city." Meredith shifted in her chair

"I would try to imagine what the city was like. My mother always showed up all dressed up, full of life. It sounded fun. I tried to imagine going with her when she left. But I had no facts to add to the story, so that ended that. She was working, she said. She was a stewardess for an airline. I couldn't go with her now, but someday she said, someday I would join her. She brought me store-bought dresses from time to time and talked about New York and Dallas and Paris and Rome. It sounded wonderful, but....then she would be gone again."

Meredith held her hands up in exasperation. "Usually, her visits involved an argument between my grandmother and my mother, and usually I felt it was about me, somehow. My mother would wind up screeching at my grandmother about how unfair she was, and then the tears would start, and Grace would wind up comforting her."

"I was an oddity in a small town, no parents, but with fancy store-bought dresses to wear. I got a lot of flack over that. Everyone else's mother sewed their clothes in the forties and fifties. It made me an outsider. Except for Amy. Amy was my one true friend." Meredith was silent for a bit, remembering. "I got beaten up one time because of my dresses." She looked around at Rachel. "Torn my dress up, pushed me in the mud. A whole gang of girls."

"No!"

Meredith nodded. "It was pretty awful at the time. Grace hugged me close and doctored all my scrapes and bruises, and told me it was just ignorance and jealously, not to let them get to me." She smiled a little. "But it did. I thought somehow,

I'd done something to cause my problems. I've read since then that's what usually happens with children in abusive situations. Children think everything is their fault somehow. But I had my grandmother, and I had Amy and I had school. My salvation. I was very good at school, so I sort of just kept my head down and went on."

"When I went away to college, I found out, by chance, really, that women with children couldn't be stewardesses back in the forties and early fifties. At first, they couldn't even be married. The next time my mother flitted through my life I asked her about it, and she explained that she was a widow since my father died in the war. And to make a long story short, she just didn't tell anyone about me. I didn't exist as far as her life was concerned."

"I told Grace about the married with children thing and she didn't say a word. She just hugged me tight and said to never mind. I think she probably knew the truth, maybe for a long time. Anyway, I was grown now. I didn't need a mother anymore. So, I moved on."

"My mother still appeared now and then. Always with a big show of money and stories about all the wonderful places she'd gone, people she knew. I hated her for that, always showing off. I just blocked her out of my life. I had my own set of problems by then." Meredith laughed softly. "And I had Grace, my rock. She kept me balanced."

Meredith patted Rachel's hand. "I married. I had you. "You were a gift from day one. I've made some mistakes in my life. I hope I haven't hurt you too much."

"Never, Mom, you never hurt me. You and Dad, you had your problems, but I never felt it was my fault. I hear horror stories from friends about growing up in a divorced family where their parents used the kids as weapons against one another. You and Dad never did that."

"Yes, your father had his problems, but he has been a good father to you."

"And you are a good mom." Rachel gripped her hand again.

Meredith smiled. "So, I got on with my life. I've made my mistakes, but overall, it was good." Meredith paused for a moment. "I saw my mother rarely. I didn't want her to be an influence on you, and she didn't seem to notice. She was busy out running around the world. When Grace got sick, I went down as often as I could, and I hired a nurse and companion to stay with her when she went home from the hospital. Once or twice, when I was down here, Audrey would show up. Same old drama. Big show of concern for any audience she could find, but she offered no actual help. Just hinted at financial problems and other commitments. Same old Audrey, except she was showing her age a little now. She had gotten all the latest facelifts and such, but she was wearing down. Grace and

I would just give one another that look that said, "She's back," and then we waited for her to go flying off again."

"One of the last conversations I had with my grandmother, she had a warning for me. Just out of the blue, one day she said, *"Meredith, when I'm gone, don't let Audrey hurt you."* I promised her I wouldn't and told her not to worry. I couldn't conceive of anything else she could do to me, not anymore."

Meredith paused for a moment, and then continued. "Grace died peacefully in her sleep. The chemo and radiation had worn her down. I knew it was coming, but it was still a shock. My rock was gone. She was 95 years old. A good long life."

Meredith took a deep breath before she continued. "Audrey showed up for the funeral, and of course, the reading of the will. Neither one of us had any idea what Grace had in the way of wealth, or what she had written in her will. Turns out she had substantial savings and investments. Sam Carter, the past president of the bank, had been Grace's friend and banker since she first came to Troubadour in the early 1900's. He had been dead for several years, but his son, Lucas, had taken over as Grace's financial advisor. He was present at the will reading, also."

"According to Lucas, her private account was a secret between a man named Charles Sternberg and his father, Sam Carter. Lucas said all his dad would tell him was that Grace had been employed by this Mister Sternberg for years, and her salary was deposited each month. Sternberg was a fossil hunter back at the turn of the century. He made some world-recognized discoveries out in the Wichita Red Beds. Sternberg was an old man by 1922, in his late 60's."

"Lucas explained that his father told him that Sternberg had hired Grace to help him with typing up his journals and field notes and organizing his storehouse here in Troubadour. He had rented a shed on Martin Durham's property. Martin was, of course, my grandfather. Sternberg told Sam Carter that Martin was against his wife working because it would appear he could not support his own family."

"Unless a woman was working with her husband in a family business, married women just didn't have jobs back then, at least not in Troubadour. But Sternberg really needed the secretarial help, he said, and Grace happened to have the training and was very interested in his work. Grace and Sternberg made a deal with Grace's husband that she could work with him, but only as a volunteer, no salary, and Martin agreed to that."

"However, Sternberg told Sam Carter, apparently, that he did not feel right about that, so he wanted to set up a secret account for Grace alone. He would place her pay in that account each month, and Martin Durham must never know. Sam Carter told his son that he knew Mr. Sternberg well and trusted what he said. He also knew Martin Durham and how strong willed and independent he was, and he didn't doubt for a minute that what Sternberg said was true. So Sam Carter set up the account and kept the secret."

"Sternberg worked out here well into his seventies and Grace was his employee. Years after Sternberg was gone, Sam still kept the secret. When Sam Carter turned the bank over to his son, Lucas, he continued to manage the account for Grace and invested it for her, land, oil leases, things like that. It did really well, survived the Depression and kept growing. After Martin died in 1935, Lucas Carter told Grace about the account. She was astonished. Had no idea. Apparently, Grace didn't touch the account though, not until she sent me to college." Meredith glanced at Rachel who sat listening in rapt silence.

"Her will stated that her full estate was to come to me, but my mother was to receive a monthly allowance and could live in the house, if she chose, for as long as she wanted, and I was not to intervene. After Audrey's death, the house and full remaining estate would become mine."

"It seemed reasonable to me." Meredith shifted in her chair. "I knew Grace wouldn't want to trust Audrey with the full amount, however she wanted to leave her something. But Audrey was furious! She immediately said she would fight it all, but the lawyer said Grace had been very clear as to her wishes, and there was no recourse."

"Audrey gave us one of her burning looks and stormed out of the lawyer's office. I figured I would not see her again, but when I got back to the house, she was there waiting for me."

"She started screeching when I came in the door, screaming how dare I manipulate my grandmother that way? How dare I steal her birthright! I tried to stay calm. I told her I knew nothing about Grace's will, but of course, she didn't listen. She screeched that the two of us never cared about her. That we never appreciated what she did for us."

Meredith laughed softly. "That really hit a nerve with me, and I shot back. I told her that I thought she had always done just as she pleased. I told her I couldn't remember a time that Grace or I ever put any pressure on her to do anything. She had her career as a stewardess, her life flying around the world. We were no impediment to her world at all. I told her I knew it was hard losing her husband in the war and being left with a baby to contend with. But all that was long passed. I told her that we should forget the past and move forward."

"Audrey stopped her screeching and just stared at me for a while. At first, I thought maybe I had gotten through to her, finally. Then a thin smile appeared in the corner of her mouth, and she started to laugh, low in her throat.

"So, you think you understand me" she said. *"You think you know me?"* She circled me like an attacking animal. *"You think you know my life?"* She laughed again. *"You know nothing about me! You or Grace either one!"* *"My husband died in the war? HA! How gullible can you be? Mother bought it hook, line and sinker! I have no idea who your father is! Some flashy guy I met in Dallas. Could have been anyone! All of a sudden, I turn up pregnant! What am I supposed to do? I can't be tied down like that. Have an abortion? I wasn't about to take the chance of dying in some sleazy place with a coat hanger sticking out of me!"*

"So what do I do? I concocted a story about marrying a soldier who was in the war. It was easy enough. Half the country was going to war and plenty of them would die. All I had to do was convince my mother, and she quickly stepped in "to SAVE me." She made quotation marks in the air with her fingers.

Meredith paused a moment. "I could hear what she was saying. Her words were hanging there in the air. My father? No idea? I guess the dumbstruck look on my face was what she was going for, because she looked very pleased, and continued.

"And another thing, since it's "TELL THE TRUTH DAY! Stewardess? You believed that one, too? You think I spent all these years padding up and down the aisle of some airplane serving drinks? Not likely, sweetheart! I'm a professional, baby! I've had the best. Hell, I've slept with CEOs and Senators, and

diplomats! The French word for what I am is a Paramour. I've been wined and dined all over the world, first class, all the way!"

"A paramour! Rachel exclaimed. "What....!"

Meredith nodded. "In French is means...."

"Oh, I know what it means!"

Meredith nodded her head and took a deep breath. "So, you never flew, I asked her?"

"And she shot back. *Oh, I flew girl! But I wasn't pushing drinks. I was being served. I've had the best! Grace always wanted me to come back to this crummy little town and play nice. I got out of here as soon as I could, and I swore I'd never come back!"*

"And, you made the choice to shut me out of your life?"

"*Yes!"* she screeched.

"And your whole life has been a lie?"

That stopped her for a second, but not for long. *"My whole life has been exactly what I wanted it to be. No one told me what to do. I called my own shots!"*

"Then I said, so now you can live with your choices." Meredith sat in silence for a few minutes and then continued. "She stared at me for a bit with a look that could have burned through steel. Then she grabbed up her bag and stormed out to her car and drove away."

"I hardly ever spoke to her again. That was thirteen years ago. I was notified by the lawyer that she was receiving an allowance as ordered by the will, and that she had moved to Troubadour and was living in this house. I made several efforts to contact her. But she hung up when she realized it was me. Finally, about five years before she died, I drove down and just knocked on the door."

"She looked terrible, very thin and unkept. It was a shock when I saw her, but nothing was changed. She mumbled a string of cuss words at me and slammed the door in my face. I waited for a bit, but she didn't come back." Meredith paused again.

"So I left, and that was the last time we spoke. She died 5 years ago, but I didn't find it out until months later. And that's the way I left it. Not until I retired and settled this last divorce, did I contact the lawyer here."

Meredith stopped talking, and the silence was deafening. Rachel stared straight ahead out into the night.

"So that's my story," Meredith said. "My sordid little story. And I think you can see why I wanted to shield you from it all these years."

"I'm so sorry, Mother. So sorry you had to carry all this by yourself."

"Oh, I was never alone, sweetheart." Meredith reached out to clasp Rachel's hand. "I had Grace. And when I was at my lowest, she was there for me. And the best advice she ever gave me was this. We cannot always choose the situations that life places us in. We can only choose how to react to them. I chose life and you and happiness."

They sat in silence holding hands as the night sounds gathered around them. Finally, Rachel rose and stooped to give her mother a kiss on the cheek. Meredith stirred and returned a hug. Then they silently went off to bed.

Grace

1920

Chapter 26

Charles Sternberg

It was just after twelve when Grace saw Martin coming up the lane. A little late for his noon meal, but she had everything on the table and a pot of stew on the stove. She called to her mother and could hear her on the stairs. She carried the stew pot to the table to fill their bowls and then looked back out the front door as Martin stopped the car and climbed out. He was not alone. A stranger climbed out behind him, and the men were talking amiably as they came up the front walk.

She quickly reached for an extra bowl and spoon and placed them on the table and then rushed to open the front door.

"Ah, there you are," Martin greeted her. "I've brought a guest today, Grace. Meet Mr. Charles Sternberg. Just Charles to us, he says." He reached to place his hand on the man's shoulder.

"Wonderful to meet you, Mr....."

"Charles," the man corrected.

"Charles." She smiled. "We don't often get guests for our noon meal. I trust a bowl of beef stew will suit you."

"Most certainly."

"This is my mother, Marie Wilson.' Her mother smiled and Charles extended his hand.

He was an older man, Grace thought. Not someone she had seen before. Possibly one of Martin's hunting companions, although she had hardly ever met any of them. He looked different than the regular crowd in the barber shop; dressed in jodhpur type pants made of some unfamiliar fabric and in tall laced-up boots that came almost to his knee. Not the usual attire for men in Troubadour.

"Charles showed up at the shop this morning, and I thought he might enjoy some of your stew. You can wash your hands here at the basin if you want." Martin poured water over his hands from a pitcher, and then handed it over to the man. Then Martin reached in his pocket and produced the newspaper. "Brought you some news today, Grace." He held out the paper. The proposal passed. Women have the vote."

"Really!" She took the paper and studied the headline. "Wonderful! And thank you for your vote!" They laughed together.

"Well, Charles, we are in for it now." Martin said. "Women with the vote!"

"Well, good! My wife will be pleased. It's a good thing, I think."

"Yes, it is. Of course now there will be lots of women out rallying the vote and making changes, I imagine."

Grace smiled at her husband. She knew he supported the bill.

"And probably a lot of changes that are needed," Charles said. "My wife has some ideas that might improve things, I know."

Grace smiled at her mother. "I guess this ends my letter writing campaign. Of course, I need to write everyone in Austin a thank you note first."

She got four napkins from the buffet and added them to the table. Then a half a loaf of bread and some butter and glasses. That looked a little nicer she thought.

"We must register or whatever we have to do," Marie offered.

"Yes, we'll have to find out about that," Grace agreed. She motioned for the men to join them at the table.

"Now enough about the vote. What brings you to Troubadour, Charles?" Grace motioned for the men to be seated and poured glasses of water.

"Well, Troubadour is my base of operation out here." The man smiled broadly, And I always stop in with Martin here for a shave and hair cut before I set out." He rubbed the back of his fingers down his cheek.

"Set out where?" Marie asked.

"The Wichita Breaks, or specifically, the Wichita Red Beds. I'm a fossil hunter."

"Charles is a famous man. He's found some ancient creatures out here from prehistoric times." Martin looked around at Charles for confirmation.

"Yes, this is a world-renowned fossil field out here, and I hope to find many more."

"How amazing! Here in Troubadour? Grace asked.

"Yes, well, nearby. About twenty miles north and west between here and the Wichita River. Are you ladies familiar with fossils?"

Yes, I'm slightly aware of them. They are bones of ancient creatures that lived on earth eons ago, I believe." Marie said.

Charles nodded. "Yes, as old as two hundred and ninety million years."

"Two hundred and ninety million!" Grace brought her hand up to her mouth in astonishment.

"What sort of creatures?" Marie asked.

"Lizards , I think you would call them. Big and small. Some quite large, and some only inches long, like my first important find here. It may turn out to be one of the first animals to leave the water and live on land. Maybe the transition to mammals."

Grace and Marie stared with mouths open, trying to take in his words.

Chares laughed. "You have much the same reaction as Martin, I see. Not a science you are familiar with, I think. "

"Martin hadn't mentioned this to me." Grace glanced at her husband.

"Slipped my mind with all that's happening, I guess." Martin glanced down.

"If you are interested, I can offer some books you might enjoy."

"That would be wonderful."

"Grace was a schoolteacher for a time," Martin offered.

They ate their stew in silence for a bit.

"This is very good," Charles offered.

Grace smiled, "Will you have another bowl?"

"Certainly. It will be quite a while before I taste food this good and filling."

"So you camp out in the breaks?" Grace said. " I understand that is a very hard country."

"Yes, all I have to eat or drink, I have to carry in with me. Supplies can get very short."

"And you work alone?"

"Most of the time. Sometimes my sons come with me.

"So where do you find these fossils?" Marie asked.

"Buried in the rock layers, hard sand really.

"Gracious!" Grace said. "How do you know where to dig?"

Charles laughed. "Yes, that is the problem, isn't. Luck or chance is a large part of it. But the color of the land gives us clues. The soil and rock are in layers. The red beds are the richest in certain types of fossils, the white layers a different sort." He studied the puzzled look of their faces. "I'll share some books with you."

The conversation drifted on. Martin asked if Charles had secured a wagon and supplies yet. That led to a discussion on the wagon he had found.

"Forrester is a good man," Martin offered. "He'll provide you properly."

Charles nodded. "I've always been satisfied before. This time I'll have room for a larger water tank. He has a freight wagon for me outfitted with some special rigging for lifting and storing the finds I make."

Grace listened to the banter back and forth between the men. They were obviously longtime friends. Another part of Martin's life she had no knowledge of.

"We'll take a look at the barn after we finish. See if it fits your purpose," she heard Martin say. He looked back at her. "Charles is needing a place to store his things and organize his collections. I think our shed off the barn might work for that.

Grace nodded and smiled. She had never really explored the shed. Never ventured out to the barn except to feed Martin's hounds, when he was away.

"Well, it has been great to meet you ladies, and the meal was wonderful. Thank you so much."

"I'm so glad you liked it. Grace responded. "And I'm so glad to meet you. I really would like to know more about your work."

"I'll get those books for you."

Charles followed Martin out the screened porch and across to the barn.

Grace and Marie watched them make their way to the corner of the barn and then turned back to clear the table.

"He seems a very interesting gentleman," Marie ventured.

After a bit the men returned. Grace could hear them conversing cordially as they approached the house.

"Charles says the shed would be just the place for his fossils," Martin announced.

"Wonderful!! So you would store the things you find here?"

Charles nodded. "And prepare them to be shipped back east. I can set up tables and shelved in there and even a bed for me, if that would be acceptable."

"Well certainly, I suppose. But you might be more comfortable somewhere else, I would think," Martin said.

"No." Charles shook his head. "I'll only be out there for short periods. Mostly, I'll be in the field, and your shed will be much more comfortable than my camp. This way I won't need to maintain a room somewhere else."

"And you can eat your meals with us," Grace added.

They all nodded, and Charles clapped his hands together. "Well, then, I'll just go about getting settled. Thank you so much for this."

Charles returned midafternoon and unloaded his things into the shed. Grace and Marie watched in glances out the window as they prepared dinner. By sundown he seemed to be settled. Martin went out to check on him when he came in from his shop. Grace had dinner on the table by the time the men came in. Audrey was installed in her chair at the table, and she stared wide-eyed at the stranger. Charles was drawn to her instantly. "Well, young lady, and who might you be?"

Audrey gave him one of her famous scowls.

"This is our daughter Audrey. She was napping when you were here earlier," Grace said.

Charles ignored the child's reaction. "Well, good! Do you have other children?"

"No, just the one."

"I have three sons myself. No girls unfortunately."

"How old are your boys," Martin asked.

"Oh, they're all grown up now. They work with me from time to time. You can meet them when they come out to help me."

Grace looked at Martin's face as he asked his question. Sons. The vacant sadness in his voice was clear to her.

"So, tell me about your work, Charles." Grace said.

"Yes, well I've been all around the Midwest, Kansas, the Dakotas. I've been principally here the last two years though. The Red Beds of the Wichita Breaks are world recognized for the Permian period, as I said earlier."

"How old did you say?" Martin asked.

"Two hundred and ninety-eight million to two hundred fifty-one million years ago. Some of the oldest fossils found so far. Back when these creatures lived in and around a string of oxbow lakes out here." He nodded toward Grace. "I brought you those books I promised. Some are textbooks, but one is my story about my travels and my finds. I hope you will enjoy them."

"I'm sure I will," Grace said.

They talked over supper and into the night. Grace tore herself away from the conversation to take Audrey up to bed. It was so good to have something new and interesting to discuss. Martin and Marie seemed as interested as she was.

Chapter 27

The books were a challenge. Grace had not read such scholarly works since her early school days. And certainly nothing as scientific and new. Paleontology, as the study was called, was very academic and most of the important words were derived from Latin she came to realize. Just keeping them straight was a major challenge, much less understand the geographic terms. She decided on a chart method that would help her keep everything straight. She listed what seemed to be key words as she found them and then created definitions for them as she read. When she made the connection with some other word or term she added it to new words to her chart. Maps from the field guides of the layers of the soil and location for fossils that had been found helped her organize her thoughts. She tackled the study as if it were her life work, spending hours reading and organizing and questioning what she had read. It was the most refreshing activity she had pursued since secretarial school. At night, once Audrey was tucked into bed, and her mother was busy with her own interests, she lay her books and charts out in the library and studied. It filled her long evenings when Martin was away at the river, or patrolling the town as marshal. He knew virtually nothing about what she was doing and showed little interest in finding out. Her mother, on the other hand, encouraged her just as she always had.

Charles Sternberg was away in the red beds for most of the time. When he was in town, he worked in his storeroom most of the day and only appeared for meals. In fact, contact between Martin and Grace centered on the times Charles was in town and eating his meals at the house. Grace had to smile at the idea that their boarder and his fossils actually provided them with a common interest.

Dinner conversation centered around the reading Grace was doing. Charles seemed eager to discuss his work, especially with Grace when he realized how seriously she was taking her studies. "I'm most impressed with your charts. That is a very original idea to organize the terms that way."

"Like I said earlier, my Grace was once a schoolteacher," Martin put in.

Grace glanced at him as he spoke. *Was that a hint of pride in his voice?* The thought gave her courage.

"It helps me keep everything straight in my mind. I mean, you must admit, Charles, that the scientists who choose these names are hardly trying to simplify the language." They laughed about that.

Martin was full of questions, also. Mostly more of a physical nature. Where exactly did Charles find his specimens? How did he get them out of the ground without destroying them? How did he preserve them and prepare them for shipment?

Marie joined in, also. Where did Charles send his shipments of fossils? "I've been reading your memoir of your travels. I find your adventures very interesting, but quite dangerous at times."

Charles laughed about that. "Well, it's not for the light hearted I suppose, but one must follow ones passion, I think, and fossils are mine."

"Keeping the records straight for each find and location must take great patience," Grace commented.

"Yes, accuracy is extremely important," Charles agreed. "I could actually use help in that quarter, but I'll have to wait until I return to Harvard, I suppose."

Grace felt a jolt as though someone had tapped her on top of her head. She straightened in her chair. "I could help you with that."

Charles paused in mid-sentence. "Yes. I believe you could. You seem to have a true inclination to the science." They both looked at Martin, who looked back and forth at the two of them as if he was just catching up to the conversation. "I would greatly appreciate the help," Charles continued. And to Martin, "Of course I would gladly pay for Grace's time."

Grace looked eagerly to Martin, but the look on her husband's face was plain to read. Realization of what Charles was proposing finally dawned on him. "My wife does not have to work, Charles. I support my own family." The offense taken by Martin was clear to Grace, but apparently Charles missed it.

"Oh, but it would be such a great contribution to my work. It would free me up for more field work."

Grace quickly added, "I could easily transcribe records, handle correspondence and such." She looked at Martin. I could do it here at the house. It wouldn't take away from..."

"I'm sure you can see that it might be an oppressive workload for Grace." Martin's voice carried over hers.

And in a flash, Grace saw that Charles, at last, had grasped the problem. "Yes, you are right, I'm sure," he conceded to Martin. "Just a thought." And to Grace, he added. "All the same, I would very much like to study the chart system you have created. And I hope you will continue your studies.

It felt as though a bright light had been snuffed out. Grace settled back in her chair and looked at her mother who had been quietly observing the conversation. The rest of the dinner was carried out in silence. Each of them lost in their own thoughts. Grace excused herself to take Audrey up to bed.

Charles left the next morning after breakfast. The idea of Grace helping him with his records was not mentioned. Martin inquired about where Charles would be working, and Charles gave him as detailed an answer as he could. Grace listened, but his direction made little sense to her since she had never seen the Wichita Red Beds. Martin, on the other hand, had hunted there over the years and seemed to know some of the landmarks that Charles offered. "How long do you plan to be out this time?"

"I hope to explore the east region of the Craddock Ranch this trip. I found a bluff there that should yield some good specimens. I'm taking supplies for 3 weeks.

"Well, I wish you a good trip." And Martin was gone, off to his shop.

Charles left for the barn to harness his mules. Grace and Marie cleared the table and watched in glances out the window as he loaded the wagon and prepared to go.

"So that's it." Grace thought. She saw no chance of changing her husband's mind. The excitement she had felt about the studies seemed a distant prospect. She would never change Martin's mind.

Her mother watched Grace move about the kitchen. "Don't give up your dreams, dear." Grace looked around with tears in her eyes. "Don't give up," Marie repeated. Grace hugged her mother and went upstairs to care for Audrey. She could see no good solution.

Days drifted by. She still read the books on paleontology and added to her charts. It was the challenge she looked forward to all day and thought about almost constantly as she went about her daily chores.

In just over two weeks Charles Sternberg appeared at the door again. Some of his food had spoiled in the heat, he said, and he had cut his work short. Also, his water tank had developed a small leak, and he could not survive without that.

I'll go back when the weather cools."

"They all walked out to the shed to see the fossils he had found on the trip. There were two fairly large burlap sacks sitting on one of the tables that Charles had installed. He carefully lifted out a smaller sack and showed them a fossilized bone labeled with some sort of code.

"This is the femur of a Dimetrodon. I believe I have almost a complete skeleton in the field. It was a fairly large fin-backed creature, you see. I have exposed the top layer of it." He flipped through a field guide to show them a drawing. I will jacket the major portion of it. Then I'll have to wait to extract it after the plaster has set."

Grace, Martin and Marie all studied the drawing. "It will be about four feet high and 10 feet long, I think," Charles added.

"My, that large! How old would you say?" Martin asked.

"About 270 to 286 million years, I believe. It is in a mid-level layer of the red clay region."

"What is this?" Grace asked as she picked up a large round shaped rock resembling a snail that lay on the table.

"That's an ammonite. One of the oldest sea creatures I've found, actually.

"How old?'

Possibly over 290 million years. They were very plentiful. Since it didn't have so many separate pieces, it has survived more easily in a fossilized state."

"I've seen these before along river banks," Martin picked up another of the ammonites

"They are very pretty," Marie observed.

"Yes, and they can be quite colorful depending on the sed-iment they were trapped in." Charles said. "Some are reddish, some white, some sort of golden if they were in the ooze that contained iron ore or oil. He pointed toward the one Grace was holding. "Take that one if you like."

Grace smiled. "I will. I'll put it by the front steps."

"So, this big creature is a major find you say," Martin looked back at the field guide sketch.

"Yes. Time will tell. The first job is to get all the pieces. If I can complete the jacketing and keep all the bones in place, I'll remove it. It's an exacting process, but usually successful.

"What do you mean, when you say you jacketed the fossil?"

"I laid strips of cloth soaked in a thin plaster over it. It's a slow process. Each layer has to dry and harden fully. I'll put many layers on before it is strong enough to remove from the ground. Here's a small one I did." He walked over to what looked like a small clam shell and picked it up. "This is a small fossil of a Diaplocaulus; a boomer-head for short. The head looks like a boomerang.

"See what I mean about the names of these things?" Grace smiled.

"Yes, the science has its own language, I'm afraid." Charles laughed softly. "I can ship it to the university like this, and it can be unpacked there. The fossilized bones are protected."

"And for a large creature?" Marie asked.

"It would look the same except much larger. It can take up to a year or more to jacket a fossil of size."

"And you are in the process of doing this now?" Martin asked.

"For a find this large I really need my sons here, however. It's not a one-man job."

"Maybe I could help you," Martin offered.

"Yes, well," Charles paused. "It's time consuming. It takes several days just to dig around the sight and add more layers of plaster."

"I'll arrange some days off. Let Luther run the shop," Martin said. "I haven't had a good adventure in a while."

"Could I come, too. I'd love to see the beds," Grace blurted out. She was shocked she had said it out loud. "Mother could care for Audrey for a few days." She quickly added as she looked at her mother, and Marie nodded. Then she looked back at Martin, and his reaction was written on his face.

"The Wichita Breaks are no place for a woman!"

Grace glanced at Charles, who was studying Martin over his glasses. He said nothing. Martin looked back at Charles, as he had clearly dismissed Grace's outburst.

"Well, I could use some help, if you are volunteering," Charles said.

"Sounds interesting. When would you want to go?"

Charles glanced at Grace, who had busied herself studying the fossils before her. "I need to wait for the weather to cool some, and..." He looked back at Martin. "I have a mass of paperwork to do here. I could use help there, also."

The silence filled the shed. Grace glanced a look at Martin, who was clearly processing what Charles had hinted.

"I truly do need help in that quarter," Charles added. "If you would allow Grace to help me in that endeavor, I would be very grateful indeed."

Grace held her breath as she watched her husband. He was conflicted, it was plain. "As a volunteer," he said after a few seconds.

"Certainly, just as you will be." Charles agreed.

Grace froze in place waiting for her husband's response.

"Would that be satisfactory, Grace? I know you are interested. I just ..."

"I would love to help," Grace said. "I would love it!"

Martin smiled. "Well, I guess my little schoolteacher needs a challenge."

And the spell was broken. Laughter flowed over the group. Relief for Grace, acceptance for Martin, pride for Marie, and gratitude for Charles.

Charles smiled at Grace. "I'll start you off with transposing my field notes. The men back at the lab complain constantly about my horrid writing. It will be your first challenge to read my script!" He took a deep breath. "It would be best if the notes could be typed up, but ..."

"I can type!" Grace answered quickly.

"Really! Well then!" Charles smiled. "Do you have a writing machine?"

"Grace shook her head. "No, no I don't, but I learned in school." Her heart sank

"Well, in that case I will find you one, and we'll get started. I'll do that first thing tomorrow!"

Grace could hardly sleep she was so excited at the prospect of her new job. Of course, she could not call it a job with Martin. It was volunteer work. But she was grateful for the opportunity.

"Thank you for this," she whispered to Martin.

"Well, Charles is a good man. He needs our help."

The next morning Grace was up at first light. As she fixed breakfast for everyone she stole glances toward the barn. Charles was the first one to arrive and when he came in the back door he was carrying a stack of field journals.

"Here's something you can get started on." He smiled. "I'll go into town and find a typing machine somewhere. Maybe the courthouse can loan us one until I can order one for you."

Grace took the books he offered. "This is wonderful. I'll do my very best."

"I know you will, dear. I see your enthusiasm for learning." He leaned in close and whispered. "I have learned a thing or two in my years. And very important one is that we cannot always control the situations we find ourselves in, but we can control how we react to them. I think you have seized on my science as a chance to fulfill your dream of somehow making a difference in this world. And you have chosen well. I will see to it that you get credit for your efforts."

After breakfast was done and the kitchen cleared, Grace and Charles sat down at the table to look at his notes. Grace quickly saw what he meant about his hard to read writing, but she could handle that. After all, she had been reading children's writing for several years. She would keep textbooks close by to check her efforts. The whole morning melted away as Charles explained the form and process for recording his papers. By noon she had a fair idea of what she would be doing. When Marie called them to lunch, she was surprised so much time had passed.

In the afternoon Charles left for town to find a typing machine, and when Martin came home that evening Charles was with him. The two men proudly carried the machine, a formidable piece of equipment, and placed it in the library. Grace immediately sat down and demonstrated how it worked, as Marie and Martin stood by in wonder.

That night after she went to bed, Grace lay awake thinking of the turn of events that had brought her this opportunity. Charles Sternberg's words stood out in her mind. *We can only control how we react to our situations.* She thought back over her life until now. Losing her father had turned her world upside down. But her reaction to that was to become a teacher and set out on her own. Then when teaching was not what she had hoped, she cut the strings and left for Ft. Worth to secretarial school. Those were choices she had made to change her life. Then meeting William and losing him so quickly. She had felt helpless, broken hearted. It would have been easy to give up. But she had chosen to strike out on her own again, to start a new life. Then just when she thought her dream of somehow being something other than just a housekeeper seemed to be gone, this opportunity opened. It seemed miraculous, but she knew it was actually a series of choices she had made along the way. Charles is right. We cannot always control the things that happen to us. We can only control how we react. And little did she realize that the truth of those words would be hammered home again.

The trouble started without warning. Telly had set his stand up on the front walk where it was a little cooler, he said.

Martin and Luther told him they wished they could move their barber chairs out there, too. They had the shop doors folded back wide to try and catch a breeze themselves. The shop was fairly busy. It was a good day. Martin saw the woman coming from the train station, walking fast, angling across the street toward the front of his shop. A stranger, not someone he had seen before. She was carrying a fancy little umbrella to shield herself from the noonday sun. Unusual for the women in Troubadour.

As she reached the walk, she stumbled slightly and began to fall, teetering on the edge of the first step. Quick as a flash Telly jumped down to her and managed to get his arm under her to keep her from hitting the brick street. Martin bolted out the door behind him and helped him set the woman back on her feet. He was laughing, he remembered later. He was glad that Telly caught her. Thinking that she was going to be very grateful for her rescue. But no, she was not.

"Get away from me!" She screamed at Telly. Don't touch me! How dare you touch me!" Her umbrella had collapsed in an awkward angle.

Telly froze and began to back away. Martin helped the woman gather up a package she had dropped. "There now, you're all better now."

The woman was still screaming. "Get away from me, get away!"

"Mam, the boy just saved you from a bad fall." Martin said. "He......"

"He grabbed me!" she screamed. Get away from me!"

A man Martin had never seen before rushed up. "Evelyn! What happened? Did you fall?"

"No, she almost did, but Telly caught her before she could hurt herself," Martin said.

"No!" she screamed again. That black boy grabbed me! I almost fell!"

The man turned his attention to Telly. "Come here, boy! You touched my wife? I'll teach you a lesson for that!'

A crowd began to gather. Telly was standing against the shop wall.

The man grabbed at the boy, and Martin stepped in the way.

"Listen fellow, you need to calm down here. Telly just saved your wife from a bad fall. You need to be thanking him.."

"Thanking him!" He began to pull off his belt. "I'll teach you to touch a white woman, boy!"

Martin pushed Telly back into the shop, then turned his attention on the man. "You need to step back, fellow. You are in the wrong here. You need to settle down!

"Who the hell to you think you are, tellin' me what to do!" the man was red in the face with his fist drawn back to swing.

"I'm the Marshal here, is who!" Martin roared. "And I'm telling you that the boy meant no harm. He just saved your wife from a fall. That's all."

"Saved my wife? Saved her? You gonna let that black boy put his hands on my wife and do nothing about it?"

"That's right. I am. Now just who are you anyway?"

"It's none of your damn business who I am!"

"Why are you here in Troubadour? I don't believe I've seen you before."

The man put his arm around the woman and pulled away toward the street. "We'll see about this!" We'll see the sheriff about this."

Martin watched the two of them huddled together, make their way back across the street toward the courthouse. He knew they wouldn't find the sheriff. He was over in Connel County at a court date.

The crowd that had gathered around the commotion were talking among themselves and watching to see what Martin would do.

"Who was that fellow? Anybody ever seen them before?"

Several people shook their heads. "I seen'em get off the train just now." Someone said.

Martin watched the couple into the courthouse, and then went back in his shop. Telly was at the back of the room huddled against the wall. "I's sorry Mr. Durham. I didn't mean no harm."

"I know you didn't Telly. I saw the whole thing. If it hadn't been for you, that woman would have had a bad fall. Don't you worry about it."

The crowd outside on the front walk was finally dispersing. Martin kept watch at the window. The man and woman never came out of the courthouse door that he could see, but they might have left from the other side.. The train whistle sounded, signaling that it was pulling out. Hopefully, those folks got back on the train and would be long gone.

The rest of the afternoon, people kept drifting by the shop and peering in as though there would be something to see. Martin acknowledged them with a nod, but most of the people sort of ducked their heads and shuffled away.

A couple men stopped in and had a comment to make or a question. "Did you have some trouble down here today? or I heard you had a little trouble."

"No, just a misunderstanding," Martin would reply.

At five o'clock, Telly folded up his stand and left. "See you in the morning, boss."

"Yeah, in the morning."

Martin closed up after Luther left and headed home. Charles Sternberg was in town for a few days, and they were planning his trip to join him out in the beds soon. He was looking forward to the adventure.

Next morning Martin got to the shop at the regular time, but Telly wasn't there. Luther showed up and made comment about it. Telly was always there before he was. Martin agreed with him. He had a bad feeling about this. The boy was never late. By midafternoon, he went looking for him, down in the black town over in the northeast side. But no one could help him out. No one had seen Telly since yesterday. Martin reported this to the sheriff but got little response. The sheriff's general manner of working was to, "let the blacks take care of their own.", he was given to saying. Martin told him about the incident at the barber shop the day before.

"Yeah, I heard about that. I was out of town, but when I got back somebody said that Telly grabbed that woman right there in front of everybody."

"Hell no! He never grabbed anybody. He saved her from a bad fall, is what he did! Who said a thing like that?!"

"Now Martin, you know how people are. You knew when you hired that boy, you were stepping over a line. You can't go changing peoples' ways." The sheriff took a deep breath. "The boy probably saw that he was in trouble by the way folks were talking and just took off. Hell, I would, if I was him."

Martin took the next day off and went back out the river to look for Telly. The people in the shacks along the river came out to look him over with suspicion in their eyes. They weren't accustomed to white folks poking around and asking questions. Especially the City Marshal.

"No sir, I ain't seen the boy since day before yesterday."

"What time of day was that?" Martin asked.

"Early, just about sunup. He was headed into town."

Martin got no satisfaction from the answers he received. "So you didn't see him last night, or early this morning?"

"No, sir." Then just a shake of the head.

"Can you tell me where he lived?"

The man looked around slowly at the other people gathered, as though he was reluctant to share the information. "Yes, sir, I guess I can. It's that last house down there on the left."

"Did Telly live alone?"

"Yes, sir. The boy didn't have no family left."

Martin looked in the door. A makeshift cot was on one wall and a table and chair set in the middle of the room. The blue shirt hung on a nail in the wall.

Martin backed out of the space. "If the boy shows up, you tell him to come see me. Tell him I'm worried about him."

The man backed up out of his way and let Martin pass.

A week went by with no word. The worry hung over Martin like a black cloud. *He had caused this. He had put that boy on the spot.*

He talked with the sheriff about it but got no encouragement. "Like I said," the sheriff shook his head. "The boy just lit out somewhere. He didn't want any trouble. Hell, I'd do the same if I was in his shoes."

Weeks, then months slide by, with no word, no answers. Martin kept looking. Talked to the railroad conductor, but the man didn't really remember the people, he said. Martin didn't know where to search, or who to else ask next.

It was midafternoon one day when Charles Sternberg showed up at the shop. He had been out in the field for a week, and Martin was surprised to see him.

"Why are you back so soon?""

Charles motioned to Martin to step out on the front sidewalk. He had no smile today. "I found something out in the breaks yesterday," Charles wiped his hand over his mouth. I'm afraid I found your shoeshine boy."

Martin felt a jolt to his body that could have been a physical blow. "What?" he managed to get out.

Charles held out his hand. "Do you recognize this?"

It was a ragged piece of red cloth.

Martin reached out to take it. Yes, it was the same. That rusty color; it had to be the shirt he had bought Telly. "Where?" He managed to get out.

Over on the Cameron section. Stuffed up into one of those ledges of limestone. There wasn't much left except bones and tattered clothes."

"Take me out there."

"We better get the sheriff in on this," Charles said. But Martin hardly heard him. He had his hat and coat and was walking away.

They looked for the sheriff and found him, feet propped up on his desk at the courthouse. He got right up when Charles related his story, but then stopped to reason out the situation, and the sheriff and Charles convinced Martin that they should not go until morning. Night would catch them long before we got there.

"We'll go at first light tomorrow," the sheriff offered.

It was Telly alright. There was enough of the shirt left to see plainly that it was him. But there was little left of the body. Someone had crammed the boy up in the rock crevasse.

Martin just stood there staring.

"I'm sorry," Charles offered, but Martin did not react.

"Well, we need to get him out of there and bury him." the sheriff said.

Martin was shocked into speaking from that comment. "We need to know how he died. He didn't come off out here on his own. We've got to find out who killed him."

"And how are you going to do that, Martin. There's not enough left to figure it out. "We best better bury him here and let it go," the sheriff said.

"He's right, Martin. You've been looking and talking to people for several of months now. There are no answers to find."

"Well, I'm not leaving him here. I'm taking him home for burial. We've got to give him a decent burial."

The other two men nodded. They would do whatever Martin wanted. They gathered the remains and placed the body in the wagon, then made their way back to town.

Martin saw to the funeral. There was lots of gossip in town about him messing in things that he shouldn't. Most were sympathetic, some were not.

The day after the burial, Martin resigned as Marshal. He could not forgive himself for placing the boy in harm's way. Martin withdrew from the town and went back to the river. Grace watched him change from the confident leader he had been to a person who trusted no one, but she could not console him. He gave up his shop and provided for his family by selling sections of his land. And though he still lived with his wife and daughter, he stayed mostly on the river much of the time and took no interest in their lives.

To the town they presented the face of a family, but at home they lived in different worlds. For the rest of his life, Martin could never forgive himself. When his health began to fail, he came home, and Grace cared for him until his death. Their lives together, and their daughter's also, were forever changed by Telly.

Meredith

2015

Chapter 28

They slept late on Saturday. Meredith was in the kitchen making coffee when Rachel came down.

"Is Angela upstairs?"

"No. I talked to her earlier. She left for her run about three hours ago."

Meredith smiled and handed her daughter her cup. They both eased themselves down at the table. Neither of them were able to get going without a shot of caffeine.

"Back down to Daniel's after her run, I guess."

They both smiled, and Rachel nodded,.

"So, what do you want to tackle today?"

"I was thinking of showing you Grace's trunk while you were here. I know you saw it when you were a child, but you probably don't remember much. It's interesting, I think, looking over the things she treasured."

"I remember the trunk vaguely."

They walked to the parlor with their coffee. Meredith raised the trunk lid and gave time for Rachel to look it over. The whiteness of her mother's letter stood out in the tray. Meredith picked it up and set it on the mantel behind a candle stick. Rachel didn't seem to notice.

"What are these?" Rachel asked, as she picked up one of the plaited hair pieces."

Meredith explained about the custom of taking a lock of hair from a deceased love one and plaiting it into a pattern as a remembrance. "This was from Graces's little brother. He died at age four from fever, Grace told me. The people back then didn't have cameras, so this was a memorial piece. The other weave was Grace's great uncle, I think." Meredith picked up the other weave. "He served in the Civil War and came to live with her parents when he was old. She was just a little girl. Grace said she remembered him as very reserved and stately. But he would sit patiently in a chair while she plated his long hair into pigtails." They both smiled at the image she described. "The black curl is different. It was from my mother's first haircut." Meredith told Rachel the story about Audrey and the lollypop and, they laughed about it together.

Meredith pointed out the other items in the tray and explained them to Rachel. Then they removed the tray and set it aside.

Rachel picked up a stack of embraided dollies. "These would make wonderful throw pillows tops."

"Take them if you are interested. That would be a good memory of your great-grandmother." Meredith said. She lifted out a completed quilt top that had never been attached to the backing. "It would be interesting to know the story of all these fabrics, I think.

"Yes," Rachel reached to touch the quilt. Important dresses, baby dresses, curtains, it's an interesting collection."

"Grace probably told me at one time, but I don't remember now. I do know that lots of this material came from flour sacks. Flour companies bagged their flour is cotton cloth sacks of colorful fabrics, and women would save the bags and sew clothes for the family out of them, especially in the 30's and 40's. Then they would save the cloth scraps for quilts."

"Really! That is interesting." They laid the quilt top aside.

Next was a woman's suit made out of cream-colored linen. It was neatly folded with tissue paper in the folds.

"This was the nicest suit my grandmother ever owned, she told me." Meredith smoothed her hand over the material. "It was a gift from her mother when she went away to school in Fort Worth.

"It's lovely, Rachel said. "Look at the piping on the collar and cuffs."

Meredith nodded. "Yes, she told me her mother ordered it from the Sears catalog. It was the first store-bought clothing she owned." Meredith laid the suit carefully aside.

At the bottom of the trunk was a book. Meredith picked it up. She could tell by the cover style and color that it was old. The title "Life of a Fossil Hunter by Charles Sternberg" was impressed into the cover. She opened it carefully. The copyright date was 1919, and on the title page was an inscription:

To Grace Durham

My loyal assistant and friend.

Charles Sternberg

"Look at this!" Meredith showed it to Rachel. This must be the man that Grace worked for. The one the banker told me about."

Rachel leaned in to read over her shoulder. "His assistant?"

"Apparently. I knew she was interested in fossils. You've seen her front walkway lined with them. The banker told us that she helped with reports and correspondence." Rachel took the book from her and turned the pages carefully.

Meredith looked back into the trunk. In one corner was a small velvet box with a hinged lid. It looked as old as everything else in the trunk, so she handled it carefully. However, the hinge opened easily, and inside was a small golden rose pendant with a tiny ruby at its center. Something more valuable than anything she had ever associated with her grandmother before. When she was small, Grace had let her rummage through the top tray, carefully of course, and touch everything there. This pendant had apparently been too valuable to leave out to be touched. Beneath the box was a packet of papers with a photograph on top tied together with a lavender ribbon. It was a stack of letters, and the photograph was of a young couple standing beside a vintage World War I aircraft. Meredith recognized Grace, but the young man, she had not seen before. However, he looked familiar to her in a way she couldn't quite grasp. He was a flyer apparently, dressed in a uniform she didn't recognize. And he had his arm around Grace in a very loving and possessive way. The man was important to Grace. She could that see in her expression.'

"What is that?" Rachel asked.

"I'm not sure," Meredith said.

Rachel studied the photograph. "Well, they are a couple. That's clear."

But Meredith hardly heard her. She was reading the first letter.

"Dearest Grace," it read. *"The training is going well. I don't expect to get leave this week, but I will come as soon as I can. I am sorry we were not able to write to your mother together last weekend, but I wrote my letter to her and told her of our plans. I'm sure you did the same. I love you dearly and think about you all the day.*
Love William."

A letter dated two days later read, *"Plan our wedding and invite your mother. We may be shipping out within the week, and I may not get another leave. But I will be back to you as soon as possible, and we will wed.*
Love, William

There were more short notes addressed to Grace, and another photograph, this one of the man, William, in full dress uniform. The caption at the bottom of the picture identified him as Lt. William Wallace of the First Canadian Air Corp. The photograph was made by Runnels Photography / Fort Worth, Texas 1916

So, Meredith thought, Grace had known and loved this man in the years before her marriage to Martin Durham. Meredith flipped through the letters and chose another to read.

Dearest Grace,

Meeting you that Saturday last Spring, was the best day of my life! I wrote my mother that you loved the pendant. She is very pleased and honored that it symbolizes our promise to each other. We will have a long and happy life.

Love, William

Meredith looked back at the pendant box. *"Yes, it was precious,"* she thought.

There were many more notes, but toward the bottom of the stack was an official looking letter much larger than the rest, folded to a smaller size. Meredith opened it carefully and smoothed the page.

To Miss Grace Wilson,

It is with deepest regret that I write this letter to you. Lt. William Wallace was involved in a tragic air collision at the field this morning. I must tell you that he was killed instantly and suffered no pain. I was his commanding officer and felt I needed to send you this personal notifica-

tion, although the official report will not be published until tomorrow. Please accept my deepest condolences and know that Lt. Wallace was a fine officer and a credit to his country.

Colonel Forest Simpson
1st Canadian Air Corp

Meredith read the letter again. *So the young man had been killed in a training accident.* She looked back at the picture. How heart breaking that Grace had lost her first love so long ago, and she had kept this letter and photograph all these years. She handed the letters to Rachel and waited while her daughter read several of them.

"How sad," Rachel whispered after a bit. "Where was she living at that time?"

"Fort Worth, the photograph says on the back. She went to secretarial school there before World War I, I think. She must have met him there."

"And they planned to marry, but he was killed in a flying accident."

"That seems to be the case."

"Did she ever speak of him?"

"No," Meredith shook her head. "But something about him seems familiar. I'm not sure what."

"Maybe she had another picture that you saw as a little girl."

"Maybe."

"What's this?" Rachel reached into the bottom of the trunk and lifted out a large folder, bound with cord. They opened it to find an old movie marque poster. Meredith studied it. The type on the page was faded but still readable. It was a movie flyer for "The Thief of Bagdad" starring Douglas Fairbanks. She looked closer. Of course, the young man named William looked a great deal like Douglas Fairbanks. Even to the thin moustache.

Grace had always vowed that Douglas Fairbanks was the world's greatest actor. She had taken her to see all of his movies when she was a little girl. She even named her cat Douglas, after him.

Rachel looked over her shoulder as she compared the poster and the photograph. "There is a strong resemblance."

She reached for the book. "So this is the scientist you talked about?" She turned to the acknowledgement page. "He lists several scientists and such who helped him with this book, but no mention of Grace." She turned another page. "Oh! Look at this!"

On a blank page by the Introduction was written a personal note.

Dear Grace,

I want to express to you my lifelong endearment and thanks to you and Martin for taking me in and providing housing for my work. Also, I will be eternally grateful to you for your hard work recording and transposing my notes and cataloging my finds. I feel that you have found your passion in this work. I look forward to working with you for many more years.

Charles Sternberg

"Wouldn't you love to be able to ask her some questions."

"Yes." They surveyed all the contents of the trunk and then, carefully began to put them back. Meredith paused over the suit. "This is what she had on in the picture."

Rachel unfolded the jacket and Meredith the skirt. It was in the style of the early 1900's, cut long to fall at the wearer's ankles. "I think I will check to see if there is a local museum," Meredith said. They might want this for display."

"Good idea."

"You know, I remember Grace counseling me as a child and especially as an adult; every time I hit a snag in my life. And believe me there were a few." She smiled. "Grace always finished with the statement that a wise man once told her that we cannot always control the situations we find ourselves in. That often things are set by fortune good or bad, disaster even. But we can control how we react to our situation. You know, give up, get angry, become a victim, or rise above it all, make the most of our chances. Maybe working for Charles Sternberg was Grace's way to rise above her lot in life. Maybe he was that wise man she always quoted."

"Nice thought. I hope so."

"Me, too."

The sound of a voices outside caught their attention. Daniel and Angela came in the front door.

"It was wonderful out there yesterday! The dig site is amazing!" was the first thing that Angela said. "Gram, did you see the picture of the large fossil Daniel has found. He says it's a Dimetrodon and about 286 million years old! I helped him put a sheet of aluminum foil over and then the first plaster strips."

"Yes, I believe I did." Meredith looked toward Daniel, and he nodded. "Did you bring it today?"

"No, and it takes some time to finish the process." Daniel said. "We'll have to put several layers of the plaster on, and it has to dry between each layer."

"That's what he's been waiting for." Angela said. "It had to be dry enough conditions to protect the fossil."

"It sounds as if you have found something important."

Daniel smiled. "Yes, I hope so. There's still a lot of work to be done."

"You should hear how he will get it out of the ground! It's an amazing process," Angela said.

"Yes, I would love to hear about that." And then to Daniel, she said, "I have just learned that there may have been a storage shed here on the place somewhere for Sternberg's work."

"Really! Do you know where?

"No, I've never heard it talked about before." "Not in the barn, certainly. I would have found it years ago."

Let's go look around. They walked out back and surveyed the area. Everyone looked in a different direction. "There's a shed thing over on this side of the barn," Angela called. "Could that be it?"

Meredith stepped over the corner of the barn and looked down the side. There was a small addition to the barn there. "Yes, I remember that now. It's always been there. They used it to store tools, I think. But it was off limits for me as a child. Always locked."

"Still is, I believe." Daniel walked back to the door and jiggled the lock. It was an old one, maybe a jailer's lock, Meredith thought. She had seen that type before, and that is what Grace might have called it.

"Do you have a key for this?" Daniel jiggled it again.

"Heavens no! I wouldn't know where to look." Meredith stepped to touch it. "But the latch doesn't look all that sturdy." She pulled at it.

"I could just knock the latch off, I think." Daniel said, "Spare that old lock that way."

"Yes, do that. Let's see what's in here."

Daniel went to his truck and retrieved a hammer. A couple of good blows did the trick. The hinge fell away and he swung the door back.

All four of them leaned in to get a look. Only Daniel was brave enough to walk into the dark interior. "It's a workshop, alright. Look at this!"

The others walked in slowly and let their eyes adjust to the darkness. Tools and brushes lay about on the table in the center of the room. There were counters on three walls with dust covered objects randomly placed.

Daniel was holding up a fossilized bone. "Sternberg's workshop!"

The women spread out to look at the counters. A small skull or two were on one counter and a large ammonite on another. Meredith picked up a chisel that was covered in spider web.

"Look at this!" Angela called. She was holding up what look like a large clam shell.

"That is a fossil casing," Daniel announced. "That's what they look like after the plaster has all dried."

" There's a fossil in there?" Rachel asked.

"Yes. It keeps it safe and intact until they can get to a lab and extract it," Angela said. She turned it over in her hands.

Daniel pointed to Angela and smiled. "She's right. The process hasn't changed much over the years."

"This is a museum," Rachel exclaimed. "It's like a time capsule!

Daniel nodded. "It needs to be preserved in a museum, certainly."

The three women walked back out into the light, but Daniel stayed behind, looking around the area.

"Well Gram, this house is turning out to be your own version of a fossil hunt." Angela said.

Meredith glanced around at her granddaughter quickly and then smiled. " I guess you're right." She reached out to hug Rachell's shoulders. "My very own fossil hunt for family secrets."

Rachel returned her hug. "Yes, I guess that's true, Mom."

"How did the car run?" Angela asked.

"Like new! I may never sell it!" They laughed at that.

Chapter 29

The girls left at one, right after lunch.

"I'll be back on Wednesday or Thursday, Gram," Angela explained. "I just need to make a few calls and collect my stuff."

"That's fine." Merddith gave her a hug. "It will be great to have a roommate." She turned to her daughter, "Thank you so much for coming. You've been so much help!"

"Well, I hope so, Mom." Rachel gave her a hug. "I'll call when we get home, and I'll be down again as soon as I can."

Meredith watched them back the car around and start down the lane. The car stopped at Daniel's trailer, and he was standing by the road waiting for them. Angela got out of the car, and they talked for a bit. Daniel leaned down to speak to Rachel through the car window and then straightened to take Angela in his arms. They kissed and then parted. Angela got in the car, and they moved on while Daniel watched. Then he turned back toward her and waved.

Meredith waved in return. She smiled to herself. *"Maybe Angela has found her passion too,"* she thought.

She hugged her arms against the chill and looked up at the sky. It was finally getting cold, it seemed. Time to unpack some warmer clothes. She went back into her house. There was work to do.

By sundown she had righted everything from her company; gathered the linens and towels for washing and straightened the kitchen. She ate some leftovers for dinner and went out on the back porch to enjoy the evening.

Settled in her rocker, she took a deep breath. Home, yes, this definitely feels like home. When the house in Dallas sells, she would tackle all the upgrades needed around here. *Call the realtor tomorrow morning, she counseled herself. And Lucas should be back from vacation this week. I'll give him a call.*

Movement caught her eye at the back door. It was the cat peering through the screen with a serious expression. She got up and opened the screen door, and again he made a cautious entrance. "So, where have you been, mister?"

The cat made a curious round of the porch again while she settled back in her chair. Satisfied with the area, he came over to her and looked up. She reached down and stroked his head. "I'm glad you came back," she said. The cat nuzzled her hand and then laid down with his paws curled under and stared out at the darkness.

"I believe I'll call you Douglas," Meredith said as she reached down to stroke the cat's fur. The cat leaned into her touch and then got up and jumped light as a feather into her lap, turned around and settled. They sat there together as the nights sound began. When she finally started up to bed, the cat moved to the screen door and waited patiently for her to let him out. "Come again," she called as he disappeared around the corner. "Don't be a stranger," she added.

The next morning, Amy called while she was fixing breakfast. I've got a meeting with the library guild today. Do you want to come?"

"Yes. I'd love to. What time?"

"One o'clock. I thought maybe we could do lunch before and then go. I know you said you were interested in the library. They are setting up next year's schedule, so you could jump in if you're ready."

"Good idea. What time?"

"Let's make it 11:30. Gives us more lunch time."

"Great!"

"See you then."

Meredith hung up the phone. *"So, I'm doing this,"* she thought. *"Joining up. Getting to know these people."* It felt right. New chapter to her new life. She went up the stairs to get ready.

When she came back down, she still had a little time. Maybe open another box before Amy got there. She looked around the parlor for a place to start. There was certainly plenty to do.

The letter on the mantle caught her eye. Standing there propped against the candle stick; it was hard to ignore.

A letter from my mother. What could it say? More excuses? More accusations?" Maybe a tearful apology after all *these years, but she doubted it.* Meredith thought about all the bottles they had hauled away. *No Audrey hadn't changed.*

And what would Grace tell her to do about the letter? What would her advice be? "You can't always control the situation you find yourself in, Meredith, she would say. You can only control how you react to it." Meredith turned the letter over in her hands.

A car horn sounded out front. Amy was here a little early. Meredith studied the envelope for a second more. Then with careful procession, she tore it in two and dropped it in a box of trash.

"There's nothing more to say, Mother. Nothing more. Some-times you just need to walk away."

Meredith gathered her purse and jacket and went out the door.

Acknowledgements

Writing historical fiction is great fun. I can weave true facts, events and locations together with my imagination to create a story. The town of Troubadour, Texas is fictional, but the problems and situations of my characters are gathered from a scattering of true people and events in the 20th Century, as well as my imagination. I cannot directly connect any of the events in the book with any one person or place, with only one exception.

There truly is a world-renowned fossil field called the Permian Red Beds, near Seymour, Texas in Baylor County. In the late 1800's, a fossil, the Seymouria baylorensis, was found there that is widely believed to be part of the evolution of mammals. Since that time many amazing finds of land vertebrates have been excavated there, and the site is recognized as one of the largest in the world for the time period.

I found out about this interesting place from a very old book that I inherited from my grandfather. He had been friends with a paleontologist named Charles Sternberg in the early 1900's in Seymour, Texas. The book is a chronology of Sternberg's work in fossil beds across the Great Plains in the late 1800's and early 1900's that included the Wichita Red Beds between the Brazos and Wichita Rivers. Charles Sternberg was the discoverer of the Seymouria.

Today there is a very interesting museum in Seymour, Texas that I recommend to all as worth your visit. The Whiteside Museum of Natural History tells the story of this ancient fossil bed and the creatures that lived there from 298.9 million to 251.9 million years ago around a string of oxbow lakes during the Permian Age. And all this took place 40 million years before the dinosaurs! Check it out!

About the author

Irene Sandell combines her passion for writing with her love of Texas History to tell the story of the people who settled and tamed Texas. A former Texas History teacher of 25 years, she enjoys collecting the "side stories of history" to enrich her novels and tell the heartfelt adventures of people woven into true places and events.

Irene also is the creator of 20 documentary films that tell the history of Texas, and she has written several nonfiction books on Texas and the United States that are presented in schools and organizations across the state.

Her novels have earned writing awards from several organization, including the WILLA Literary Award from Women Writing the West and the Will Rogers Medallion Award for best Western Fiction.

She and her husband live in Plano, Texas.

Also by Irene Sandell

Untamed Texas Frontier: Land of blood and hope

(English and German) (Previously published title: *Beloved Over All*)

Stella Carter and her husband left the racial strife of Kentucky searching for a safe haven in Texas. Benjamin Walters came west seeking to escape the violent secrets of his past in Missouri. Henry Prescott was one step ahead of the law when he left Arkansas for the cattle range of the Southwest. Unimagined hardships, Indian wars, captivity, and outlaws await these pioneers in the maelstrom of events that engulf the Texas frontier following the Civil War. The lives of buffalo hunters, Indians, soldiers, cowboys and settlers intertwine in the struggle to find their place in this beloved land. Based on true characters and events, this novel weaves an action-packed saga of the American frontier.

In A Fevered Land

Lon Prather and his cousin Emory Campbell are determined to escape the drought and financial ruin of cotton farming during the Great Depression. They follow promises of money and adventure to the oil field towns of Wink, Kilgore and Odessa. Their quest leads them to the boisterous life of the Texas boomtowns where they find love and hatred, hope and regret, failure and success.

River of the Arms of God

Kate Walters believes she is escaping her controlling father for the life of her dreams when she hastily marries Colby Walters and moves to his ranching empire, Pantera. But she soon finds that the wide open lands of West Texas have a host of their own secrets that hold her captive. Only when she is shown the strength to stand on her own by Sarah Graham, a youn woman who lived along the Butterfield State Route and walked the same ground 100 years before, does Kate find true freedom.

The life lessons that both women learn lead them on journeys that reach across the years and span the continent.

The House on Swiss Avenue

Robyn Merrill hopes that starting a new life in a new place will help to heal her broken heart, but the path she chooses and the people she encounters touch her life in ways she could never have   expected. Secluded in her family mansion, Adeline Sinclair has spent a lifetime devoted to memories and to the history of her family only to question her choices in her twilight years. Her historic house on Swiss Avenue brings the two women to together to solve mysteries from the past.